STAGE FRIGHT

STAGE FRIGHT

Glenn Ickler

CYNTOMedia
CORPORATION

Pittsburgh, PA

ISBN 1-56315-358-0

Trade Paperback
© Copyright 2005 Glenn Ickler
All rights reserved
First Printing—2005
Library of Congress #2004117518

Request for information should be addressed to:

> SterlingHouse Publisher, Inc.
> 7436 Washington Avenue
> Pittsburgh, PA 15218
> www.sterlinghousepublisher.com

SterlingHouse Publisher, Inc. is a company
of the CyntoMedia Corporation

Art Director: Jonah Lloyd
Cover Design: Jonah Lloyd
Typesetting & Layout Design: N. J. McBeth

All rights reserved. No part of this publication may be reproduced, stored in a retrieval system, or transmitted in any form or by any means—electronic, mechanical, photocopy, recording or any other, except for brief quotations in printed reviews—without prior permission of the publisher.

This is a work of fiction. Names, characters, incidents, and places, are the product of the author's imagination or are used fictitiously. Any resemblance to actual events or persons, living or dead is entirely coincidental.

Printed in The United States of America

Chapter 1
Sandbagged

Ker-whump!

A forty-pound gray canvas sandbag thudded to the stage six inches from the right foot of the flame-haired young woman who was just opening her lips to say, "Dahling, are you theah?" in her best fake British accent.

What came out instead was, "Jesus H. Christ!" as she staggered backward and did an arms-akimbo, legs-apart pratfall that an Olympic judge would have scored 5.8 on the 6.0 scale. This exclamation was followed by, "That fucking thing could've killed me!"

In my seat at the back of the theater, I performed a sitting high jump that would have done a kangaroo proud. The balding, egg-shaped man on my left who was directing the play rehearsal leaped to his feet and waddled down the aisle shouting, "Son of a bitch! Where the hell did that come from?"

A young man who had been waiting at stage right to make his entrance stepped forward and pointed toward the ceiling.

"Schmuck!" bawled the director. "I know it came from up. What I want to know is how the hell did it get there?"

The actor shrugged and blushed and moved toward the terrified woman who was still sprawled on her elbows and derriere at center stage. The director, Duncan Dunworthy Bell, who was better known as Ding Dong Bell, tried to hoist his stubby, 250-pound carcass directly onto the stage. After one try, he decided to use the steps at stage left instead. Ding Dong and the actor, whose name was Norman Rogers, almost collided at the fallen woman's head while six other members of the cast of *Long Night's Journey Into Day* emerged from the wings and crowded around her, yammering things like, "Are you okay, Alice?" and "What the hell happened?"

With notepad in hand, I trotted up the aisle to get a closer look. I'm Warren Mitchell, better known as Mitch, and I'm a general assignment reporter for the *St. Paul Daily Dispatch*.

General assignment means I get sent to cover everything from accidents in autos to zebras in the zoo. I had been interviewing the famous guest director, Ding Dong Bell, at the Glock Family Theatre, near the west-central Minnesota city of Alexandria, for a Sunday feature story.

Accompanying me, as he often does, was *Daily Dispatch* photographer Alan Jeffrey. Al, who had performed a sitting high jump almost as Olympian as mine, followed me up the aisle with his camera bag slung over his shoulder.

Expecting to experience nothing more stimulating than a group of actors struggling with a work in progress, we had accepted Bell's invitation to watch the evening's rehearsal. Now I had a news story as well as a feature. I could see the headline: "Mysterious missile barely misses bagging Alexandria actress."

Alice, whose last name was Prewitt, allowed Ding Dong and Norm to pull her to her feet. Amid the hubbub, I heard Alice say she was okay except for the bruises on her ass but that she would like to get her hands on the throat of the asshole who had left that sandbag hanging above her head. It struck me that her recitation was an anatomical tour de force, beginning at the bottom and working its way up, then down, and then up again. We writers revel in spontaneous prose like that.

Once assured that the damage was limited to Alice's posterior and pride, all eyes turned upward, seeking the source of the bomb. I vaulted onto the stage (I'm six inches taller, sixty pounds lighter and thirty years younger than Ding Dong) to get a better look. Al, who is three inches shorter than I am, but more muscular and athletic, followed me on the first bounce.

Because the Glock Family Theatre was built beside a large scenic lake, its height was restricted to the equivalent of two and a half stories. This means the fly area above the stage was much shallower than the soaring lofts in large professional theaters. Still, the rows of steel rails supporting the lights, drop curtains, and teasers were 15 feet above the actors' heads. A forty-pound sandbag falling that distance can gather enough momentum to flatten the skull and compress the spine of any person unlucky enough to catch such a missile on top of the head. If Alice had taken one more step to her right before the sandbag dropped, she could well be a candidate for another sort of bag — the kind in which dead bodies are removed from the scene.

Ding Dong's question about how the bag got up there was logical. These bags normally are on the floor, where they're used as weights to secure set pieces that can't be fastened permanently with stage screws or nails. People milling around me on the stage were asking how the bag had been hoisted, who could have done the hoisting and why.

I moved in for a closer look and discovered that the bag was attached to a long piece of rope. Someone had slung the loose end of the rope over one of the steel rails in the rigging above the stage and hauled up the bag. But how had the hauler secured the rope and how was it released when Alice Prewitt walked into position to deliver the opening line of the second act?

"Do you have any idea who might have done this?" I asked Ding Dong.

"It had to be somebody who knows the blocking," Ding Dong said. "If the son of a bitch wanted to hit her, he miscalculated the landing spot. Maybe he just wanted to scare the shit out of her — and also everybody else in the cast. This ain't the first weird thing that's happened, but it is the worst."

"What else has been weird?" I asked. I smelled an even better story than "Mysterious missile barely misses bagging Alexandria actress."

"Not now, Mr. Mitchell," he said. "Talk to me later after I calm these people down and maybe figure out how that son of a bitch was rigged."

I had finished my interview with Ding Dong, and we were planning to drive the 120 miles back to St. Paul after watching the rehearsal, but Al and I decided that this conversation was worth waiting for. It wouldn't be the first time we rolled into our respective domiciles at sunrise after chasing a hot news story.

Seeing Ding Dong in action was better than watching the play, which was a silly British farce set in a London whorehouse. The man was sixty-seven years old, had been working with actors since his college days, and, of necessity, had become a master psychologist. He displayed this talent by having the entire cast and crew sit along the edge of the stage while he stood on the floor with his face at the level of their knees and spoke in a silk-smooth voice just loud enough to be heard. After a few soothing sentences, he advised them to go home, relax with a drink of whatever calmed them best and get a good night's sleep. He finished with, "I'll see you at the usual time tomorrow evening. Good night, everyone."

Everyone echoed his "good night" and filed out. Everyone, that is, except Jimmy Storrs, the technical director, who stayed to help Ding Dong solve the mystery of the plummeting sandbag. Al and I walked around with them, but he kept his camera out of sight and I took mental notes rather than written ones because we both figured discretion was the better part of valor at this point.

"The story is that there's a ghost in this theater," Ding Dong said to us. "Some bullshit about it being built on the ground where the Indians used to worship the spirit of the lake."

"There's a ghost in every theater, isn't there?" Al asked. Even the huge Guthrie Theatre in Minneapolis had acquired a ghost before it was ten years old.

"Well, a lot of us have died onstage more than once," said Ding Dong. "But it sure as hell wasn't any ghost that did this."

Jimmy hauled out a ladder and climbed up to examine the steel rail above the point of impact with a flashlight. He announced that he could see where the rope had disturbed the accumulation of dust on top of the rail. Then he climbed down, moved the ladder and looked at the next rail. With a succession of moves, climbs, and looks, Jimmy traced the rope to where the opening of a door would release the free end from where it had been secured. It was the door that Norman Rogers was supposed to have opened for his entrance after Alice spoke her first line.

"Somebody rigged up the sandbag before the rehearsal and tied it off somewhere so it didn't fall during the first act run through," Jimmy said. "Then during the break between acts, he moved the end of the rope to the bedroom door at stage right so the bag would fall when Norm opened it."

"Son of a bitch!" Ding Dong replied in a voice no longer silky. "I saw Norm open the door to take a peek just before his cue. If he had waited to open it when he was supposed to, Alice might have walked right into that goddamn sandbag when she turned to see him. Son of a bitch!"

"Jeez, it could have killed her," Jimmy said.

"Goddamn right it could have," said Ding Dong. "Up until now it's been goofy games, but this is getting serious."

"What do you mean, goofy games?" I asked.

"Oh, you know. Crazy little things, like furniture breaking or doors not working right or pictures falling off the wall. Stuff that pisses you off and makes you wonder what the hell is going on. But nothing that could hurt somebody. Son of a bitch!"

"Got time to tell us about it now?" I asked.

"Oh, I suppose," said Ding Dong. "But you gotta be careful what you put in the paper. The wrong kind of publicity could scare the audience away and wreck this show."

"On the other hand, the right kind of publicity might bring in a bigger audience," I said. "People are always fascinated by ghost stories. And if the ghost is an Indian from the tribe that lived around here, so much the better."

"Let's sit in the parlor while we talk," he said.

The parlor was in the center of the stage set. It was the area where the madam greeted the bordello customers and sat them down to wait for their evening companions.

"Fine, as long as you promise nothing will fall on my head," I said.

"I don't promise a damn thing, but Jimmy didn't see any more sandbags so I guess we don't have to put on our hardhats."

Al reached into his camera bag and pulled out a cell phone. "I'm going to call Carol and tell her we'll be home later than expected," he said. Carol was Al's wife. She had been subjected to more than one lonely night of waiting.

"Want me to call your apartment too?" Al asked. He knew what the answer would be.

"Don't bother," I said. "Sherlock isn't taking any calls tonight."

Sherlock is a large, black-and-white tomcat whose full name is Sherlock Holmes. Except for a persistent colony of ants below the sink, Sherlock is the only living creature sharing my one-bedroom apartment.

"You should train him to pick up the phone," Al said. "He'd be the purr-fect answering service."

"Really the cat's meow," I said.

Al shook his head, made a brief call, and joined Ding Dong Bell and me on the plush burgundy sofa at left-center stage. The first preview performance was scheduled for the following Thursday, only eight days away, and the set was complete except for some finishing touches.

Talk about being surrounded by doors! The bordello set was exactly what one expects in a free-for-all, sex-filled farce, with five doors and a French window at floor level, a flight of stairs with a door halfway up on the landing and a balcony with two more doors. The French windows and the door to the outside world were up center. On the stage-right wall were doors to a pair of bedrooms used by the ladies and their customers. On the stage-left wall were doors to a walk-in closet and the madam's living quarters. The door on the landing led into a bathroom, and the two doors on the balcony were for additional bedrooms (or playrooms, as the madam described them).

"So what's been going on?" I asked. I had reloaded the tiny tape recorder I always carry in my shirt pocket, and I turned it on as Ding Dong replied.

"This whole thing's been fucked up from the start," he said. "You know about the deal we've got."

I did, having been told during the interview that Ding Dong was directing this show as a favor to the theater's owner, Herman Glock. Ding Dong and Herman had been close friends since college days, when they were almost the only Jews attending a prestigious Lutheran school. The college had lured them in with scholarships because the administration was trying to diversify the student body. This effort had been hugely unsuccessful because the Lutheran students universally ignored the non-Lutherans, and the tiny groups of minorities mustered individually as isolated camps of Methodists, Catholics, and Jews instead of joining forces.

Glenn Ickler

After graduation, Ding Dong went to New York City, spent the requisite time waiting on tables, and eventually emerged as one of Broadway's premier theater directors. Herman also loved the theater, but he went into business with his father, who owned a resort consisting of a rustic lodge and some log cabins in Minnesota's lake country. Hoping to lure more family trade, and to provide an outlet for his wife Ingeborg's dramatic desires, Herman built an attractive little theater and filled the summer seasons with light comedies and musicals. Herman kept the cost of the productions down by using amateur talent from nearby towns. This pleased the locals, satisfied the audiences and kept the box office busy for twenty-one prosperous years.

But times had changed. Despite the low overhead, Herman Glock's theater had lost money for three consecutive summers as attendance drifted downhill. In an effort to spark renewed interest in his theater as it began its 25th season, Herman called upon his old pal Ding Dong Bell to make a guest appearance as director of the silver anniversary season opener. Herman was hoping to fill the house from mid-June to mid-July with this production. All this information was going into the feature story I'd be writing for the Sunday edition of the *Daily Dispatch*.

"So what's been going wrong?" I asked.

"Well, it started with auditions," said Ding Dong. "I don't know any of these people, so I asked Herm to get somebody familiar with the situation to sit beside me as my audition assistant. I wanted somebody to clue me in on personal things — like who was pissed off at whom, who might have strange sexual preferences, and who was banging somebody else's wife — stuff like that. I like to have a cast that gets along with each other if at all possible, so I try to stay away from putting people together who might hate each other for whatever reason."

"That makes sense," I said.

"The problem was that Herm sent me a girl from the local community college who didn't know from Adam any of the local schmucks auditioning. So all I could do was cast people according to how they fit the part and hope they'd get along. I found out I'd made some big mistakes when I showed the list to Herm."

"What kind of mistakes?"

"First off, I cast a dame as the madam and a guy as the madam's husband who turned out to be recently divorced from each other because she popped into his office one day and caught him getting a blow job from his secretary. Sort of like the former president and Monica, only this chick didn't bother to hide under the desk. The dame auditioned on Sunday, the guy came in on Monday, and they were both perfect for those roles. What did I know? Then I find out they don't speak to one

Stage Fright

another offstage except to fight, and I see them keep shooting each other nasty looks onstage. It's a real bitch working with those two."

"I'll bet it is," Al said.

"And I also cast two schmucks as regular johns who in the real world have been taking turns screwing the same woman — who, of course, is also in the show as one of the whores. You can imagine how cozy that is for everyone concerned," said Ding Dong.

"Sounds like you didn't miss a single opportunity to make your directing job tougher," I said.

"Oh, but I haven't even mentioned the gay guy and the homophobe schmuck I cast as inseparable brothers who always come in together to patronize this cat house," said Ding Dong. "Herm tells me all this shit the day after I've called these people and they've all accepted their roles."

"Sounds like you've got a lot of headaches," I said.

"The only headache I didn't get was Ingeborg Glock. She didn't audition, thank God, or I'd have had to cast her and there's no role in this show for her. She ain't tough enough to play the madam, and she's way too old to be a whore."

"I sympathize with you, but there's nothing in your casting problems for a story. Tell me about this supposed ghost — or what the spook has been doing."

Ding Dong leaned back and took a deep breath while he thought about how much he wanted to tell me. Before he could tell me anything, the door at the rear of the auditorium swung open, and a loud voice called out, "Ding Dong?"

"What'cha want?" asked the director.

"I want to know what the hell went on here tonight," said Herman Glock. He walked up the aisle to the edge of the stage, pointed at Al and me, and said, "And who are these guys?"

"These are the guys from the St. Paul paper that are doing the piece about my being here," Ding Dong said. "They were here when Alice almost got beaned, and I'm telling them about the other shit that's been happening."

"Like hell you are!" Herman said. "We don't need any of that in the paper."

Again Herman pointed at Al and me. "It's time for you guys to leave. I need to talk private to Ding Dong."

I'm not one to lose a story without putting up a fight, so I said, "Ding Dong has agreed with me that a properly told ghost story could sell even more tickets to your opening show."

"Well, Ding Dong doesn't own this theater, and I don't want any ghost stories being told about it, properly or otherwise," said Herman. "Much as I appreciate you coming all the way out here from the Cities to do a write-up on Ding Dong, I need for you to leave now so I can talk to my director."

Herman had that certain look in his eye — the look that means vamoose or I'll vamoose you. He was a short, wiry, gray-haired man in his late sixties, but I wouldn't bet against him in an arm wrestling match, and I had no desire to provoke him. Although I'm persistent when pursuing a story, I also know when it's time to say good-by, which is what Al and I said right then.

But good-by is not farewell, and I was making plans to return by the time our front tires hit the blacktop at the end of the gravel driveway. I had some vacation time coming, and Herman Glock's resort looked like an interesting place to spend a few days fishing for walleyes in the lake — and for ghosts in the Glock Family Theatre.

Chapter 2
Fishing for Favors

In Minnesota, it is common practice for families to go either "up north" or "to da lake" for their vacations. However, this has not been my custom. I don't relish being fodder for black flies and mosquitoes, and I have little desire to park my ass on a hard boat seat all day hoping to catch a fish that's big enough to be worth cleaning.

Knowing my feelings about fishing, my kindly city editor, Don O'Rourke, gave me the fisheye Thursday morning when I told him I'd like to take the next week off because I wanted to indulge myself in this so-called sport at a resort near Alexandria.

"What the hell makes you so hot to go fishing all of a sudden?" Don asked.

"I saw the way they were biting up there when Al and I went to do the story on the theater director," I said.

There was truth in this. We did see several nice catches of walleyes brought into the dock that day. Don's expression told me he was not convinced.

"If I'm lucky, I might also hook a story for the paper while I'm there," I said.

"What kind of story?" Don asked.

"There's something funny going on at that theater, but the owner shut the director up before he could tell me about anything that happened before we arrived."

"And you think you can come up with something by staying at the resort for a week?"

"I can hang around the theater when I'm not pursuing the wily walleye. If the director can't talk, one of the actors might. Or I might see another sandbag fall."

"If you do come up with a story, I suppose you'll want the paper to pay for your vacation," said Don. He had a nasty habit of guarding the company's exchequer as if the money were his own.

"I wouldn't turn down an offer to pay for my room and meals," I said. "I don't expect to draw a double salary for working during my vacation, though."

"I'm glad to hear that at least your expectations are realistic." He opened his computer to the vacation files, discovered that nobody else would be away during the week in question and gave me his approval.

Glenn Ickler

"Thanks," I said. "I'll stay in touch all the time I'm there."

"You damn well better if there's a story worth printing," Don said.

I decided to stick my neck all the way out. "So, what about paying for my room and meals?"

Don looked at me the way a dog owner looks at a pet that has just pooped on the living room rug.

"Get the goddamn story and I'll think about it," he said.

After calling the Glock Family Resort and reserving a cabin for the week beginning Sunday, I needed to find a shelter for Sherlock Holmes. I sometimes filled his food and water dishes and left him alone for a weekend, but I couldn't bail out for seven days without providing for his care and feeding.

"Hey, Al, want to take care of some pussy for a week?" I asked on our way to lunch.

"My darling wife might object to me consorting with strange women," he said.

"Not that kind of pussy, you filthy-minded sex fiend. I'm talking about Sherlock Holmes. He needs a home away from home next week. From Sunday on, actually."

"Care to tell me why old tuna-breath will be needing outside care?"

When Al heard my plan, his response was unexpected. "You can't go ghost hunting without me!"

"Carol won't like you taking off for a week — especially if it's a week of your vacation time."

"Carol and the kids can come along. School lets out tomorrow, so both Carol and the kids are free until next fall."

Carol taught at a junior high school, and their children, Kristin and Kevin, were in the seventh and fifth grades, respectively.

"That would be great, providing your other boss — the one on the photo desk — will let you go and the resort still has a vacant cabin big enough to hold your family."

"I'll work on both my photo desk boss and the resort right after lunch. I know my home boss, Carol, loves boat rides, and the kids get a kick out of trying to catch fish."

"You probably don't want to take Kristin and Kevin to see *Long Night's Journey Into Day*, however. Unless you plan to explain the facts of life very clearly between now and opening night."

"Kevin and Kristin can watch TV that night, providing that show ever opens," Al said. "Another sandbag falling out of the rigging might send the whole cast scurrying away for good."

Stage Fright

"You're right. Before that happens, I've got to find out what's going on in that theater," I said.

"Correction, we have got to find out what's going on in that theater. This is now an ensemble production, not a Warren Mitchell soliloquy."

"You're assuming that the resort will have a place waiting in the wings for all four of you."

"I'll wing it alone if they don't."

"Be careful about that. It could be curtains for your marriage if you exit from St. Paul without Carol."

Al was able to get both a week off and a reservation for a cabin with a double bed, a single and a rollaway. This pleased me because I knew I would enjoy their company, but it did not solve my cat-sitter problem.

My mother, who lives on a farm in southeastern Minnesota, is allergic to cats, so I couldn't ask her. That left me with only one possibility.

Martha Todd is a black-haired young woman, partially of Cape Verdean descent, with a sweet smile, long legs and the most beautiful ass in all creation. She lives in my building, in an apartment at the other end of the ground floor.

Martha and I see each other as often as possible because we enjoy each other's company, but our relationship would drive most people up a wall. After knowing each other for almost a year, we were still at the "just good friends" stage for a couple of reasons. One was that Martha was having a hard time recovering from a violent marriage and a venomous divorce. The bastard she married inflated his ego by beating her up and dragging her around the kitchen floor by her hair. While Martha's physical scars had healed and the hair she had shaved off in self defense had grown back, the emotional wounds were still raw and bleeding.

The other impediment to romance came from my side. I had not regained the ability to completely give myself to anyone of the opposite sex since being given an out-of-the-blue heave-ho the previous summer by a woman I had hoped to marry.

Oh, Martha and I could hug each other and play some minor league kissy-face, but we seemed to be incapable of unleashing ourselves from our emotional bygones. Every time we got within a zipper's width of graduating from friends to lovers, one of us would get cold feet thinking about commitment and the moment would slide by. It was a frustrating situation, but I really liked Martha and wanted to keep working toward a time when we'd both say to hell with everything and take the plunge.

Glenn Ickler

Sherlock Holmes was as fond of Martha as I was, and Martha loved Sherlock. She had taken care of him the previous summer when Al and I were sent to the Massachusetts island of Martha's Vineyard to cover the story of a missing St. Paul banker, so I was sure she would say yes. I would rather have had her agree to share that lakeside cabin with me for the week, but, chicken that I am, I couldn't work up the courage to ask. Or could I? I was asking myself that question as I knocked on Martha's door that evening.

"Of course I'll take care of your kitty for a week," Martha said. That's all I had asked her to do after discovering, the moment the door opened, that I didn't have the balls to invite her to join me for a week of fun and frolic in a cabin by the lake.

"I am most appreciative," I said. "And so is Sherlock. I think he actually prefers your company to mine."

"It's the way I rub his tummy," she said.

"Yes. I'm jealous."

"You're jealous because you think that Sherlock likes me better than you?"

"No, I'm jealous because of the way you rub his tummy."

Her Cape Verdean heritage had blessed Martha with a soft, coffee-with-cream complexion that sets off a smile that makes new-fallen snow look dingy. She smiled that smile and said, "You never lay on your back and purr."

"Is that the secret?"

"You could try it."

I started to lower myself onto her carpet.

She laughed and said, "But not right now."

I straightened to my full six-foot-one, twisted my short brown moustache in my best imitation of a stage villain's twirl, gave a devilish wink with one brown eye, and asked, "Okay, when?"

"When the time is right," she said.

Her smile gave me the courage to stick my neck out a little further.

"I've reserved a cabin with two beds near Alexandria," I said. "We could bring Sherlock Holmes along, and you could take care of him up there."

"And what about my two jobs down here?" she asked. Martha was putting herself through law school at night by working days as a clerk for a lawyer and non-school evenings as a waitress. Her schedule was a third reason our relationship wasn't progressing very rapidly.

"You're right," I said, hoping I didn't sound relieved. Still, having summoned the courage to broach the subject, I didn't want to blow the opportunity. "How about the weekend? You could come up Friday night and see the play, and we could go fishing or riding around the lake or something Saturday."

Again Martha smiled. "With or without Sherlock Holmes?"

"You could leave him in my apartment for that short a time."

"Stay in touch and I'll think about it. Now I need to go to class." She stretched up and kissed me ever so lightly on the lips, turned me around and gently propelled me out the door.

Oh, I would stay in touch all right!

Chapter 3
Up to da Lake

On Sunday morning, I delivered Sherlock Holmes to Martha Todd, told her I would call her early in the week, and drove to the Glock Family Resort, arriving at the 2:00 P.M. check-in time after stopping in Alexandria for a cheeseburger and fries.

Minnesota is the Land of 10,000 Lakes — it even says so on the license plates — and at least a dozen lie within a twenty-five-mile radius of Alexandria, a city of about 8,800 souls. The waters filling these glacially scoured basins run clear and cold, creating a prime habitat for pan fish, pike, and the king of Minnesota fishes, the walleye.

Herman Glock's father, Gerhard, started the family's resort by building a lodge of pine logs within the proverbial stone's throw of a freeform lake about twenty miles from the city. He built his dock at the base of a sheltered inlet, from which boaters can gain access to broader, deeper waters by passing between two wooded points of land about half a mile out.

When vacationers began flocking to Gerhard Glock's lodge in such numbers that it was filled all summer, he began building one- and two-bedroom log cabins to handle the overflow. These cabins were sprinkled amid the pines and birches that covered the fifty-acre complex.

Gerhard eventually retired and turned the reins over to Herman and Herman's wife, Ingeborg. When the family fishing vacation trade declined, Herman added the theater, also of log construction, and business boomed again for more than a score of years. Now a ghost, or something more substantial, was endangering the future of the Glock Family Theatre. How could any warm-blooded reporter stay away from a hot story like this?

My cabin stood on a knoll about fifty feet from the lake, and was shaded by thirty-foot-tall, second-growth pines. The interior, which was about twenty by fifteen feet, was divided into three spaces — a kitchen-dining area, a bedroom, and a bathroom so small that my knees rubbed against the door if I closed it when I sat on the john.

The kitchen-dining area occupied the first ten feet inside the door and ran crosswise the full width of the cabin. Jammed against the wall that separated this

Stage Fright

room from the bedroom was an overstuffed armchair that looked out of place in this confined space.

The bathroom was on the left and the bedroom on the right at the rear of the cabin. The ten-by-ten bedroom contained a four-drawer pinewood dresser and two single beds, one on each side of a nightstand with a chipped blond veneer finish. Upon opening the drawer, I found the requisite Gideon Bible. Hallelujah!

The place wasn't listed on the AAA register of luxury accommodations, but it looked and smelled clean. I had noticed this virtue in the main lodge and even in the theater the previous week while I was interviewing Ding Dong Bell. It was obvious that my host and hostess, Herman and Ingeborg Glock, were sticklers for cleanliness.

I stuffed the contents of my suitcase into the two bottom drawers of the dresser, hoping that the top drawer would be filled the following Friday by Martha Todd, and ambled downhill to conduct a more thorough exploration of the main lodge. When I checked in, I was told that the lodge contained a dining room, where lunch was served at noon and dinner could be purchased from 6:00 to 8:00 P.M., and a bar. The latter was opened Monday through Saturday at 11:00 A.M. and closed at 1:00 A.M. in accordance with Minnesota law. Since I don't drink alcohol, my main interest was the dining room. However, I figured the bar might be the best place to find members of the cast for *Long Night's Journey Into Day* after a rehearsal.

What I found immediately upon entering the lodge was Alan Jeffrey and family, who were just checking in. I got a hearty hug from Carol, a polite greeting from Kristin and Kevin, and a request for physical assistance from Al.

"We got a shit load of stuff to unload," he said, pointing to his twelve-year-old, brown-and-rust-colored Chevy van.

"I'm not licensed to do menial labor," I said. "How well do you tip?"

"He's the world's worst tipper," Carol said. "If I were you, I'd tiptoe away."

"If I do that, Al will tip over and make you carry all the heavy stuff," I said. "Lead me to your luggage."

The Jeffreys had a two-bedroom cabin a stone's throw from the lake. I know this measurement is accurate because the first thing Kevin did was chuck a rock into the water from the foot of the front steps. The land sloped gently from those steps to a strip of sandy beach that led to the boat docks. Beyond the twin points marking the inlet, the lake spread out over several square miles.

The name Minnesota means "land of sky-blue waters," and the water in this lake fit the description to a T. A summery breeze from the southwest was ruffling the surface into a slight ripple that flashed multiple reflections of the sun, creating a scene that could have graced a postcard.

The scene inside was not quite as utopian. The Jeffreys' living quarters were slightly larger than mine — there was even a rocking chair that fit in one corner — but the bedrooms were so cramped that an adult had to turn sideways to walk between the dressers and the beds.

Carol looked around the bedroom that she and Al would be using and said, "There aren't any closets to hang things in."

Because I hadn't brought any clothes that needed to be hung on anything more spacious than a doorknob, I hadn't noticed this shortcoming.

Part of the Glock Family Resort package was the use of an aluminum fishing boat with a six-horsepower motor. At the urging of their children, Al and Carol decided to take a boat ride on the lake after they finished unpacking. I declined their offer to ride along and instead went looking for Ding Dong Bell.

On my previous visit, I had learned that Ding Dong was in room 203 in the main lodge. I called that number on the house phone and got no answer. I located the bar and peeked in to see if he was there. No luck. Finally, I walked over to the theater, found a side door near the back of the building that wasn't locked, and let myself in.

I was in the scene shop, off stage right. The door between the shop and the backstage area was open and I could hear two male voices coming from the other side of the flats that formed the set. I cocked an ear and listened. The voices were muffled by the flats, but neither of them sounded like Ding Dong's.

Were these the Glock Family Theatre ghosts? They didn't sound that spooky, but there was only one way to find out. I cracked open a door — the same one that had been used to let loose the sandbag — and peeked.

The voices were coming from tech director Jimmy Storrs and another man in khaki coveralls whose back was toward me. They were wielding paintbrushes, putting some final touches on the set. Thinking that maybe they could tell me where to find Ding Dong, I opened the door, stepped through and said, "Hi."

I might as well have fired a shotgun directly over their heads. Jimmy dropped his brush as he whirled ninety degrees to face me, and the other man spun around, took a step back and kicked over the bucket of paint.

Jimmy's eyes were open so wide that I could almost look through and see inside his head.

"Jeez, don't sneak up like that!" he said. His cohort was staring at me the way a raccoon crossing the road looks at a truck just before the wheels squash him into the pavement.

"Sorry," I said. "I didn't mean to shake you up. I was just hoping you could tell me where the director is."

"You're the guy from the paper, aren't you?" asked Jimmy.

"I'm the reporter from the *St. Paul Daily Dispatch*," I said, emphasizing the word "reporter." "The guy from the paper" is too generic a description to suit me.

Jimmy stooped to retrieve his paintbrush. "We weren't expecting no company."

The other man blinked out of his trance and turned to pick up the overturned paint bucket. A beige puddle was creeping like a volcanic lava flow across the floor toward the edge of a circular oriental rug that covered the middle of the stage. The man dropped to his knees, blocked the puddle's progress with his paintbrush and called to Jimmy for help. Together they began sopping up paint with their brushes and squeezing it back into the can.

"Can I do something?" I asked.

"There's rags and paper towels in the scene shop," Jimmy said.

I hustled out, found a roll of paper towels, and joined the cleanup crew.

"I'm really sorry," I said as I stretched a strip of paper towels between the paint and the Oriental rug. "I had no idea I'd shake you up like that."

"It's just that there's been so much shit going on," said Jimmy. "Everybody's nerves are on edge."

"What kind of shit?" I asked. "More falling sandbags?"

"Nothing that bad. Just a lot of shit. We ain't supposed to talk about it. Orders from on high."

"From Herman Glock?"

"You got it."

Figuring that this meant I would get nothing from Jimmy, I asked where Ding Dong Bell could be found.

"He's gone on down to Minneapolis until tomorrow night," Jimmy said. "Said he needed to get away and spend some time in the city. He'll be back for tomorrow night's rehearsal at seven."

"How's the show coming?" I asked.

"It's not that bad — considering that everybody's so up tight. We got a free preview for the folks from the Alexandria senior center coming up Thursday night, and we got our first paying audience coming in on Friday. I just hope nothing else goes wrong on them nights."

"What could go wrong?"

17

Glenn Ickler

Jimmy shook his head. "Like I told you, we got orders not to talk about any of the shit that's been going on."

"Far be it from me to get you fired. Maybe I'll go talk to Herman."

"Good luck. Herman's so worried about the show flopping and the theater going down the toilet that I don't think he'll give you the time of day."

"Well, I'll see if he's wearing a watch. Sorry again for causing all this trouble."

"That's okay — it could be worse," Jimmy said.

I made my exit, stage right, and went to hunt up Herman Glock. I found him in the dining room, overseeing the set-up for the evening meal.

"You're the guy from the paper, aren't you?" said Herman after I introduced myself.

"I'm the reporter from the *St. Paul Daily Dispatch*," I said, again emphasizing the word "reporter."

"So what brings you back here? I thought you were done talking to Ding Dong."

"I was. That story is all written, and you can read it in this morning's paper. I liked your place so much that I booked a week in one of your cabins. I'm on vacation."

"Does being on vacation mean you won't be snooping around asking questions about the theater?"

"I can't promise you that. I am interested in your ghost, or whatever it is that's causing problems with the rehearsals."

"There aren't any problems with the rehearsals."

"How about the falling sandbag I saw nearly clobber an actress?"

"There's been nothing like that since. Everything's normal."

The temptation to call him a liar was offset by my concern for Jimmy Storrs's job security, so I played it cool.

"I'm glad to hear that," I said. "Are you sold out for opening night?"

"We're sold out for the whole opening weekend — Friday and Saturday nights and the Sunday matinee. Once the word gets out that we've got a terrifically funny show, we'll sell out the rest of the run."

I wondered if he really believed what he was saying.

"That's great," I said. "It's a problem for me, though, because I was hoping to get four seats for Friday night."

"Why four seats?"

"The photographer who was with me last week when I talked to Ding Dong is also here on vacation. His wife is with him, and I'm hoping to have a guest."

Stage Fright

"I'll find you some seats," Herman said. "We can set up some folding chairs if we have to. But if you write anything, you have to lay off this crap about a ghost. As you know, this is a make-or-break production for us."

"I promise to exercise the utmost discretion," I said. "I'd hate to see your theater go belly up because of anything I wrote."

This was true, but it didn't mean I would abandon my quest. Ding Dong had complained about weird happenings and Jimmy had talked about a lot of shit going on. I wanted to find out what all the weird shit was and who or what was causing it. Once I had the facts, I'd decide what to write.

Ding Dong would be back in about twenty-four hours. Until then I could amuse myself with some light reading, some heavy eating and maybe a modicum of walleye fishing. I had taken the precaution of bringing along a cushion for the boat seat.

The cushion was put to use that evening. Al suggested that the adult males in the party do some after-dinner walleye fishing, so I grabbed the cushion, a casting rod, and my tackle box, and joined him for what turned out to be a sunset cruise.

It was close to the summer solstice, when the sun doesn't disappear until after nine o'clock in western Minnesota. This meant we could fish for more than an hour and still return to the dock in daylight. At least that was the plan.

The fishing went fine. We even caught a couple of keepers. It was the return trip that got us into trouble.

With Al running the little, six-horse motor, we went out of the inlet on which the resort was located, passed a heavily wooded point of land on our left and cruised into a broad bay, where we let out our trolling lines. At about 8:30, we decided it was time to reel in and head for home.

Al steered toward the point with the thick grove of trees and gradually increased our speed. We rounded the point about ten yards from the shoreline, which was much closer than we had been going out. The bay we had been fishing in disappeared from view behind us and we saw the light come on at Herman Glock's dock ahead of us. Suddenly there was a grinding, scraping sound beneath us that rattled the fillings in my teeth. My ribs banged against the side of the boat as we screeched to a halt. At the same time, the tiller bucked and bounced out of Al's hand as the propeller hit bottom and the motor quit running.

Our boat was standing still atop a bar of sand and gravel that extended into the lake on the Glock Family Resort side of the point. We had been far enough away from the woods to miss this unseen hazard to navigation on the way out, but now we were aground on the gravel without engine power.

"We snapped a shear pin," Al said after a quick look. "It's a good thing or we would have wrecked the prop on Herman's motor."

Fortunately, Herman's boats also came equipped with oars. I moved from the bow to the middle seat and pushed against the bottom with one oar, poling us slowly forward. A few additional shoves and we were off the bar and floating free. I picked up the other oar, inserted both into the oarlocks and started rowing toward the light.

"I knew I brought you along for a reason," Al said. "You're a lot better rower than either one of my kids would be."

"I always like to get my oar in," I said.

"Should I sing 'Row, Row, Row Your Boat?'"

"If you sing anything but 'Far, Far Away' I'm going overboard."

It took much longer to cover the distance to the dock when propelled by one manpower than it did with six horsepower, so it was a good half hour past sundown before we reached our destination. We were greeted by Herman Glock, who had been summoned by Carol when we didn't arrive home before dark. Carol and the kids were also there.

"Bet you hit the sandbar around this side of the point, didn't you?" said Herman. "I should have warned you about it but I clean forgot."

"We knocked off a shear pin," Al said. "But it looks like the prop's okay."

"No problem. I'll fix it up and have you ready to go back out in the morning. Sorry I didn't tell you guys about that sandbar."

"I guarantee you we'll remember that it's there," I said.

Chapter 4
The Other Shoe

"Have you seen yourself in our paper?" I asked Ding Dong Bell when Al and I found him in the dining room at suppertime on Monday.

"No, I haven't," he said, taking the Sunday Arts section from my hand. "Do you schmucks always travel a hundred miles to deliver your stories to the subject in person?"

"Not hardly," I said. "We're here for a week's vacation. We both liked the place so much that we came back to relax and do a little fishing. We're also hoping you don't mind if we sit in on your final week's rehearsals."

"Why the hell would you want to do that?"

"I've done community theater myself, and the process fascinates me," I said.

"I think it would be fun to watch a real Broadway director at work," said Al. "I'll even shoot some pix of the scenes, if you'd like."

"You're not writing any stories while you're on vacation are you, Mr. Mitchell?" Ding Dong asked.

"I don't usually work on my own time," I said, dodging his loaded question with a truthful reply.

"Tell you what," he said. "I'll read what you wrote about me in this paper, and if my ego is satisfied I'll let you sit through as many rehearsals as you can stand without being bored out of your mind — and God knows that won't be many. Come around at seven o'clock, and I'll either invite you to sit down or have your asses thrown out of the theater and into the lake."

"Fair enough," I said. "And one other thing while we're talking. Now that the story is in print, will you tell me how you got your nickname?" Ding Dong had refused to reveal this during the interview because he didn't trust me to keep it out of my story.

"You swear to me that this is off the record?" he asked.

"I swear it on a stack of style books," I said.

"Okay. When my parents, God rest'em, named me Duncan Dunworthy Bell, they were hoping that my two rich grandfathers, Duncan Bell and Herbert Dunworthy, would look to me as their favorite grandchild and that this feeling of favoritism would be reflected in what they left me in their wills. As for me, I came to hate that name because all through grade school the kids would call me either Dunky or Dummy, so when I went away to boarding school in the eighth grade I signed all my registration forms as 'D. D. Bell.' So what happens? First day of school, the son of a bitch math teacher looks at my name on the roll call sheet and says, 'D. D. Bell. I'll bet that stands for Ding Dong.' Well, you better believe the little schmucks in my class picked that up in a hurry, and it's been nothing but Ding Dong ever since."

"Well, it is unique. Did your grandfathers come through for you in their wills?"

"Son of a bitch, no! Papa Bell left all his money to a shelter for retired greyhound racing dogs, and Granddad Dunworthy willed his fortune to a pretty-boy television evangelist that lured him away from the Jewish faith. I think the schmuck used Granddad's money to buy crystal doorknobs for his thirty-seven-room mansion in the Hollywood hills."

"That's a shame," Al said. "But you've done very well for yourself without their money."

"I can't complain," said Ding Dong. "Now I'm gonna go read this paper and see if I should complain about that. See you schmucks later."

As we walked back to our table to join Carol and the kids, Al said, "I hope you flattered the shit out of him in that story."

"How could I not?" I said. "The man's an award-winning, big-time director who is doing a wonderful favor for an old friend. When he reads my piece, his ego should have a veritable feast."

"Well, wherever ego, we go," Al said.

"Id figures," I replied.

Ding Dong did not have us thrown into the lake when we appeared in the theater a few minutes before seven. He shook hands with both of us, said my story was "much too kind" and thanked Al for pictures that he said made him look "ten years younger and fifty pounds thinner."

"Some son of a bitch at the *New York Times* wrote that I looked 'porcine,'" Ding Dong said. "Your pictures make me look portly instead of porky, don't you think?"

"Absolutely," I said. "That New York writer is a fathead."

"Hey, I like that," Ding Dong said, with a smile still lighting up his face, which really did remind me of Porky Pig. "Sit anywhere you want." We were about to park ourselves on the aisle about halfway back when Herman Glock walked in from the foyer accompanied by two men who looked like they were entering a funeral home at the beginning of a wake.

"Oh, oh!" said Ding Dong. "Herm's board of directors is here."

"He has a board of directors?" Al said.

"Yeah he does. He told me that the law required him to set up a board in order to incorporate the theater as a separate business from the resort, which he wanted to do in case the theater didn't fly."

Herman and his duo of doleful board members took seats in the back row without coming forward to say hello to Ding Dong. Herman said something in a half-whisper, and the two board members turned their eyes toward Al and me. Seeing no welcoming smiles, we both decided not to wave a cheery hello.

"The schmuck on the left is the chairman of the board, Oscar Olson," Ding Dong said. "He owns that big new car dealership you passed on your way out here. The one in the dark gray suit is Gordon Glanz. He's president of the biggest bank in town."

"I'm impressed," I said. "Apparently the big money powers in town are giving this theater a lot of support."

"They're also giving Herm a lot of shit about losing money for the last three years. He's sure that the majority of the board will vote to close the theater if this season is another loser."

"They could do that?" I asked.

"Herm says the board has the power to shut down the theater by majority vote. But I shouldn't be telling tales to a reporter, so I'm going to shut my trap and start my rehearsal. Like I said, sit anywhere you want." He rumbled down to the front row, sat down, clapped his hands, and yelled, "Places for act one, please!"

Where we wanted to sit was as far as possible from Herman Glock and his two tight-ass companions. We chose the third row, center, and watched the action unfold in the fancy brothel that Jimmy Storrs and his crew had created.

We saw obvious improvement over the previous week's rehearsal. Some rough spots in the timing had been smoothed out, and the actors were more comfortable with their lines and blocking. The bawdy slapstick script was genuinely funny, and the cast was doing an acceptable job of bringing it to life. Yet we could sense tension in the air — a feeling that everyone on stage was waiting for something to happen, something that wasn't in the script. This feeling was so pervasive that Al and I looked at each other midway through the first act and Al whispered, "I feel like I'm waiting for the other shoe to drop."

"You're not the sole worrier," I said. "The whole cast is laced up tight."

"You're right. It's a wonder their tongues work at all."

Act One ended without incident, and Ding Dong told the cast to "take five." We went forward to talk to him and noted, as we faced the rear of the theater, that the members of the executive trio were staying in their back row seats.

"Doesn't look too bad," I said to Ding Dong.

"They're doing fine," he said. "It would be a great show if the people could just relax and have fun with it."

"I get the feeling that they're expecting an unpleasant surprise, like a falling sandbag," said Al.

"You won't see anything like that," said Ding Dong. "I've got Jimmy checking for sandbags every night."

"What will we see?" I asked.

"Nothing but what the playwright wrote, I hope."

"How is the cast getting along?" I asked. "Last week you said you'd made some mistakes in who you picked."

"You don't see much friendly chit chat during the breaks, but so far there haven't been any fist fights or hair pulling," said Ding Dong. "There does seem to be something extra cold going on between Angela and the two guys who were banging her."

"Which one is Angela?" I asked.

"The frizzy-haired blonde with the really big tits who's playing the whore called Sheba. Her full name is Angela Maguire. Those two guys, Eric and Andy, used to hang all over her, but now it's like none of the three are speaking to the other two."

I had noticed Sheba. In addition to the really big tits, she had extra-long sun-tanned legs that were connected to a generous ass that curved exactly where a woman's ass is supposed to curve. All of these goodies were being displayed in an over-stressed white T-shirt and a butt-hugging pair of red shorts that barely reached the bottoms of her buns. Her well-tanned face, which was framed by a fashionably-frizzy mop of blonde hair with dark roots, featured two dazzling dark eyes fringed with long lashes, a short, upturned nose, and a pouty mouth that always looked ready to be kissed. I estimated her height at six feet even and her age at about twenty-two or three. Oh, yes, I had noticed not-so-little Sheba! And I could see why Eric and Andy would want to hang all over her.

"Okay, it's time to get this show back on the road," said Ding Dong. "Places for act two, please!"

Alice Prewitt, otherwise known as Tania, opened the second act with the line, "Dahling, are you theah?" and nothing fell from the ceiling. The rehearsal rolled on,

Stage Fright

and after about ten minutes I was actually getting a feeling of relaxation from the actors.

Then the other shoe dropped.

Rhonda Lapierre, who was playing Mamie, the madam, was built like an old-time opera soprano — low and wide. In fact, Al's description of her to Carol was, "If she was an inch taller, she'd be perfectly round." If I had to guess her weight, I'd say it was a few pounds over 200. I'd guess her height at an inch or two over five-feet.

Mamie's line was, "I'm taking a firm stand on that." She then plopped herself down solidly onto a straight-backed wooden chair. We were stunned to see all four legs snap and splay out around the falling seat like rays around the sun.

After the seat-full of madam hit the stage with a thud, the only sound heard was Rhonda's cry of pain. While the people on stage stood frozen in a tableaux of suspended animation, Ding Dong leaped from his seat and rolled up the steps shouting, "Son of a bitch! Rhonda, are you all right?"

"My back!" Rhonda said. "I think I broke my back!"

Ding Dong's hand was on her shoulder. "Don't move!" he said. "Don't try to get up. Somebody call for a doctor."

A voice from the back of theater said, "I'll get an ambulance right away." Herman Glock ran out through the swinging double doors to use the phone in the foyer. His two companions had risen from their seats. They stood in the aisle shaking their heads and looking even gloomier than before.

The next ten minutes dragged as Rhonda sat with her stubby legs sticking straight out in front of her, all the while uttering a steady stream of groans and expletives. Ding Dong tried to comfort her while the rest of the cast members, including Norman "Frenchy" Lapierre, Rhonda's ex-husband, stood around staring and looking uncomfortable. Those who were on speaking terms occasionally whispered to each other, but mostly they just stood and stared until two burly (thank God) EMTs came down the aisle with a gurney and a backboard.

They slid the backboard carefully down behind Rhonda. Next they asked for help, and with the assistance of the two sturdy young men I figured were Eric and Andy, they tipped the chair gently onto its back. The EMTs slid the backboard onto the collapsed gurney, popped up the legs, and following Ding Dong, wheeled Rhonda off the set and out through the ground-level scene shop door.

We heard the ambulance roar away, and Al said, "This might be the straw that broke the camel's back." He was nodding toward Herman and the two board members, who were huddling at the back of the house.

"Let's hope it didn't break Rhonda's back," I said. "Ding Dong could never replace her this close to opening."

"This could go down in theater history as the show that closed before it opened."

"And this could be the company that closed its season before opening night."

Chapter 5
Fishing for an Angle

"What really pisses me off is that it has to be some son of a bitch inside the group that is doing this shit," said Ding Dong. Al and I had found him in the dining room shortly after noon on Tuesday, and we sat ourselves down at his table in hopes of picking up some more information.

"It's gotta be somebody that knows the script," Ding Dong continued. "Those chair legs were cut just right to bust when Rhonda plopped herself down full force. Six other people sat on that chair last night before she broke it, but they were all a hell of a lot lighter than Rhonda."

"You said Rhonda and her husband just went through a nasty divorce. Could he have booby-trapped the chair?"

"I don't think Frenchy knows enough about carpentry to make the right kind of saw cuts. And I also don't think this was personal. I think some son of a bitch is trying to wreck this show."

"Okay, that theory fits with the sandbag bomb," I said. "But why would somebody involved in the show be trying to wreck it?"

"I'll be a son of a bitch if I know," Ding Dong said. "All I know is that if this show doesn't fill the house, Herm could lose his theater. But you can't print that I said that, Mr. Mitchell! Do you hear me?"

"I hear you. And you're right. I can't print it without getting information from Herman and from the chairman of the board. What was his name again?"

"Oscar Olson. But I doubt like hell that he'll talk to you about finances and I know Herm won't tell you anything. This ain't the kind of shit anybody wants to see in the paper."

"There are two sides to that question," I said. "It's possible that going public with a story about sabotage, if that's what it is, could scare off the saboteur and at the same time create more interest in the show."

"Yeah, that's what they tell you in New York, too, right before they fuck you over royally on the TV or in the paper," said Ding Dong. "I've already told you more than I should have, so I'm shutting up. If you want to talk to Herm or to that Olson guy, be my guest." He turned his attention to the sandwich on his plate.

"I do want to talk to them. And I hope we can sit in on tonight's rehearsal."

"I got no objection to that," he said through a mouthful of pastrami on rye. "Tonight's their first time in full costume. Tomorrow it's costumes and full make-up. Then Thursday, if we've still got a cast, we do a free performance for the people from the senior center."

"Speaking of the cast, how about Rhonda?" Al asked. "How bad is her back?"

"Her back ain't broke, but it hurts like a son of a bitch," said Ding Dong. "I talked to her this morning, and she said they gave her a shit load of pain pills and told her to stay off her feet for a week. That will be a pretty short week because it will end Thursday night when the audience walks in. Until then, she'll be sitting in a chair and saying her lines."

"Will you have Jimmy checking all the chairs along with the overhead rigging?"

"I'll have Jimmy checking every son of a bitching thing I can think of."

I had to find a story angle, so I decided to bait Herman and see if I could get a nibble. I found the resort owner sitting in a boat that was tied up to the dock. He had taken apart a balky, twenty-horsepower outboard motor and was examining the pieces.

"You really have to be a jack of all trades to operate this business," I said for openers. "Mechanic, carpenter, fishing guide, innkeeper, restaurateur, theater producer, board chairman …" I left the sentence dangling, and Herman grabbed the hook.

"Not board chairman," he said. "That was the board chairman and the treasurer who were with me at the rehearsal last night."

"Oh, really?" I said in my best imitation of innocent ignorance. "Ding Dong mentioned something about them being on the board, but I assumed you would be the chairman since it's your theater."

"That's not the way it works. I'm the CEO, but I report to the chairman of the board. We had to do it that way for fiscal reasons. But I'm sure you're not interested in the boring details."

Like hell I wasn't. "Your whole operation here is interesting," I said. "I just assumed that the theater was an integral part of your resort."

"Well, it's not. How come you're not out fishing on a beautiful day like this?"

It was a beautiful day. The sun was high in an intense blue sky that was decorated with puffy white clouds, a soft, early summer breeze was blowing from the west, and the temperature was in the mid-seventies. "My fishing buddy is out with his family right now," I said. "We're going out after walleyes later this afternoon when his wife decides she's had enough sun."

Stage Fright

"Actually, the best time for walleyes is at dusk and after dark," Herman said. "Instead of wasting your time at Ding Dong's rehearsal last night you could have been out catching some big ones."

I wanted to say that there was an even bigger one who needed catching in the Glock Family Theatre. Instead, I said, "I'm more of a theater buff than I am a fisherman. I don't consider watching Ding Dong put the finishing touches on this production to be a waste of time."

"Well, whatever floats your boat," Herman said. He was bending over the motor, putting the pieces together and talking with his back to me, clearly hoping I would leave.

"I hope I'm not a jinx, though. Both times I've been at a rehearsal something bad has happened."

"It's not just you," he said. "I think Ding Dong already told you that there's been other things on other nights."

"He has mentioned that, but he's never said what they were."

"That's because I told him not to." Herman tightened the last screw, gave two unsuccessful pulls on the starter rope, and turned toward me with a satisfied look when the motor popped to life on the third try. "And I'm practicing what I preach, Mr. Mitchell. You're not going to get any more information out of me, either."

"Not even to help save your theater?" I had to shout over the roar of the motor to make him hear me.

He gave me a look that would ice a whole stringer full of walleyes, shut down the motor, and said, "My theater doesn't need saving, Mr. Mitchell."

"You've lost money for three years in a row, and you said yourself the board of directors is in control. Doesn't that worry you?"

"Not in the least," he lied. "My board would never close this theater just because it was losing a few dollars a year."

"I hope you're right," I said. "But it might depend on how many of those few dollars a year you were losing."

Herman pasted on a smile that reminded me of a bride's father greeting the 200th guest in the receiving line. "Enjoy your afternoon, good luck with the fishing, and have a good time at tonight's rehearsal if that's what you're planning to do," he said. "Now I have to go tackle my next project. I'm a jack of all trades, you know." He climbed out of the boat and walked away, leaving me adrift on the dock.

It was time to interview Oscar Olson at his auto dealership. I decided to let my fingers do the initial walking and checked out the yellow pages. The number for Oscar Olson Motor Sales, Inc., was easy to find — they had a half-page ad. I punched in the number, and waded through the menu of press one, press two, press three. Eventually I encountered a live female voice and asked to speak with Mr. Olson.

"I'm sorry, but Mr. Olson is in a meeting right now," said the live female voice. "May I take a message?"

Knowing the frequency with which corporate presidents return calls to newspaper reporters, I explained that I would be "in and out," said it might be better if I tried to call again later and asked what time Mr. Olson might be available.

"He probably won't be out of the meeting before 3:30," she said. "And even then he has a full schedule of appointments until he leaves at five. Would you like to schedule an appointment for tomorrow?"

Since a face-to-face meeting was what I really was angling for, I said yes. She found an opening at 1:30 P.M., took my name and the number at which I could be reached and instructed me to "have a good day."

I hung up wondering what would happen in the morning. Would Oscar Olson recognize my name and have his secretary phone me with a reason we couldn't meet? Would he welcome me with a line of bullshit about the financial condition and future prospects of the Glock Family Theatre? Or would he tell me the theater was in as much trouble as Ding Dong Bell believed it to be? Well, I'd find out tomorrow, wouldn't I? Meanwhile, there were walleyes to be teased.

Al and his crew were piling out of their boat when I walked down to the dock. In the lead was an excited Kevin, who was holding up a stringer decorated with six yellow perch the length of a dollar bill and shouting, "Look, Uncle Mitch! Look what me and Kristin caught!"

"Kristin and I," said teacher Carol to her son. To me, she said, "We're going to clean them — or, I should say Al is going to clean them — and have them for breakfast tomorrow. Care to join us?"

I looked at the six little fish, tried to picture them minus heads, tails and fins and decided that French toast and bacon in the lodge dining room was a more promising choice. Carol's expression showed that she agreed.

After the dutiful father had cleaned his children's catch, Al and I relaxed on wooden lawn chairs in the shade, and I told him how little I had learned. Shortly before the time we planned to go fishing, a blanket of dark clouds rolled across the sun, accompanied by a northwest wind that chilled the air and turned the mirror-smooth surface of the lake into a ragged array of choppy waves. We were wondering whether it would be wise to leave the dock under those conditions when the first rank of icy raindrops smacked us in the face and settled the question.

Stage Fright

Margie was an uncompromising perfectionist and an incurable worrywart, she seemed always to be less than five minutes away from a nervous breakdown. I could imagine what an ass-reaming over a bounding bunny would do to her.

"I'm surprised Margie is still with the show," I said.

"She like went home bawling, but she came back the next night," said Angie. Another gulp and she was halfway through her second drink. I began to wonder what her capacity was and whether I would wind up carrying her home.

Still seeking information, I asked, "Do you remember any other incidents?"

She scrunched up her face so that her eyes closed and her nose tilted skyward. "Oh, yeah! Like I almost forgot to tell you about the phone call."

"What about the phone call?"

"You know the scene where I'm in the living room and the phone like rings and I pick it up?" I nodded and she continued. "Well, just the other night I picked up the phone and like put it up to my ear and I felt something gooey — and it smelled bad. Would you believe that some asshole had like smeared the phone with dog shit? Jeez, I almost puked right there on the stage!" The memory of the moment caused her to chug-a-lug the remainder of her rum and coke.

After pressing my fist hard against my lips to stave off a laugh, I said, "I take it you don't think the doggie-do came from the ghost?"

"This was no ghos'," she said. "This was like Ding Dong said, some sumbitch tryin'a wreck the show."

The fact that Angie had begun blurring her plosives and glottal stops alarmed me. I wanted her to be able to make her way home without my assistance. She was holding herself upright on the stool by propping her arms on the bar, and her eyes had the glassy look of someone who isn't quite focusing on the landscape. I decided it was time to stop baiting the sucker and head for dry land.

"Well, it's time for me to turn in," I said. "It's been nice talking to you."

"You not gonna buy me 'nother li'l drinkie poo?" Angie said.

"It's past my bedtime, Angie. Gotta get up and go chasing after walleyes bright and early in the morning." Still, I felt I had to be polite and make the offer, so I added, "Can I walk you home?"

"No thanks. Gonna have 'nother drinkie poo, even if you're like too cheap to buy me one," she said, waving at the bartender. "This girlie needs one more for the road. Like set'em up, Joe!"

That scared me. "You're not driving somewhere are you?" I asked.

Angie shook her head with such vigor that the momentum almost toppled her off the stool. "Walkin'," she said. "Got a cabin here 'til rehearsals are over. Me an'

Julie took this week off from work an' we're like sharin' a cabin." Julie was playing Salome, the third prostitute in the show.

"Where do you work?" I asked.

"At the bank."

"Which bank is 'the bank?'"

"Douglas State Bank, of course, silly," she said. "I'm like a cus'omer service specialist. This week the goddamn cus'omers aren't bein' serviced." She giggled at her own double entendre.

"That wouldn't be the bank where Gordon Glanz is president, would it?"

"Yeah, it is. You know Mis'er Glanz?"

"No, but I hope to meet him soon," I said. "Maybe you can introduce me sometime." I started to say good night, but another question popped into my brain. "Does Julie work at the bank too?"

"Oh, no," Angie said. "Julie works at Oom."

"Julie works at where?"

"At Oom. Tha's what we call Oscar Olson Motors. Don't'cha get it? O-O-M spells Oom."

"Got it. And with that, I think I'll say good night. See you tomorrow."

"Swee' dreams," said Angie. "Don' take no wooden wampum from no ghos'!"

Ah, yes, the ghost. Tomorrow morning Al and I would have to discuss the best way to spy on a spook.

Stage Fright

"See you at supper," Al said as he started toward his cabin at a trot.

"Yeah, see you!" I replied as I began running for my front door. I almost made it before the clouds burst open and the wind-driven rain poured down with the intensity that my dairy farmer uncle always described as "like a cow pissing on a flat rock." The thirty-second drenching I received before I reached the cabin fit my mood perfectly.

The rainy weather did not improve during that evening's dress rehearsal, but my damp, dreary mood did. First, the addition of costumes brightened the stage and seemed to energize the actors, even though the air of anxiety could still be felt. The whores were all enticing in their scanty outfits, especially Angela Maguire in a red teddy that was a smidgen too short on both ends.

Second — and this was the big one — the rehearsal went off without any unscheduled events. No falling sandbags, no breaking chairs, no deviations either from the playwright's script or the director's blocking. No pranks by any ghost, Indian or otherwise. As the lights went down at the end of the second act, I could feel the tension drain from my body, and I heard Al give a long, relieved sigh.

The lights went back up, and a jubilant cast gathered on stage for the director's notes. As for Ding Dong, he wore a smile as wide as Alice's Cheshire cat. After his notes, which were brief and positive, the actors went to the dressing rooms with light steps and happy faces. There was even some buzzing chitchat in place of the stunned silences and concerned babble of questions Al and I had heard during our previous visits.

Ding Dong's smile was still stretching from one ear to the other when we approached him. "Son of a bitch!" he said. "This is what we needed! I can't remember the last time we made it through a whole rehearsal without some kind of fuck up."

"We've seen two of them," I said, hoping to catch him off guard. "What were some of the others?"

He opened his mouth to answer but stopped to look at me, then at Al, and finally back at me again. "Nice try, schmuck," he said. "But you know I ain't talking to you about any of that shit."

"Maybe it's over," Al said. "What can it hurt to tell us what's been going on?"

"Maybe yes and maybe no," Ding Dong said. "How much did Herm tell you?"

"Not even as much as you have," I admitted. "In fact, your friend Herman seems very confident that the board will not vote to close his theater no matter what happens."

Ding Dong's expression told me that he still believed otherwise, but he stayed loyal to his pal and the party line. "Good! If Herm says there's no problem, then there's no problem," said the director. "Now I'm going to talk to the costume people about making some minor fixes. Until tomorrow, gentlemen."

"Don't let them do anything to that red teddy that Angela's almost wearing," I said as he walked away. He raised his right hand and gave me a thumb's up.

Al and I adjourned to the bar, where he consumed a draft beer and I sipped a cold ginger ale with no ice. You get more that way.

"Do you really think Ding Dong's troubles are over?" I asked.

"I think this was the lull before the storm," Al said. "I think whoever is messing with these rehearsals laid off tonight because he has a real show-stopper planned for Thursday or Friday night, and he didn't want to scare away the cast before then."

"I have that same feeling. Somebody needs to catch the bastard before then."

"The only way to do that is to set a twenty-four-hour ghost watch in the theater."

"Ding Dong told me that he suggested that after the sandbag incident, but the board wouldn't approve the cost of hiring enough people to work around the clock."

"Maybe we could take turns," Al said. "I've always wanted to be a stage star."

"That's a stellar idea," I said. "We could take turns watching for the ghost."

Al yawned. "Let's figure out a watch list in the morning," he said.

He went off to bed, leaving me sipping the last of my ginger ale and wondering why an Indian ghost would wait twenty-five years before haunting the Glock Family Theatre and who I could persuade to tell me about some of the other so-called "weird shit" that had gone on at *Long Night's Journey Into Day* rehearsals.

My straw was making that slurping noise at the bottom of the glass when the answer to my second question appeared on the bar stool next to me in the long-legged, full-breasted form of Angela Maguire.

Chapter 6
Pumping Angela

Angela was wearing a scarlet muscle shirt that ended two inches above her navel and showed so much cleavage that I could almost get another view of the aforementioned belly button by looking down through the top. Her bottom was covered just to the point of public decency by the abbreviated red shorts she had worn during the Sunday rehearsal, and her painted toenails gleamed like two rows of rubies through the tips of a pair of shiny red sandals. She seemed to have a thing for red, which was appropriate considering the role she was playing.

"Hi," she said. "You're the guy from the newspaper, aren't you?"

"I'm the reporter from the *St. Paul Daily Dispatch*," I said, punching the word "reporter" especially hard. "And you're the whore called Sheba? Right?"

"That's who I'm playing. My real name is Angie, and I'm a really nice girl."

"My real name is Mitch, and I'm a really nice guy."

"Would a really nice guy buy a really nice girl a drink?"

"Why not?" I summoned the bartender. Angie ordered a rum and coke, and I asked for another ginger ale, no ice.

"You're drinking ginger ale?" Angie asked.

"Can't have booze," I said. "I'm an alcoholic."

"That's really the shits. Can't you even like have one to keep me company?"

"If I have one, the only thing I'll be keeping company is the floor after I finish the sixth drink and pass out. No, I can't keep you company with alcohol, but I'll be happy to keep you company any other way you can think of."

"Ooh!" she said with a little squeal. "I can, like, think of lots of fun ways for a guy to keep me company."

I was sorely tempted to say something about the fun way two members of the cast were keeping her company, but I had more important fish to hook. As the drinks arrived, I said, "Tonight's rehearsal went pretty well, didn't it?"

"Yeah, it did." She took a hearty swig of the dark liquid in her glass.

"No sandbags falling, no chairs breaking," I said. "Must be a relief."

"Yeah, it is. There's been like a lot of shit happening because of the ghost."

"What's happened besides the sandbag and Rhonda's chair?" I was keeping my tone casual and my face blank, but when she looked away to pick up her drink again I reached into my shirt pocket and turned on the tape recorder.

"Oh, like it seems that something's been happening almost every night. Doors that are supposed to open one way get reversed, so they like swing the other way. The phone like rings when there's no cue for it to ring. Pictures like fall off the wall in the middle of a scene. Crazy shit like that."

"Nothing else as dangerous as the sandbag or the chair?"

"Oh, like one night the damn curtain came down in the middle of the second act and almost conked Andy on the head." The Glock Family Theatre had a proscenium stage with a heavy, roll-up curtain attached to a three-inch-diameter, wooden pole at the bottom. Normally this was dropped only at the end of every act. "It came right down behind him real fast while he was like telling the madam what a great lay I was — or, you know, Sheba was."

Passing up the obvious response, I said, "That would have given Andy quite a headache."

"It would have like knocked him colder than the ice cubes in this drink," she said, taking another healthy swallow from her glass. "Andy goes 'holy shit' and falls flat on his ass, the way Alice did when the sandbag almost landed on her head."

"Scary. Anything else you can think of?"

She did a bottoms up with the rum and coke, rattled the remainder of the ice cubes around in the bottom of the glass, and said, "Maybe there is. If you like buy me another drink."

"My pleasure," I said, signaling the bartender once more.

Angela waited until the fresh rum and coke was in her hand before she resumed her summary of rehearsal events. "One night the rabbit got loose," she said. "It like came hopping on stage right when Andy and Alice are in that big clinch and he's patting her on the ass and like telling her how soft and cuddly she is."

The rabbit normally was carried by a third whore named Salome, who talked continuously about using the bunny while servicing her customers. Thankfully, the script never specified how the long-eared lapin was involved in this activity.

"I know the scene," I said. In fact, I had been envious of Andy during this scene because Alice had an ass worthy of patting. "Ding Dong must have gone bullshit when the rabbit made it a threesome."

"He was pissed. He like yelled 'son of a bitch,' the way he always does, and gave Margie holy hell." Margie was the stage manager. She had bustled about the Glock Family Theatre in that capacity without pay for the last fifteen years. Because

Chapter 7
Haunt Hunting

The force with which Carol Jeffrey slapped two blueberry pancakes onto my plate made it plain that she was not pleased with my table talk. Al had invited me to have breakfast with his family in their cabin, and I had broached the subject of setting a port-and-starboard watch for the Glock Family Theatre ghost.

"I thought we were all here for a nice vacation," Carol said as she plopped two pancakes onto Al's plate with equal gusto. "Don't you two clowns ever think about anything but work?"

I confessed to having had an ulterior motive from the beginning.

She responded with the logical question. "You're the writer — why do you need Al? He's not going to take a picture of a ghost, is he?"

"He might," I said. "But the main thing is that one person can't watch the theater all day and half the night."

"I'll bet one person could if that one person was a reporter looking for a story."

Needing time to think of a response, I filled my mouth with a large chunk of fluffy blueberry pancake. In addition to being much too pretty and intelligent to be married to Al, Carol is one hell of a cook.

While I was chewing, Al came to my rescue. "Mitch and I need to work together on this," he said. "He would go even nuttier than he already is if he tried to stake out the stage all by himself. I'll take you guys out during the morning and evening hours when the fish are biting, and I'll hide in the theater in the heat of the day when the fish are dozing way down deep."

I swallowed my food, licked a smear of syrup off my upper lip, and said, "Al is right, although I'm not sure I agree wholeheartedly with his characterization of my current mental state."

"You plan to spend hours and hours of your vacation sitting in a dark empty theater and then you deny acting nutty?" asked Al.

"Insult me all you want to — I won't crack."

Carol grimaced, but she relaxed when I said I'd stand the first watch so the Jeffrey family could take advantage of the fabulous fishing weather. The sky was an unblemished blue as far as the eye could see, and a soft warm breeze from the west was raising rows of ripples that sparkled in the sunlight like crystal glasses in a detergent commercial. To complete the idyllic picture, a great blue heron stood motionless amid a patch of lily pads, watching for his breakfast to swim within range of his serpentine neck, not more than fifty feet from the cabin.

At nine o'clock, I wished the late-starting fisherpersons luck and walked casually toward the side door of the Glock Family Theatre, the one that opened into the scene shop. This time the damn thing was locked. So was the stage door at the rear of the building. I decided to be gutsy and try the twin glass doors at the front entrance. These, too, were locked. This was not in my plan. This was frustrating. This called for subterfuge.

At the front desk of the lodge, I asked the whereabouts of Herman Glock. The young woman on duty said he was repairing a washing machine in the laundry shed. I found him there, peering into the mechanism at the back of a machine that had been disconnected and turned 180 degrees. I explained to Herman that Al had left a camera in the theater after Monday night's rehearsal and had asked me to retrieve it while he took his family out fishing.

"I don't have time to run over there just now, Mr. Mitchell," Herman said.

"No need for you to waste your time," I said. "Just loan me a key for a few minutes. I'll get the camera and bring the key right back."

Herman's face said he didn't want to part with his key ring, but he unhooked it from his belt and held it toward me. From a jumble of at least two dozen jangling keys on the ring, he pulled one out and said, "This one opens the door to the scene shop."

"Thanks," I said. "I'll bring these right back." I did, too, after letting myself into the scene shop, navigating by the light of the open door to the rear stage door, and unlocking it to facilitate my return visit. I was even devious enough to grab my Nikon out of my car on the way back to the laundry shed. The Nikon was dangling from its strap in my hand when I gave the keys back to Herman and thanked him one more time.

As I had hoped he would, Herman spotted the camera. "Your friend is lucky that his camera was still there," he said. "Things have been known to disappear when they're left laying around that place." He took the keys with a greasy hand and went back to tearing apart the guts of the washing machine.

Taking care that nobody was within eyeshot, I slipped around behind the theater and let myself in. When I closed the door, I was plunged into almost total darkness. Not having any idea where to find a light switch, I waited until my sun-shrunken pupils widened enough to see the back of the cyclorama, followed it around to

Stage Fright

the end, slipped between the cyc and a teaser and found myself behind the set. Here I could see a bit better because of the daylight filtering in from the windows in the foyer.

My next problem was finding a hiding place. If the ghost appeared, would he, assuming the culprit was male, mess with something onstage or would his target be backstage? Where could I station myself to cover both areas?

I decided on a dark corner backstage near the entrance to the scene shop, my thought being that I would see anything that moved backstage and hear any movement that took place onstage. I dragged a folding chair out of the scene shop and sat down to wait, wishing there was a way to encase myself in an invisible lighted bubble and read the morning paper.

It turned out that my biggest problem was staying awake. After an hour in the semidarkness, my head began to droop and pop up in a steady rhythm. The only sounds breaking the dusky monotony were the inexplicable creaks and groans routinely made by an empty building. At noon, having seen and heard nothing ghostlike, I gave up and went to find Al, leaving the stage door unlocked.

The Jeffreys' angling expedition had actually resulted in the capture of eight edible-size sunfish and one rather handsome yellow perch. The entire catch was hooked by Kristin and Kevin, the walleyes having ignored Al's casting plugs and Carol's silver shiners. All four were devouring peanut butter and jelly sandwiches when I knocked on their cabin door.

"Your turn to stand ghost watch, as soon as you finish eating," I said to Al. "I'm going to have lunch and then pay a call on Oscar Olson. I want to hear what the chairman of the board has to say about the future of the Glock Family Theatre."

"Is there a ghost of a chance I'll see anything happen in the theater?" Al asked.

"Don't get spooked if you do," I said.

"Never fear. If the ghost really is an Indian, I'll wampum."

Having a choice of a heart-healthy tuna salad sandwich in my cabin or a quarter-pound greasy cheeseburger and fries in the lodge dining room, I naturally opted for the latter. When this feast was set before me, I found myself wishing I could wash it down with a cold beer, but my beer drinking days were years behind me. Booze had become my emotional refuge of choice after my wife and infant son were killed in a car crash six years earlier, and only a tough and expensive tour at the Hazelden Rehabilitation Center had hauled me out of an alcoholic hell.

After lunch, I dragged out the cell phone and called Martha Todd, hoping to check on Sherlock Holmes's welfare and Martha's plans for the weekend. She was often home in the early afternoon, but the only answer was her dusky voice on the machine, instructing the caller to leave a message after the beep. I obeyed this command, left my cell phone on so she could return the call, and took a ride into Alexandria.

The building that housed the sales and business office of Oscar Olson Motors, Inc., was behind a sprawling, multi-colored sea of sedans, SUVs, and pickups. Feeling like a beggar at a royal feast, I drove my Honda Civic, which had been assaulted by the street salts of eleven Minnesota winters, through this sunbathed expanse of unblemished glossy metal and nosed into a parking spot marked VISITOR.

Inside, I encountered a chubby, middle-aged receptionist wearing a too-tight white blouse, a knee-length black skirt, and a telephone headset. She uncovered one ear, listened to me announce that I was here for my 1:30 appointment, and said that Mr. Olson was in conference until approximately two o'clock. Since this was only thirty minutes away, I told her I would wait, and she promised to notify me when Mr. Olson was free. I wandered among the new cars on display in the showroom until I attracted the attention of an overzealous salesman, who swore that he could offer me top dollar for my trade-in on the royal purple pickup I was examining. Resisting the temptation to ask for a bid on my vintage two-tone, blue-and-rust sedan, I told him that I was just killing time and retreated to a chair near the receptionist's desk.

Two o'clock came and went. So did 2:30. Finally, at almost quarter to three, the receptionist's phone buzzed, she spoke briefly into her little microphone, turned to me and said, "Mr. Olson will see you now. Down the hall and third door on your right."

Oscar Olson was not your stereotypical round little Oscar. When he rose to shake my hand, his eyes were level with mine, which put him at six-foot-one, and his body had the lean and hard look of a man who exercised and watched his calories. His yellowish-white hair was retreating from his forehead, and his glasses were bifocals. I guessed his age as right around fifty-five.

"What can I do for you Mr. Mitchell?" he said in a hearty voice after motioning me toward a chair. "You're the fellow from the newspaper, ain't you?"

"Yes, Mr. Olson, I'm a reporter for the *St. Paul Daily Dispatch*," I said, once again emphasizing the word reporter. "I'm the one who did the interview with Ding Dong Bell. Maybe you read it in Sunday's paper."

"Every word," said Oscar. "Awful nice piece. Should help bring in some audience for the opening production."

Stage Fright

"I hope it does. And that's what I'd like to discuss with you as chairman of the board — the opening production and the audience."

"What can I tell you?"

"There is a rumor going around the theater that the board of directors might close it down if this season loses money the way the last three seasons have."

"Really? Where did you hear that rumor?"

"From various members of the company," I said, not wanting to get Ding Dong involved. "Herman Glock says it wouldn't happen, but I'm wondering what the board really has in mind."

Oscar frowned and thought a moment before he said, "Since we're not a publicly owned corporation, what the board has in mind really is nobody's business. But for the record, I will say that we are hoping for a more financially rewarding season than we have seen in the last three years."

The folksy tone was gone, and he was talking like a big city corporate executive. I had to admire his skill. The guy was so elusive he could have been a politician.

"What are the possible consequences of another financially unrewarding season?"

"I believe the board will deal with that question when, or if, it comes before us," Oscar said. "At the moment, we are concentrating all our efforts on producing a well-received, money-making show under the guiding hand of a world famous Broadway director."

"What about the incidents caused by the so-called ghost? Are you concerned that they might spoil the show? The cast is very edgy, as you must be aware."

Oscar took a moment to form the answer in his mind before speaking. "The board is confident that these incidents have run their course and that the production will go off without any unscheduled events," he said.

Remembering how confident he and Glanz had looked at the Monday night rehearsal, I said, "But what if there are more — as you call them — unscheduled events? What if something like that sandbag falling from the sky happens during a performance? Is the board prepared to deal with that possibility?"

"The board has discussed it, Mr. Mitchell, and I'm sure you understand that it would be unwise for us to expound on our plan in the newspaper."

"Do you think the so-called theater ghost reads our paper?"

"Who knows what ghosts do, Mr. Mitchell? I'm just saying it wouldn't be wise for us to air our dirty linen in public print."

"I get the impression that you think the ghost may be more corporeal than spiritual," I said. "Do you have a plan to combat a real-life saboteur?"

"Once again, I'm not free to discuss how the board would handle a situation that frightened the audience away. I would rather talk about positive things than the possible negative effects of a ghost or, as you put it, a real-life saboteur."

"Okay," I said. "What's in store for the Glock Family Theatre if this production is a howling success financially? Will a profitable run guarantee the theater's future?"

"Again, this is a matter for the board to discuss when the time is right," he said.

Oscar continued to play dodge ball with my questions for another five minutes before I decided to say thank you and good-by. He rose and shook my hand again when I stood up to leave. The board chairman didn't hide his pleasure at my departure, but he was polite enough not to say, "Don't let the door hit you in the ass when you go out."

Back in the car, the message light on my cell phone was blinking. I pressed the required buttons and heard Martha Todd's voice saying that she was sorry to have missed me, that she was changing clothes to go to work, that Sherlock was well fed and happy and that it looked like she would be joining me on Friday afternoon in time for dinner and the show. "Hope you've got a place for me to sleep," she said.

Well, I did have one in mind. I could only hope that her mind would be in tune with mine. Those twin beds in my cabin were not nailed to the floor. They could be slid together to create, should we say, "a more intimate" arrangement.

My first stop at the resort was the stage door at the back of the Glock Family Theatre. I slipped in, groped my way to the cyclorama in the darkness and said, in a stage whisper, "Al! Are you there?"

From out of the gloom came his voice: "Who goes there? Are you the ghost of productions past?"

"No, Mr. Scrooge, I am the ghost of productions yet to come," I said. "Where the Dickens are you?"

"Over here in the corner, making myself as small as Tiny Tim."

"God bless us, every one!"

After reporting that nothing was stirring except the rabbit in his cage, which was kept in the scene shop between rehearsals, Al went to join his family for a couple of hours on the lake. Seated back in my dark corner, I opened a paperback mystery and illuminated the pages with a miniature flashlight purchased in Alexandria. There would be no boredom or dozing on this watch.

The actors' call to begin getting into costumes and makeup was for 7:00, so I planned to slip out the back door about 6:45. I figured anyone setting a booby trap would do it before the cast straggled in, and I wanted to be sure to avoid any early arrivals.

An hour went by, and I became so deeply immersed in the whodunit that I almost didn't hear the footsteps on the stage. When the sound registered on my brain, I clicked off my reading light and tiptoed to the back of the flats at stage right. The footsteps had stopped but I thought I heard water running. Ever so slowly, I eased open the upstage right door about a finger's width and peeked through the crack.

On the set at downstage left there stood a bar that was used by the madam when she offered a patron a drink. In the dim light, I could see the dark figure of a person — I couldn't determine which sex — standing at the bar with his or her back to me. The sound of running water ceased and the person set something — possibly a bottle — on the bar.

I stepped quietly through the door, took a couple of steps toward the figure in front of me and said, "Okay, ghost, your haunting days are over."

With a shriek that topped high C, the person spun to face me. Even in that dim light, I could see it was Angela Maguire.

Chapter 8
Got'cha!

"Oh, my god, you like scared the living shit out of me!" Angie said in a voice an octave higher than normal. "What the hell are you doing here?"

"I might ask you the same," I said. "I'm here looking for the Glock Family Theatre ghost, and right now you're the leading candidate for that title."

"You're full of shit!" she said. "You don't think I've been setting up the weird stuff at rehearsals, do you?"

"What were you doing right now?"

She was holding a coffee can in her right hand, and she looked down at it as she replied. "That's different. This is like the first time I've done anything."

"What was in the can?"

"That's like none of your business, newspaper man."

"It will be Ding Dong Bell's business when I tell him I caught you messing with the bar. What were you pouring?"

"Oh, jeez, don't tell Ding Dong. He'll be bullshit if he finds out what I did."

"Then I'd suggest you tell me what you did and maybe undo whatever it was."

"Promise me you won't tell Ding Dong?" She moved toward me and dropped to her knees at my feet. "I told him I needed something from the dressing room and like mooched his key to get in here. He'll kill me!"

I caught a whiff of urine and wondered if Angie had been so startled that she'd wet her pants. She was wearing black spandex bicycling tights and the light was too dim for me to see if they were darkened at the crotch. "Do you swear to me that this is the first thing you've done?" I asked.

"Yes. I swear to God, yes!" Angie said. "This is personal. It has nothing to do with all that other shit."

"Okay, I won't tell Ding Dong. But you have to undo what you did."

"I'll do anything you want me to as long as you don't tell."

That was an interesting proposition, especially with her kneeling in front of me with her upturned face at the level of my belt buckle. But there was business to attend to, so I pushed back my lascivious thoughts and asked again, "What did you do?"

Stage Fright

"I like put something in the bottle that Eric pours his drink out of in the first act."

"What kind of something?"

She took a deep breath and said, "Piss!"

"Did you say piss?" I was having trouble computing this response.

Angie rose and looked me in the eye. "Yes, I said piss. I found out that it was Eric that put the dog shit on the telephone, so I like decided to get even. I peed in this coffee can and like poured it into the whisky bottle that Eric uses." Well, that explained the essence of urine drifting in the air.

"Eric smeared the dog poop on the phone?"

"Alice said she like heard him bragging about it in the bar the other night. He's like really pissed off at me, so he decided to do something really nasty."

"Why is Eric really pissed off at you?"

"I don't want to talk about that. That's like super personal."

"Okay, we won't go there. But you're saying that Eric is responsible for at least one of the things that have messed up your rehearsals?"

"He did that one anyway," Angie said. "Do I really have to pour the piss back out of that whisky bottle?"

Now she had me. My moral self told me that I should insist on her cleaning the bottle thoroughly and refilling it with tea. The devil in me said it would be highly entertaining to see Eric, who in his out-of-character moments had impressed me as being a self-important little prick, take a swig of Angie's bodily waste in retribution for the phone poop caper.

After wrestling briefly with the angel of my conscience, I pinned the little sucker and said, "Okay. We'll let it be our little secret."

Angie flung herself at me, wrapped her arms around my neck and her legs around my waist, gave me a quick, hard kiss on the lips, and said, "I knew you were a good guy."

I don't know when I've looked forward to an evening of theater with more enthusiasm than I did that night. Of course, I had to pass along the secret of Angie's revenge to Al, so we were both primed for the drinking scene, which came about ten minutes into the first act. We looked at each other and actually giggled in anticipation when Mamie the madam said, "What's your poison Antonio?" Antonio was the name of the sleazy whorehouse hanger-on that Eric was playing.

"Straight bourbon," said Antonio. "Mind if help myself?"

Glenn Ickler

"Be my guest," said Mamie and Antonio went to the bar. With a grand gesture, he picked up the ice tongs, lifted the lid of the ice bucket and clinked three ice cubes one-by-one into a lowball glass. I chanced a glance at Angie, who was standing stage right, and saw her cover her mouth with both hands.

When I looked back at Eric, he was pouring amber liquid from the whisky bottle into his glass. He recapped the bottle, picked up the glass and hesitated a second as he brought it to his lips.

"Oh, damn, he smells it," I whispered to Al.

But no. The pause was merely the preliminary gesture to an arm's length salute with the tinkling glass full of ice cubes and tinkle. "To Mamie and her beautiful girls!" he said and tossed down the entire liquid content of the glass in one gulp.

The expressions that crossed Eric's face immediately thereafter far outdid anything I had seen produced by his limited acting skill. First, there was a look of curiosity — a sort of "what the hell was that I just swallowed?" look. Then came a look of realization as the flavor registered on his tongue. This was followed by an open-mouthed, wide-eyed look of horror as the message of taste was translated into a descriptive noun by his brain. Then Eric threw up on his shoes.

After a shout of "son of a bitch!" from behind us, where Ding Dong Bell was sitting in the last row of the house, and a ten-minute pause to give Eric time to wash out his mouth and settle his stomach, the rehearsal was restarted from the beginning. This time, Eric sniffed the new bottle produced by the props mistress before he poured from it and the entire show went off without a hitch. However, every time Eric and Angela were on stage together Al and I could feel the tension reverberating all the way to our seats in the 15th row. We were pretty sure that Ding Dong felt it too, and wondered what he would say when the rehearsal was over.

The director surprised us by saying nothing about the incident. Instead, Ding Dong gave a post-rehearsal speech praising the entire cast and crew. He told them they all were performing marvelously and that they had a wonderful show. He finished by reminding them that although Thursday night's senior citizen audience wouldn't be paying admission they were entitled to the best performance the cast could give them. Everyone except Eric was smiling when Ding Dong ended his upbeat recitation and bade the cast and crew good night.

Outside the theater, the warm fuzzy feeling engendered by Ding Dong Bell's pep talk was dampened by a Minnesota mid-June drizzle. The temperature had dropped into the fifties, and the raindrops felt like tiny ice cubes as they splattered on our cheeks.

Stage Fright

"No fishing in the morning if this keeps up," Al said. "The kids will go stir crazy if they have to stay in the cabin all day." As if in response, the drizzle intensified until it became a shower.

I reminded him that there were ping pong and pool tables in the lodge and said "nighty-night." I thought about revisiting the bar, but the raindrops were increasing in size and volume so I decided I didn't need to pump any of the actors for more information. I headed for my cabin, breaking into a trot because several years ago I read about a study that proved a person who runs through rain is struck by only 70 percent as many drops of water as a person who walks.

Whatever percentage splashed on me during my dash through the dark was enough to soak my shirt and the front of my khaki pants. I removed the wet items and stood shivering in my skivvies for a minute, wondering whether to sit up and read or go to bed and sleep. I decided to read, so I wrapped myself in a blanket because the cabin had no heater and sat down in an armchair next to the brightest lamp in the room. Inside the blanket, I was as snug as a butterfly larva in its cocoon. The shower had become a near downpour, and the rhythm of the raindrops drumming on the roof was hypnotic. The book grew so heavy that my hands couldn't hold it and it fell into my lap. Soon my eyelids became so earnestly attracted to each other that I could no longer keep them apart.

A steady hammering at the cabin door snapped me back to consciousness. I looked at my watch and discovered that it was 1:15. Why in hell was somebody banging on my door at this hour?

I figured it had to be Al. But what did he want? Had he captured the ghost? Had his cabin caught fire? Had the kids wandered away into the dark, rain-drenched woods?

The knocking continued while I cleared the fog from my brain. With the blanket still wrapped around me, limiting the length of my steps like a woman's narrow skirt, I shuffled toward the door. As I passed the phone, I noticed that the message light was blinking. No use calling the front desk at this hour, I thought. When I opened the door, I was confronted by a very tall blonde woman who looked half drowned, with rainwater dripping from her long stringy hair and nipples the size of my thumb almost poking through her saturated T-shirt.

"I'm so druckin' funk I can't find my cabin," said Angela Maguire. "Can I come inna yours?"

How could a gentleman say no? I stood back and she sloshed in. I could hear her feet squishing inside her mud-smeared sneakers and a puddle had encircled her on the floor by the time I closed the door and turned back to view the wreckage.

"It's a really shitty night out there," she said. "An' I'm a really shit-faced girl."

"I never would have guessed," I said. "Why don't you go into the bathroom, take off your wet clothes and dry yourself off? I'll slip some dry things through the door."

"Baffroom is a good idea," Angie said. "I gotta pee so bad my teeth are floatin'." She staggered forward in the direction I was pointing and disappeared into the bathroom. I unwrapped myself from the blanket so I could walk at a normal pace and went into the bedroom, dug through the dresser drawers and pulled out a pair of sweat pants and a heavy-gauge T-shirt.

"Jussa minute," Angie said when I rapped on the bathroom door and announced I was bearing dry duds. When she opened the door, her T-shirt was rolled up far enough to reveal her bare belly, and she said, "You gotta like help me get my shirt off. It's so wet it sticks to me all over."

Never one to shirk my duty when a fair damsel calls for assistance, I grabbed the bottom of the T-shirt, and with me pulling and Angie writhing like a cobra, we pried it up over what I was guessing were size 40-D boobs. Freed from the shirt and unfettered by a bra, those twin torpedoes popped out like they were spring-loaded and came to rest against my bare chest. Despite this considerable distraction, I managed to yank the stubborn T-shirt over her head and peel it off of her upstretched arms. I dropped the soggy bundle onto the floor, and Angie dropped her arms onto my shoulders. She wrapped her clammy hands around my neck and breathed into my left ear as she said, "Thanks for the help. I couldna' done it without you."

"You're more than welcome," I said, looking down at where our naked chests were pressed together. "Thanks for the mammaries."

The pun didn't register because her brain was as sodden with vodka as her clothes were with rainwater. "You gonna like help me with my pants, too?" she asked.

Now if Angela Maguire was sober, the answer would have been an enthusiastic "yes." However, Angela Maguire was in an alcoholic haze so thick you could almost see the droplets of fog around her head. There was no way I would undress a woman who was so far gone, so I said, "I think you can get those off without my help." Reluctantly, I undraped her limp arms from around me and separated the skin of my upper body from hers. "See you when you're wearing something dry," I said, and I ducked out of the bathroom and went to find the blanket so I could rewrap myself.

"You got no clothes on," she said as I was shutting the bathroom door. "Why do I needa get dressed?"

"Because it's cold in here," I said through the door. "You'll catch pneumonia if you don't get dry and get into something warm." I knew this was an old wives' tale, but the first old wife I ever heard it from was my mother, and who am I to argue with her?

Securely wrapped in the blanket, I waited in the chair while Angie struggled with the wet jeans encasing her lower limbs. I could hear her swearing and banging into the wall, but I resisted the temptation to go back and help pull them off. After all, she had previously gotten her jeans down far enough to use the toilet. At least I hoped she had taken them down before she peed. Finally she emerged from the bathroom, wearing my sweatpants but not the T-shirt.

"T-shirt rubs too hard on my nips," she said. "Anyway, it ain't that cold."

"I'll get you a blanket," I said.

"Jus' lemme like get into yours with you," Angie replied.

"I'm afraid I'm not up to that, Angie."

"I bet Angie can get you up." She plopped herself onto my lap and tried to kiss me, but I rolled to one side and held her face tight against my right cheek.

"You might if you were sober," I said. "Like you said when I opened the door, you're too druckin' funk to do anything."

"Yeah, I can't funk nobody on accounta I like got a dose of herpes, but I give great head. Wanna see?" She was pulling on the blanket at my crotch, but I was sitting on the loose end so she couldn't uncover her target.

Her statement about herpes made me all the happier that I hadn't helped remove her pants. "You say you've got genital herpes?" I asked, looking for confirmation.

"I got 'em from Andy and didn' know it," Angie said. "So I like passed 'em along to Eric. Tha's why he's so pissed at me, and we're both pissed at Andy, the dirty, rotten son of a bitch."

Well, that explained why Ding Dong had noticed that the atmosphere around this trio now resembled a winter night in Antarctica.

"That's why Eric put the dog shit on your telephone?" I asked.

"Tha's why. But I got that asshole good tonigh', didn' I?"

"You sure did. Now why don't you crawl into one of the beds in there and get some sleep. I'm ready to call it a night, too."

"I can give you really good head," she said. "You can like play with my tits while I'm givin' you a ..."

I put a hand over her mouth and said, "Not tonight, Angie." I wrapped my right arm around her bare shoulders, being careful not to touch the offered flesh, and stood us both upright. Together we lock-stepped to the bedroom, where I pulled back the covers on the bed I wasn't using and deposited her therein. I pulled the covers up to her chin and said good night.

"Hones', honey, I give really good head," she said in a dreamy monotone as I crawled into my bed. The next thing I heard was a snore.

A gray and gloomy daylight was visible out the window when I heard the next sound, which was another knock on my front door. I looked at the bedside clock and discovered it was nearly 9:15. Raindrops were still splattering against the windows. The knocker knocked again.

Well, this one had to be Al. Nobody else would be hassling me on a rainy morning. He probably wanted to discuss who would take what hours hiding in the theater today. I rolled out of bed and went to the door wearing only my tiger-striped boxer shorts. When I opened the door, there stood Martha Todd, wearing a hooded, ankle-length, yellow plastic slicker and carrying an unhappy-looking black-and-white tomcat.

Chapter 9
Just the Purr-fect Friendship

"Can a girl and her pussy cat come in out of the rain?" asked Martha.

When she said that, I realized my mouth was hanging open, and I was standing in the doorway staring at them like they were from some distant planet instead of inviting them in. "Oh, sure," I said, stepping back out of the way. "Sorry. I wasn't quite awake and I'm not exactly dressed for girls and their pussies ...I mean for company." My god, I was babbling like an idiot!

"Must be tough, sleeping in until after nine on a weekday," said Martha as she handed a damp Sherlock Holmes to me.

"I'm on vacation, remember?"

"Well, you're dressed casually enough to be on vacation." She was grinning as she gave my sporty-looking skivvies the eye.

"Oh, shit!" I said in my most eloquent manner. "This is what I was sleeping in." I looked around the room for the damn blanket, then remembered that I had unwound my self from it in the bedroom. I sure as hell didn't want to go back in there at this particular moment. Luckily, I spotted my khakis, still damp from the night before, draped over a chair at the dining table. I hastily pulled them on while Martha watched with an amused grin on her face.

"I never dreamed you were so bashful," she said. "I was enjoying the view." She had pulled her hood down and was unsnapping the front of the raincoat while I was trying to think of something to say that would get us out of the cabin before Angie woke up. Martha had just finished unsnapping, but I was nowhere near finished thinking when a voice from the back of the cabin said, "Who's out there, Mitch, honey?" And there she came, strolling out of the bedroom still wearing nothing but the sweatpants.

Martha stared for a moment at the expansive display of bare bosom bouncing toward us before she said, "Sorry. I guess there's no room for me here."

I tried to grab her arm as I said, "Martha, this is not what it looks like."

"It never is!" she said. She whirled and was gone with a slam of the door, leaving me with an armful of moist tomcat with his ears laid back and an angry look in his eyes.

"Friend of yours?" asked Angie.

"She used to be," I said as I deposited Sherlock Holmes into the armchair. "Your grand entrance took care of that very nicely."

"Sorry," she said. "If she's like pissed off at you, I can always be your friend. I give really good ..."

I cut her off by shouting, "I know! I know! I know what you give! Now I'd appreciate it if you'd let me figure out how I'm going to explain this to Martha."

"Well, you don't have to be rude, you know. Where are my clothes? I'll put them on and like never bother you again." She pulled down the sweat pants, giving me a beaver shot and confirming my suspicion that she was not a real blonde. She stepped out of the sweats, turned around, and walked away toward the bathroom with a little more swishing of her bare butt than I thought necessary.

"If your clothes are still wet, you can wear the sweatpants, and I'll find something to wrap around your ... to cover your top," I said.

"Don't let me stop you from chasing after your pissed-off girlfriend. I'll be like fine in these old grubby wet things."

God, how women can guilt you! "You don't have to go out in wet clothes," I said. "It doesn't take any more time for you to get into something dry."

She emerged from the bathroom wearing her jeans and T-shirt, which had dried just enough so they weren't dripping. In one hand she carried a strip of shiny crimson cloth that I couldn't identify until she held it up and said, "I ain't going to put on these nasty wet panties. Thanks for the use of the bed, Mitch, honey." She waved the panties in my direction like Queen Victoria flicking her hankie to acknowledge the obeisance of a gaggle of commoners and marched out the door.

With Angie gone, my only thoughts were of Martha. I had to catch her before she drove away. I was wondering why she had appeared a day early and unannounced as I pulled a fresh T-shirt over my head. Still wearing the damp khakis, I opened the door and found myself facing Alan Jeffrey, whose right fist was poised to knock.

"You got some kind of a sixth sense that tells you when somebody's at your door?" he asked.

"I was just on the way out," I said. "And I'm kind of in a hurry."

"Don't let me stop you. I just came by to tell you that I picked up this message at the front desk a minute ago." He handed me a slip of paper on which the desk clerk had written that Martha Todd had called at about 8:30 Wednesday evening. She said she had been unable to reach me on my cell phone but that she had an extra day off and would be arriving sometime Thursday morning instead of at the original time.

"You look a little pale around the gills," Al said.

Stage Fright

"That's because a whole lot of trouble has just come down the pike," I said.

"Is there something fishy going on?"

"I don't have time to stand here and carp about it," I said, stepping out and slamming the door behind me. "I need to cast around and find somebody."

Al stepped aside, but before I could take two steps toward the lot where Martha would have parked her car, Carol Jeffrey came striding up the path carrying a black umbrella. She planted herself in front of me like an airport security guard about to demand a strip search.

Carol did not flash me her customary smile as she said, "What did you do to Martha? I just saw her getting into her car, and she was bawling like a baby. I took her over to our cabin, and she's sitting in there dripping tears into a cup of coffee. Did you two have a fight?"

"There wasn't time for a fight," I said. "You wouldn't believe what happened."

"Try me." I could never disobey Carol, especially when she was anchored squarely in front of me with her nose less than a ruler's length from mine, and her tipped umbrella dripping rainwater on my head. I invited them both to come in out of the rain and, snug and dry inside my cabin, I tried her.

When I finished my explanation, leaving out a couple of minor details, Carol said, "You're right, Mitch. I don't believe you."

"Carol, it's the god's truth!" I said. "Angela came to the door soaking wet and falling down drunk, so I gave her some dry clothes and let her sleep it off in the other single bed."

"Martha said you had a naked woman in your cabin."

"Only from the waist up! She wouldn't wear my T-shirt because she said it rubbed too hard against her ... well, you know what I mean."

"Do you really expect Martha to believe a bullshit story like that?" In the twelve years I had known her, I had never before heard Carol Jeffrey use that word, or any similar obscenity.

"She has to!" I said. "It's absolutely true. Go ask Angela if anything happened."

"I might just do that," Carol said. "But right now, I'm going to go back and try to calm Martha down. And you stay far away from her until further notice!"

I sort of squeaked out a "yes, ma'am," as Carol wheeled and took off out the door.

When I turned around, Al was looking at me the way my father did when I was sixteen and told him that his car, which I had borrowed, was standing motionless in a downtown parking lot when the radiator got smashed in. "Did you really not touch that bimbo?" Al asked.

"There was some incidental, accidental contact while I was helping her get her wet T-shirt off, but we spent the night in separate beds after I turned down an offer that most guys couldn't refuse," I said.

"Well, good luck convincing either Carol or Martha that you didn't spend all night in that babe's saddle. I believe you because no man would ever admit to passing up a chance like that unless it was true, but women think we always lead with our dicks and never tell the truth. Come to think of it, why did you refuse Angela's offer?"

"Because she was so damn drunk she could barely walk and talk. And actually, even if she had been sober I might have sent her home because this is not a woman I want to get mixed up with. Oh, and as a side bar to my feature story, Angie told me that Andy gave her a gift of genital herpes, and she passed them along to Eric, which is why she and Eric are playing those disgusting little tricks on each other."

"Why doesn't she go after Andy?"

"I'm not so sure she won't," I said. "If I was Andy, I'd be damn careful after seeing Eric gulp down a tumbler full of Angie's bladder cocktail."

"Which brings us to the topic of the day," said Al. "Who's going to sit backstage at what time — and how do we get into the theater today? I assume whoever locked up last night took care of the door we were using."

"Since you can't go fishing in the rain this morning, I was hoping you'd take the early shift. As for getting in, Angie told me that the door she used yesterday will be unlocked all this week so that the set crew and props people can get in anytime they need to do some finishing work."

"Okay. I'd just as soon stay out of our cabin until Carol gets Martha settled down any way, so I'll go to the theater now. Make sure you relieve me in time for lunch."

"I'll relieve you as efficiently as that much-advertised heartburn remedy. Meanwhile, I will roll on some dry pants and aid my stomach by catching some breakfast in the dining room." And although I didn't say it, keep an eye on Martha Todd's car. There was no way she was going to leave the Glock Family Resort without listening to my explanation of Wednesday night's watery fiasco.

As we started for the door, I saw the message light on the phone still blinking. I picked up the receiver and punched "0." The woman who answered informed me that there had been a message waiting for me at the front desk since 8:30 last night but that my friend, Mr. Jeffrey, had picked it up this morning.

Al headed off to the theater, and I managed to catch the last scoop of scrambled eggs as the kitchen crew was clearing away the breakfast buffet. For all I tast-

Stage Fright

ed them, the eggs might as well have been made of cardboard. The coffee didn't seem to have any flavor either as I sipped it at a window table while keeping an eye on a white Honda Accord that I recognized as Martha's.

The rain stopped while I was mentally rehearsing the third silent draft of my explanatory oration. As I started on the fourth draft, Martha, Carol, and the two Jeffrey kids came trooping to the Accord. Oh, god, I thought, she's getting ready to leave and there will be a trio of Jeffreys eavesdropping on my plea for understanding — and, yes, forgiveness — even though there really was nothing to forgive.

Audience or no, I had to make my pitch. I raced to the door and was about to hail them when I saw that Martha was opening the trunk instead of the driver-side door. She pulled out a suitcase and a backpack and slammed the trunk lid down. With the women in the middle and a child at each end of a line of four, they marched like a color guard back to the Jeffreys' cabin.

Wondering when I would find out what this was all about, I went back to my cabin to spend the rest of the morning reading the local newspaper, which I picked up in the lobby. At least, Martha wasn't going back to St. Paul this morning.

Upon opening the cabin door, I was greeted with an enthusiastic "meow" by Sherlock Holmes, who was probably thinking that everyone he knew had deserted him. Sherlock performed his customary circle of my ankles and hopped into my lap a split second after I sat down.

"Hi, old buddy," I said. "At least I have one friend left in the world."

"Purr!" said Sherlock and his motor kept running as he settled down for a nap.

At noon, I was forced to disturb my slumbering companion because it was time to relieve my — I hoped — wide awake compatriot in the gloom of the Glock Family Theatre. There was no cat food in the cabin, but I put down one dish filled with water and another holding the remains of a huge walleye and wild rice dinner I had brought back from the dining room the night before. The walleye was half gone by the time I said good by.

The open door was on the far side of the theater, off stage left. As I stepped inside, I heard sounds on the stage — a couple of footsteps followed by two thumps, one louder than the other. With the stealth of a burglar, I crept to the back of the set, opened the down-left door a crack and peeked through.

A man was standing near the sofa at center stage with what looked like a cave dweller's club in his right hand. Stretched on the rug at his feet was another man, who was not moving. The light was dim, but I could see well enough to determine that the motionless man lying face down on the floor was Alan Jeffrey.

Chapter 10
On the Fur Side

As I was taught in the Navy, I paused briefly to review my options before taking action. There weren't many. I could charge through the door and challenge the man with the club to physical combat. Or I could stay behind the door and try to talk to the man with the club. Or I could run like hell to the lodge to get help. None of these seemed particularly attractive, but I was damned if I could come up with anything more appealing.

My dilemma was dissolved when the man dropped his weapon onto the sofa, took a cell phone out of his pants pocket, punched in a number and said, "Mr. Glock, can you come over to the theater? I just bopped an intruder with a belaying pin, and I might have whacked him a little too hard." The voice was familiar. It was Jimmy Storrs.

Jimmy's words sent me flying through the door like Angie's tits popping out of that wet T-shirt. "What do you mean you might have whacked him too hard?" I yelled at Jimmy as I knelt beside the inert photographer.

"I didn't mean to knock him cold," Jimmy said. "I finally caught the ghost who's been screwing up our rehearsals, and I just wanted to make sure he didn't run away."

"This is not a ghost, you idiot!" I said, feeling for a pulse in Al's wrist. "This is the photographer from the St. Paul paper, and he's a paying guest at this resort."

My pulse was hammering away at about 150 thuds a minute because I couldn't find any sign of Al's. Just as I was about to go into my personal version of cardiac arrest, Al let out a groan and tried to turn his head to one side.

"Don't move," I said. "Let's make sure your neck is okay."

Jimmy was kneeling beside me. "Jeez, man, I'm sorry," he said. "The guy was standing in the middle of the stage looking around. I thought he was getting ready to sabotage something else, so I grabbed a loose belaying pin and bopped him." The belaying pins were used to secure backstage ropes that controlled the height of teasers and light bars.

"What happened?" Al said in a voice muffled by the carpet.

"You were kayoed by a sneak punch in the first round, Rocky," I said. "Just don't move your head for a minute." I ran my fingers along the vertebrae in his neck

Stage Fright

and everything felt normal. I laid one finger in the palm of Al's right hand and instructed him to squeeze it, which he did successfully.

"Can you wiggle your toes?" I asked.

"They're wiggling."

"Okay, I guess it's safe to roll you over. But there's a lump sprouting on the back of your head that you might not want to press against the floor."

With Jimmy and me helping, Al rolled over and sat up. We dragged him to the sofa and propped his back against it. Al was gently fingering the expanding knob behind his right ear when we heard footsteps and looked up to see Herman Glock running down the aisle. He bounded up the stairs onto the stage and asked, "What the hell's going on?"

Considering this to be a fair question, I replied. "Al was on the stage looking at the set and checking the lighting angles preparing to shoot some pictures before the performance tonight. Your man here thought he was the ghost that's been dropping sandbags and sawing through chair legs. He decided to shoot first and ask questions later, which is why Al has a big lump on his head — and you have a possible lawsuit on your hands." I tossed in the bit about the lawsuit because I firmly believe that the best defense is a good offense.

Picking up my cue, Al emitted a groan that sounded like a rutting stag and said, "I won't know whether my skull is fractured until I see a doctor."

"I'll call an ambulance," said Herman. "We'll get you to the hospital right away."

"Just get a bag of ice to put on that bump. I'll get my car and drive him to the emergency room," I said, pleased that my diversionary tactics were working so well.

Herman told Jimmy to run to the kitchen and get a large bag of ice. "Then you can explain to me why you're sneaking up behind people and clobbering them over the head," he added. Jimmy disappeared and I went to get my car, leaving Al with Herman to discuss the possible repercussions of his possible concussion.

"Poor old Herman thinks we've got him by the short hairs," Al said on the way to the hospital in Alexandria. "He's so worried about a lawsuit he didn't even question that goofy story you told him about me checking the lighting angles on an unlit stage."

"Best to keep him in the dark about what we're doing," I said.

"Right. He wouldn't take it lightly if he knew we were shadowing the spook."

"The one I'd like to shine a spotlight on is Jimmy Storrs. What was he doing in the theater at noon, seven hours before the call for tonight's show?"

"He is the tech director. Maybe he was going to work on something."

"But what was that something? Think about it. Who's in a better position to sabotage the set than Jimmy Storrs?"

"But Jimmy has been acting as puzzled as anybody else when he cleans up after a so-called accident."

"Maybe 'acting' is the key word there," I said. "He might be putting on a better performance than anybody in the cast."

"Well, we don't lack for suspects," Al said. "We know that Eric and Angela have been responsible for at least two of the incidents, and one of them might have had a hand in the others. And now we have Jimmy Storrs, who has the know-how and the access to everything on, above and behind the stage. Ooh!"

The "ooh" was because I hit a pothole in the hospital parking lot and jarred the ice bag Al was holding against the tender spot on the back of his head.

"Sorry. You'd think they would take better care of the parking lot next to the emergency room," I said. "Imagine hitting that pothole if you had a fractured leg."

"The mere thought of it cracks me up," Al said.

"Obviously that whack on the head didn't affect the punny part of your brain."

"We can discuss that gray area later, after I've had my head examined."

Carol was emerging from the front door of the main lodge carrying some sheets and towels when we returned to the resort. "Where have you been?" she asked Al. "We got tired of waiting for you and ate our lunch."

"We went to the hospital," I said. "They examined Al's head and found nothing."

"That I believe," Carol said. "But why on earth did you go to the hospital?"

"Let's walk slowly over to our cabin and sit down, and then I'll tell you what happened," Al said. "I've got a lump the size of a baseball and a headache that would pop the seams of a basketball."

Carol said okay, put an arm around Al's shoulders, looked at me and said, "I can't invite you to join us, Mitch. Martha is in our cabin and I don't think she'd care to see you just now."

"How long will I be the outcast?" I asked.

"You're lucky you're only an outcast," Carol said. "Martha would just as soon make you a castaway."

"You've been living with Al too long," I said and headed toward my cabin. At least Sherlock Holmes wouldn't cast me out.

Stage Fright

It was almost dinnertime when a knock on my door roused me from a deep coma in the armchair. I opened the door to find Al standing there with a pile of sheets, towels, and assorted items of wearing apparel in his arms.

"What's this all about?" I asked.

"Your former friend Martha is sleeping in my bed, and I have been exiled to the bunk where Angela spent last night in bare-breasted but allegedly lonely splendor."

"Are you shittin' me? Carol made you move out so Martha could move in?"

"It's her motherly instinct."

"Isn't Martha a little old to be treated like Carol's daughter?" If I was guessing Martha's age correctly, Carol had only two or three years of seniority.

"Age doesn't matter," Al said. "I am married to a universal care-giver — sort of a Nordic Mother Teresa."

"I could use somebody like that myself right now," I said.

"Don't look at me, old buddy. I am not the type to go around binding up the knife wounds in a love-fractured heart."

"It's a good thing you're not a writer, either," I said. "The copy desk would have deleted that last sentence after copying it into their journal of mixed metaphors. And as long as we're talking about mixed-up things, how's your head doing?"

"I took two Tylenol, and now the man swinging the maul inside my skull is merely pounding on my brain instead of splitting it." Al deposited his armload on the bed most recently occupied by Angela Maguire and went back to his cabin for supper. Since I was now unwelcome at the Jeffreys' table, I ate dinner alone in the lodge and adjourned to the theater to observe the free geezer performance. Al joined me there a minute before curtain time and said the women and kids were driving into Alexandria to see a "family type" movie.

"Has Martha mentioned my name?" I asked.

"Not in polite company," Al said.

As the opening scene of *Long Night's Journey Into Day* began, the actors were wound so tight they were walking like marionettes. But as the action moved along without any unscheduled activities, and the audience (Al and I guessed the average age as 75) began to laugh in the appropriate places, you could almost feel the players gradually tossing off their tension and beginning to enjoy themselves.

Some of the old farts in the audience laughed especially loud at Salome's references to her use of the rabbit as a stimulant for her less vigorous customers, and I began to wonder if I had missed something in my high school sex-ed classes.

During the intermission, we wormed our way through the crowd in the foyer to congratulate Ding Dong Bell. "Son of a bitch!" he said. "It does look good so far."

"Maybe your troubles are over," Al said.

"I ain't counting my chickens until the fat lady sings," said Ding Dong. I'd have to pass that comment along to the keeper of the copy desk's mixed metaphor log.

As the lights went up for Act Two, I noticed that I was sitting up straight with every muscle taut and, although my lungs were puffed with oxygen-depleted air, I wasn't releasing a single atom. Glancing sideways at Al, I saw him frozen in the same ramrod posture. But when no sandbags fell near Alice as she opened the second act, we both sat back with audible exhalations and prepared to enjoy the rest of the evening.

The bathroom on the landing three steps above the whorehouse parlor floor is seldom used during the show. In the first act, the room is used once when Andy hides from his wife and again when another of the johns, the one played by Norman Rogers, says he has to go to the john. When Norman comes out, he reports a problem with the flushing mechanism, which sets up a bit early in the second act where a plainclothes policeman who is investigating the brothel pretends to be the plumber summoned to repair the toilet.

The bogus plumber goes into the bathroom and emerges during a chaotic moment when the parlor is filled with men spouting sexual innuendoes. The plumber tops them all by shouting, "Your ball cocks are shot! They have to be replaced."

Al and I were both thoroughly relaxed when, about three minutes into the action, the plumber appeared at the front door right on cue. He was steered to the bathroom by Mamie the madam and he opened the door to go in. Before he knew what hit him, the plumber was nearly swept off his feet by a flood. But it was not water flowing over his shoes. Oh, no. The startled man found himself ankle deep in fur.

Out of the bathroom poured a torrent of rabbits. Gray rabbits, brown rabbits, white rabbits, spotted rabbits — there must have been two dozen of the damn things hopping all over the stage. The audience went crazy with laughter and, after recovering from their initial open-mouthed state of shock, so did the people on stage. Rhonda Lapierre actually collapsed on the sofa she was laughing so hard. Randy Rhodes, the homophobe, and Norman Rogers, who was glaringly gay, were hugging each other for mutual support, and Angela Maguire was shaking so hard with laughter that those twin turrets nearly popped out of the top of her teddy.

Stage Fright

The scene began to lose its humor when some of the rabbits hopped off the stage and began mingling with the audience, where people were starting to realize that the lapin invasion was not in the script. The laughter was replaced by shrieks from women who didn't appreciate the feeling of fur brushing against their ankles and shouts from men who were trying to shoo the bounding bunnies away.

From the back of the theater came a familiar voice shouting a familiar refrain. "Son of a bitch!" yelled Ding Dong Bell as he charged down the aisle toward the stage. "Son of a bitch! Son of a goddamn bitch!"

Al and I joined the cast, crew, and director in the main lodge bar after the show. It had taken twenty minutes to round up the rabbits and restore order, and during that time, forty-eight members of the audience got on their bus and went back to the Alexandria senior center. Ding Dong had the cast reopen the second act and the performance finally ended with the actors taking their curtain call to the applause generated by a half-dozen family members, two octogenarian gentlemen, Al, me, Ding Dong, and 300 empty seats.

"I'll never leave New York again," Ding Dong said as he gulped a scotch on the rocks and set the glass on the bar for a refill. "Never, never again!"

"How could somebody sneak all those rabbits in there between acts?" I asked.

"After the crew cleans up the set, everybody either goes to the dressing room or the green room," Ding Dong said. "Everybody except the son of a bitch who stuffed that cage full of those furry little bastards into the bathroom. He opened the front of the cage and jammed it against the bathroom door so they couldn't get out until Freddy yanked it open. Then, whoosh!" Ding Dong tossed down the second scotch and motioned to the bartender to pour him a third.

"Can't say I blame you for wanting to get back to New York," Al said. "This show would drive anybody away."

"I get nothing but shit from the minute I come to the theater until something screwball happens on stage," Ding Dong said. "Every night before the rehearsal I got to listen to that homophobe son of a bitch Randy Rhodes telling crude jokes about gays and keep those two schmucks, Eric LaFlamme and Andy Anderson, away from each other so they don't start throwing punches and referee a shouting match between Frenchy Lapierre and his ex-wife, Rhonda. Then the show begins and I got to sit there and wonder what will fuck everything up tonight. Son of a bitch!"

"I didn't realize you had all that action going on in the dressing room," I said.

Glenn Ickler

"It's one big son of a bitching pain in the ass. That damn Frenchy and Rhonda are the worst. I wish to hell I'd known about their divorce before I cast them. I'd have left one of them out."

"Which one?" Al asked.

"I don't know. They both look perfect for their roles. I guess I'd have probably cast Rhonda and left out Frenchy, even if he does look like the perfect pimp." Ding Dong gestured toward the object of this description, who was sitting at a corner table with Alice Prewitt and Angela Maguire. Even off stage, Frenchy could pass for a pimp. He was small and wiry, about the same height as roly-poly Rhonda but a good sixty pounds lighter. Frenchy slicked his long, black hair straight back and sported a thin, black Salvador Dali-style moustache under a long, pointy nose, so that the overall effect reminded me of a weasel.

"Do you think Frenchy might have set up the collapsing chair for Rhonda?" Al and I asked in unison.

"She's accused him of it about twenty times," Ding Dong said. "Of course he keeps saying he didn't. How the hell do I know? Where's that son of a bitch bartender? I need another drink!"

"Think we should add Frenchy's name to our growing list of candidates for theater spook of the year?" Al said as we walked away from the agitated director.

"Your resident ghost writer has already done so," I said.

"That's the spirit."

Our next stop was at the table occupied by Frenchy Lapierre, Angela Maguire and Alice Prewitt. Neither of us had ever had a conversation with Frenchy, and this seemed like an opportune time. As we arrived, Frenchy was delivering the punch line of a very old joke: "And the first little old lady said, 'I know, but this one is eating my popcorn!'"

Frenchy rolled with laughter at his own joke. When the women finished their polite giggling and Frenchy recovered from almost falling out of his chair, I said, "Hi. Mind if we join you?"

"Gentlemen of the press!" said Frenchy. "Pull up a chair and I'll tell you guys the story I just finished telling these lovely ladies."

"If it's the one about the duck, I've heard it," I said, trying to be diplomatic.

"Tenth grade," Al said, with his usual disregard of diplomacy.

This putdown did not sit well with Frenchy. However, the trio did some chair shuffling so we could sit down, and I wound up next to Alice, who was several inches shorter and several bra sizes smaller than Angie. Alice was wearing a yellow tank

Stage Fright

top that revealed a well-tanned and surprisingly muscular set of shoulders and upper arms in addition to a small U-shaped patch of cleavage.

To myself, I said this is a woman who lifts weights. To Alice, I said, "You guys gave us another exciting show tonight. The explosion of the rabbit population wasn't quite as scary as the falling sandbag, though."

"I still have nightmares about that sandbag," Alice said. "Every night I check the rigging before I walk out for the second act."

"Any theories about who's doing these things?" I asked.

Before Alice could respond, Frenchy said, "It's the Ojibway Indian ghost. Didn't anybody tell you about that?"

"We've heard something about an Indian ghost, although the tribe hasn't been specified," I said. "What do you know about this ghost?"

"All I know is that the theater was built on the spot where the Ojibway used to camp when they came to perform ceremonies to honor the spirit of the lake," Frenchy said. "Ask Herman Glock. He'll tell you the same thing."

"Ding Dong Bell doesn't think it's any ghost," Al said.

"What does Ding Dong know?" Frenchy said. "He's from New York. People around here all know the Ojibway used to camp right where the theater is."

"So why has this Ojibway ghost waited twenty-five years to get pissed off about the theater?" Al asked.

Frenchy rolled his dark eyes and shrugged. "Who can tell about ghosts? Or Indians, either, for that matter." He drained the remaining tap beer from his mug and waved the waitress over to our table. "Buy you guys a drink?"

"Why not?" Al said. "Tap beer for me."

"Ginger ale with no ice," I said. This provoked a more comedic double take from Frenchy than he had ever performed on stage, but he recovered his equilibrium in time to say, "Another round of the same for the three of us."

"So, you're convinced there really is a ghost?" I asked Frenchy.

"Gotta be," he said. "Nobody in the show would do this kind of shit. Could have killed Alice, for Christ's sake."

"Ding Dong says it has to be somebody who knows the script," I said.

"So, if the ghost watched a few rehearsals, he'd pretty soon know the script."

I turned to Alice, who was slurping on a mudslide, and asked, "What do you think? Do you buy the supernatural Native American haunt theory?"

"I guess I believe in the ghost," she said. "There's been so many things go wrong that it's hard to imagine a person doing them all."

Of course, I knew that "a person" had not done them all. At least two of the incidents had been set up by two different people, Eric and Angie, but this was not the time to go public with that information. When Al and I sat down, Angie had made an exaggerated show of looking away from me, but I could feel her eyes boring holes in my head while she waited for my response.

"It's kind of hard to imagine a ghost hoisting a forty-pound sandbag into the rigging and stringing the rope around the set," I said. I glanced at Angie and she spun her head away.

"That's true, but like I said, I don't see why a real person would do all this."

"Ain' no ghost!" said Angie. This probably was only her second rum and coke, and she was already slightly sloshed. I decided that Angela Maguire was a cheap, but altogether too frequent, drunk.

"You think it's somebody in the cast or the crew?" Al asked.

"I sure as hell do. An' I think I know who it is, too."

That brought all four of us to attention. Al got the word out first: "Who?"

"I'm lookin' at the sneaky bastard right now," Angie said.

We followed her gaze, which was focused on the front door. A tall man with brown hair that almost brushed his lumberjack-size shoulders, dressed in jeans and a T-shirt that said "Coed Naked Canoeing" on the back, was passing under the EXIT sign.

"You think it's Eric Laflamme?" Frenchy asked.

"I'd bet my ass on it," said Angie.

"I'll take a piece of that bet," Frenchy said. He was still rocking with laughter at his own unscripted humor when Al and I excused ourselves and walked out into the night. The rain clouds had moved east, toward the Twin Cities, and the sky was flecked with thousands more stars than were visible under the halo of ambient light in St. Paul.

"Your last night's bed partner seems to think the ghost's identity is as clear as that sky," Al said.

"She was not — I repeat, not — my bed partner last night, and she was sloshed tonight," I said. "But drunk or sober, I don't trust anything Angie says about Eric."

"Okay, so Angie was half in the bag when she pointed her finger at Eric la former flame. But he does look like he could lift a full bag of sand without any problem."

"Let's hit the sack," I said.

Chapter 11
Another Opening, Another Show

Al rolled out of the sack early Friday morning, barreled into the bathroom for a couple of more pain killers to soothe his throbbing head, and said he was going off to snag some walleyes with his kids. The morning plans of Carol and Martha were unknown, but I was pretty sure they didn't include Warren Mitchell, so I snoozed a while longer before indulging myself in a large breakfast in the dining room, accompanied only by the morning newspaper.

After stuffing myself with bacon, scrambled eggs, and toast in preparation for whatever new difficulties the day would dish out, I wrapped up some leftovers in a napkin and took the package back to the cabin for Sherlock Holmes. While he mewed in gratitude for his breakfast, I mused in puzzlement over my double dilemma: how to placate the distressed Martha Todd and how to handle the unpleasant story that was unfolding at the Glock Family Theatre.

Martha was the more immediate concern. I hadn't written a line about the goings-on at the Glock Family Theatre since "Mysterious missile barely misses bagging Alexandria actress," but I was officially on vacation, so Thursday night's rabbits, although they were fair game, could wait awhile. And, I thought, who knows? There might be an even more hairy story to write after the official opening night performance, which was only eleven hours away.

My fear was that Martha would decide to go back to St. Paul without giving me a chance to explain Angie's presence and state of semi-dishabille. I didn't blame Martha for being hurt and angry, but damn it, the least she could do was listen to my side of the story. I would march straight to the door of the Jeffreys' cabin and demand an audience with the lady.

Demand? Better make that "request." I was well enough acquainted with the guardian of the gate to know that demands got you nowhere with Carol Jeffrey. A polite, politic approach was more likely to produce the desired result.

Carol answered my knock, and I explained my mission as coolly as a diplomat angling for ice fishing rights in February. She stepped outside, led me to the picnic table beside the cabin, and offered me a seat facing the lake. She sat across from me and over her shoulder, about fifty yards offshore, I could see Al and his kids anchored near the lily pads where the sunfish and perch waited for their worm-laden hooks. Apparently they had forsaken the pursuit of the wary walleye and were concentrating their efforts on hooking a sure thing for the frying pan.

"First of all, you have to know that Martha is terribly hurt," Carol said. "She tells me she was just reaching a level of trust with you after having been through a horrible marriage to a man who lied, cheated, and beat the crap out of her."

"I know all about that," I said. "Her memories of the way that bastard treated her have been a major pothole in our road to romance."

"Well, you can understand her disillusionment then when she walks into your cabin and finds a naked woman coming out of your bedroom."

"Only half-naked. She was wearing my sweatpants."

"Whatever. Martha said it looked like a pair of twin torpedoes coming straight at her. She probably didn't check below sea level."

Not a bad description of Angie's unfettered tits, I thought. Aloud, I said, "Damn it, Carol, I told you exactly what happened that night! Even if you don't believe me, it's the absolute god's truth, and I need to explain that to Martha before she bails out for home and never speaks to me again."

Carol's blue eyes locked onto mine, and our gaze held steady for a good sixty seconds, during which I somehow managed to avoid blinking. Finally, she said, "You really do care for this woman? Beyond sleeping with her over the weekend?"

"Yes, damn it, I do," I said. "It kills me to have hurt her, and I want to repair the damage if it's at all possible."

"I'm not sure it is, but I'll talk to Martha. I'll let you know if I can arrange for you two to discuss a peace treaty later today. I have managed to persuade her to stay and see the show tonight, so she won't be — as you put it — bailing out for home before tomorrow morning."

"Anything you can do will be greatly appreciated. Maybe even by both of us."

Carol reached across the table and squeezed my hand, the first gesture of sympathy she had given me since her initial encounter with a weeping Martha. "Okay, Mitch," she said. "I'll give it the old college try. Meanwhile, don't let any more drunken actresses into your cabin — especially if my husband is there with you." She walked back to the cabin, leaving me to contemplate the glorious expanse of sun-sparkled ripples dancing on the blue waters of the lake. No wonder the Ojibway would come here to pay homage to the aquatic spirits.

Back at my cabin, I pondered my other problem: To write or not to write, that was the question. I had more than enough anecdotes for an immediate story, but would it be nobler in the mind to wait until tonight's official opening, when the

Stage Fright

slings and arrows of outrageous fortune could possibly deepen the theater's sea of troubles?

Could possibly? Hell, it was a sure thing. I decided to wait.

While waiting, I watched Al and the kids scale and fillet a dozen sunfish and hung around their cabin hoping that Martha would come rushing out, announce that all was forgiven, and throw her arms around my neck with wild abandon. Eventually I gave up on that futile flight of fancy and went to the lodge for something more tangible — a cheeseburger and fries.

I spotted Ding Dong Bell and his stage manager, Margie Hansen, at a table by the front windows. As I walked past them, I said hello and gave them a "poor me" tale of being all by myself at lunchtime. Margie took the bait and invited me to join them. I graciously accepted, even though Ding Dong did not utter any welcoming sounds.

Without looking up at either of us, the director confessed to being badly hung over. His rapid consumption of alcohol had continued until the bar closed at one o'clock, and he was suffering the consequences eleven hours later. For lunch he was having tomato juice and dry toast, a combination he said would still the thudding hammer in his head and soothe the roiling demons in his gut. It would have made me even sicker.

The director and stage manager had met to discuss the upcoming opening performance. Hangover and all, Ding Dong was double-checking every light and sound cue, the placement of every prop, and the timing of the set cleanup between acts.

When they finished, I broached the subject I knew they didn't want to hear. "Are there any clues about the instigator of last night's rabbit caper hopping about?"

"Nothing," Ding Dong said.

"Too bad you didn't take roll call in the dressing room during intermission," I said. "If you knew who was absent, you might have a lead."

"We'll be counting heads tonight," Margie said.

"You have any idea who wasn't accounted for last night?" I asked.

"No," she said. "I went outside, myself, for a smoke after we cleaned up the set."

"Too bad," I said, mentally adding Margie to our ever-expanding list of possible ghosts. She was, after all, in an excellent position to perpetrate any of those acts of sabotage, although I wondered if she was strong enough to move a cage full of rabbits onto the set or to hoist the sandbag that nearly sent Alice Prewitt to the hospital or worse. Margie was only about five-foot-two and probably weighed a pudgy one-thirty, but she might have a helper with biceps.

"What about before the opening?" I said. "Is anybody guarding the stage today?"

"Jimmy Storrs will be there all day," Ding Dong said.

"And I'm going in to take his place for a couple of hours so that he can eat dinner and go over the tech cues," Margie said. Oh, great, I thought. Two of our prime candidates for foxhood will be guarding the chicken coop.

"I hope everything goes according to the script," I said, firmly believing that wouldn't. "Is the house sold out?"

"Opening night is always sold out," Margie said. "It's the rest of the run we worry about. There's a reviewer coming from the local paper, so we need a good show in order to get a good write-up."

"Are they sending a staff writer who is qualified to review a play or is it some stringer with no training?" I asked. Maybe this sounded like newspaper snobbery, but it could make quite a difference in the review.

"Usually it's the drama professor from the community college," Margie said. "He's a pretty good writer, and he's always been good to us." I wondered how the good professor would have handled twenty-four bunnies bounding out of the bathroom — and I wondered what unrehearsed dramatic development he might be faced with describing to his readers after opening night.

Opening night at the Glock Family Theatre had always been a dress-up affair. I learned of this tradition while interviewing Ding Dong Bell for the Sunday feature story, so my vacation wardrobe included one suit, one button-down collar shirt, one paisley-print tie and one pair of shoes made of leather that could be polished (although it seldom was). Herman Glock and his board of directors would be decked out in tuxedos, but we mere ticket buyers weren't required to go to that extreme.

I had showered and was just pulling on my skivvies when I heard a knock on the cabin door. Who's there now, I wondered, figuring that Al would just walk in. Since it could be a stranger, or, God forbid, Angela Maguire, I quickly pulled on my pants and trotted barefoot and shirtless to the door, zipping up my fly as I went. I was glad that I had made this conservative gesture because the knocker was Martha Todd.

"Hi," she said, with a forced, self-conscious half-smile. Spurts of sweat surfaced in my armpits, and I returned the awkward greeting while she gave my state of semi-undress the once-over. "Are you alone?" she asked.

Stage Fright

I assured her that there was nobody here except me and a snoozing Sherlock Holmes and invited her in. This time it was my feline companion who came trotting out of the bedroom to greet her. Martha scooped him up and snuggled him against her face, causing him to purr and me to wish that for the next few minutes I could be a cat.

"Did you come back to take custody of Sherlock Holmes because I'm an unfit guardian for a tomcat?" I asked.

"I came back because Carol and I talked to that frizzy-haired bimbo who spent the night naked in your bed," Martha said.

"She wasn't naked; she was wearing my sweatpants," I said. "Anyway, what did she tell you?"

"She said she thinks you're gay. She said she offered you the best — well, you know what she offered you — and you turned her down cold. Are you gay, Mitch?"

"I would be more than happy to demonstrate that I'm not."

"At this point, a simple yes or no will suffice."

"No, Martha, I am not gay. I turned down Angie's offer of unmatched erotic stimulation because (a) she was drunk as the proverbial pole cat and (b) I have absolutely no desire to get physically involved with that woman."

"Is there any woman you do want to get physically involved with?"

"There is one," I said. "If you want to see her, there's a mirror in the bathroom."

Martha's coffee-with-cream face actually darkened with a blush. "Okay, let's drop the subject," she said. "Since the story you told Carol more or less matches what Angela said about your response to her freewill offering, I'm here to apologize for not giving you a chance to explain."

"You don't need to apologize. I can imagine how it looked from where you were standing when Angie came bouncing out of the bedroom."

"Bouncing is an understatement. Those boobs are incredible."

Having been skin-to-skin with those boobs, I could confirm that assessment. However, I was not interested in getting any deeper into a discussion of Angie's physical high points, so I passed up the opportunity to say that boobs that big would be hard to handle. Instead, I changed the subject. "Does this visit also mean that you're willing to accompany me to tonight's performance of *Long Night's Journey Into Day*?"

"Actually, Carol, Al, and the kids and I are going to dinner at the lodge before the show and I came here to invite you to join us."

"Do I have time to finish dressing?"

Glenn Ickler

"You'd better take time. The sign on the dining room door says no shoes, no shirt, no service."

"I'm three for three in that category," I said. "Why don't you and Sherlock have a seat while I become appropriately attired?"

"Okay. But we're all hungry, so hurry it up."

"Keep your shirt on," I said.

"Bet you never said that to Angela," said Martha. God, women certainly do know how to hurt a guy!

The theater was already more than three-quarters full when our party of four arrived after dropping Kevin and Kristin at the game room, which was supervised by an adult on performance nights. Our seats were in the center section in the middle of Row E, and I ran interference, mumbling "excuse us" while bringing a pair of seated couples to their feet so we could pass. I was followed by Martha, Carol, and Al, in that order.

In the seat on my right was a mid-thirtyish woman with a ballpoint pen in her hand and a press kit on her lap. As I sat down, she acknowledged my presence with a curt nod of her curly brunette head, which barely came to the height of my shoulder.

"You reviewing the show?" I asked.

"I guess," she said. "I got sent here at the last minute because the guy who usually does this came down with a case of galloping GIs."

That's really the shits, I said to myself. To the woman, I said, "What paper are you working for?"

"The *Alexandria Daily Times*," she said. "I'm a reporter, not a theater critic."

"So, just report what you see and hear on the stage."

"It's not that simple. My editor expects me to analyze the damn play and tell the readers whether it's any good or not."

"Just tell them it's a laugh-filled, wonderfully entertaining farce."

"Why haven't you got a press kit? You sound like a reviewer."

"Like you, I'm a reporter. Only I'm on vacation."

"From what paper?" I told her my name and where I worked. She looked properly impressed, stuck out her right hand and said, "I'm Heather Rondeau. I'd love to work for a paper as big as the *Daily Dispatch*."

"Maybe you will some day," I said. As I shook the proffered paw, the house lights began their slow, pre-curtain fade into darkness.

In the gloom, Heather sighed and said, "I hope this won't be a waste of time."

"I've been watching rehearsals, and I can guarantee you that it won't be," I said.

Halfway through the first act, my guarantee became solid gold.

The stage was occupied only by Angela Maguire, otherwise known as Sheba, and Andy Anderson, playing the john known as Georgie, who had emerged together from a room at the head of the stairs. With a moonstruck look on his face, Georgie took Sheba by the shoulders, gazed soulfully into her eyes and said, "Sheba, baby, this has been the most exciting night of my ... what the goddamn hell?"

Chapter 12
Let there be Light

Georgie's mid-sentence ad-libbed expletive was motivated by a sudden loss of illumination. Every cavity in the building — stage, auditorium, light booth, foyer, what have you — had been plunged into an impenetrable blackness. Even the eternal flame of the EXIT signs that glowed red over the doorways was extinguished.

Being in a blacked-out theater with 310 people is an experience that stays in one's memory. First, in stereo, I heard simultaneous shouts of "Oh, my God!" from Martha on my left and Heather on my right. A split second later, the ebony air was filled with a cacophony of women's shrieks, men's expletives, and the inevitable "son of a bitch" from Ding Dong Bell's seat in the last row. Mingled with this, and all but drowned out, were repeated requests from Herman Glock to "please remain calm."

Nobody paid the slightest attention to poor Herman. I could hear people colliding, swearing, and pushing as they tried to get to the aisles. I couldn't imagine what they planned to do once they got there, with no light to guide them toward an exit. Our little group was going nowhere, as I heard Al saying, "Just hang tight," on one side and Heather saying, "I'm not moving until I can see" on the other.

The bedlam was reduced to the proverbial dull roar by the appearance of a flashlight beam, arcing across the audience from the lip of the stage. From behind the waving light came the voice of stage manager Margie Hansen, begging for calm, quiet, and patience while technicians were looking into the problem and attempting to restore power. Lulled more by the light than by Margie's voice, people stopped trying to shove each other out of the way and the communal writhing — but not the bitching — subsided.

"What's the matter, Herman, didn't you pay the light bill?" shouted one oh-so-clever and original comedian in the second row.

"Where was Herman when the lights went out?" yelled another.

"In the dark," somebody replied.

"This is better than the frickin' script," said a female voice at my right elbow. It was Heather, making her first critical observation of the evening.

"Let there be light!" I said. And to my amazement, there was light.

Stage Fright

"Hey, that's pretty good," Heather said. "Do you have a direct connection to somebody upstairs?"

"If, by upstairs, you mean the lighting booth, I might have."

Before Heather could respond, Herman Glock came charging down the aisle, ascended the steps onto the stage and looked down into 310 unsmiling faces. "Somebody threw the main switch," Herman said. "Obviously, it was an accident, and I apologize for the inconvenience. Now, if you'll all just take your seats, we will resume the show from where the lights ... from where we left off."

"I'm takin' my seat home," said a man in the front row.

"Me, too," said another and suddenly there was a stampede of asses toward the exits. Herman stood at the edge of the stage, pleading with the people to stay and see the rest of the show, but at least half the seats were empty when the ebb tide stopped flowing through the exits and Angie and Andy assumed their starting positions on stage.

At the intermission, I turned to Heather and said, "Well, you'll have more than the quality of the production to report on."

"That was scary shit," she said. "People could have been trampled, and somebody could have been hurt really bad."

I nodded and wondered if she had heard about any of the rehearsal incidents. "It was different," I said. "Even kind of spooky in a way."

"I doubt if the spook had anything to do with it," Heather said.

"There's a spook?" I asked, with a tone of utmost ignorance.

"Oh, we've heard some stories at the paper about this theater being haunted because it was built on an Indian ceremonial ground. Personally, I think it's bullshit."

"You don't believe in ghosts?"

"I don't believe in anything I can't see with my own eyes and have verified by two other reliable sources. Just ask yourself, if this spot is so frickin' sacred, why would an Indian ghost wait twenty-five years to start haunting the theater?"

"I have asked myself that," I said.

"Oh, then you do know about the ghost stories," Heather said.

Before I could remove my foot from my oversized mouth, the lights dimmed and the second act began. The performance finished without further incident, but there was no feeling of exaltation coming from either the stage or the auditorium as the cast members stiffly took their bows and the remaining customers mechanically applauded.

"You going to write anything for your paper?" Heather asked as we moved toward the aisle.

"I guess I'll have to," I said. "Like I said, I'm here on vacation, but it's hard to pass up reporting an opening-night theater blackout with a full house."

"I'll be looking for your story," she said as she turned away and began pushing and weaving her way toward the lobby.

"Yeah," I said. "I'll be watching for yours, too."

Al's kids were in bed and we four adults were sitting around the kitchen table in the Jeffreys' cabin at eleven o'clock. Each of us was sipping the beverage of his or her choice. Al had a beer, the women had white wine, and I had my usual ginger ale.

"So what are you going to write?" Carol asked when I said it was time for me to go back and pull out my laptop.

"I'm going to say that the blackout was the latest in a series of troubles that have beset this production right from the start of the rehearsal period and then list some of the previous incidents. Maybe I can pull in some bits about plays that are supposedly jinxed, like Macbeth, for example."

"What's with Macbeth being jinxed?" Martha asked.

"It seems that somebody in the cast always gets hurt when Macbeth is produced," I said. "In order to stay safe, you're not supposed to mention the title or say the last line on stage until the opening performance."

"Sounds like a lot of crap," Al observed.

"Hey, I was in a production in which the guy playing Macbeth got his hand slashed open to the tune of twenty-some stitches during the big sword fight with MacDuff at the end," I said. "Macbeth took his curtain call with a bloody towel wrapped around his hand. We had to do an additional benefit performance to help the guy pay his emergency room bill because he didn't have insurance."

"You were in a production of *Macbeth*?" asked Martha.

"Is that so surprising?" I said. "I've actually done quite a bit of community theater. That's the only Shakespeare, though."

"I had no idea you were an actor," she said. "Maybe I should reevaluate your story about the bare-breasted blonde in your bedroom."

"That was not an act," I said. "Now, ladies and gentleman, I absolutely have to exit to my cabin and write a story for the morning edition, the early-run deadline for which is less than an hour away. Who's going to be joining me there tonight?" I looked hopefully at Martha, who pointed to the beer drinker on my left.

Stage Fright

"Al is," Martha said. Seeing my undisguised disappointment, she added, "It's not that I'm still mad at you, Mitch. It's just that every time I walk into that cabin I see those twin torpedoes bearing down on me from the bedroom. There's no way I can spend a night in there."

"What if I get a different cabin?"

"Go write your story and I'll see you in the morning." She offered her lips for good night kiss but didn't leave them in position very long. I could still feel their gentle brush, however, while I was writing my story about the events leading up to this night's adventure and wondering what Saturday night's performance might add to the lore of *Long Night's Journey Into Day*.

When I entered the dining room to have breakfast Saturday morning, I saw a doleful Ding Dong Bell sitting all by himself, sipping from a freshly-filled cup of coffee. I greeted him, got no response other than a nod, and asked if I could join him. This evoked another wordless movement of his head, so I plopped myself down and inquired about the condition of said noggin.

"I ain't hung over, if that's what you're asking," Ding Dong said. "I was so goddamn frustrated and pissed off and sick to my stomach that I didn't even have a drink last night. I just sat around until after midnight with Herm and a couple of his board members and tried to figure out a way to put an end to this shit."

"And did you?" I asked.

"Not really. The board chairman — you know, the car salesman — thinks Herm ought to bring in an Ojibway medicine man to do sort of an exorcism in case there really is a devilish Indian ghost raising hell in the theater."

"What do you think about that?"

"I think it's bullshit, but it ain't my theater. If something happens tonight, which I think is more 'when' than 'if,' I'll bet that Herm will be desperate enough to call in the medicine man."

"And what will Herman do when that doesn't work?"

"Who knows? But whatever happens during the rest of the run, it ain't my worry. I'm on a plane to New York tomorrow afternoon."

"You're leaving that soon?"

"My work was done when the curtain went up opening night," said the director. "It's up to the stage manager and tech director to run things for the next three weeks."

"Aren't they the two chief suspects to be the Indian ghost?" I asked.

"They're in the best spots to be setting up this shit, but there's others who could be doing it. Almost any son of a bitch in the cast or crew could have pulled the switch last night with only two people on stage."

"So, you're saying that only Angie and Andy are in the clear?"

"And Fred Sorenson, who I know was in the light booth. He had just made a lighting change right on cue, so he wouldn't have had time to run down to the basement and throw the main switch."

"Is there any way of eliminating people by figuring out who was in the dressing room and who was backstage waiting for an entrance or picking up props?"

"Those pain-in-the-ass Lapierres were supposed to be entering from opposite sides of the stage, but who knows if both of them were in place? And every single person we talked to after the show gave us a different list of who was in the dressing room and who was outside having a smoke or in the can taking a piss when the lights went out."

The waitress arrived with a couple slices of buttered toast for Ding Dong, who winced when he heard me order a mushroom, ham and cheese omelet with hash browns and whole wheat toast. I promised to hide the plate behind my water glass and the small bouquet in the center of the table and asked him if he thought that the car salesman, Oscar Olson, really believed a ghost was slinging sandbags, cutting up chairs, hauling in a 200-pound cage of rabbits, and turning out the theater's lights.

"It's hard to figure him out," Ding Dong said. "Also, the banker guy pretty much backed him up when he talked about the ghost. They both seem like smart people, but smart people sometimes have really wacky ideas, so the schmuck could be serious."

"Or he could be blowing smoke," I said. "But if that's the case, he would seem to be putting off finding the real guilty party. Why would the chairman of the board be doing that?"

"Makes no son-of-a-bitching sense to me. But, then nothing else does either."

We sat in silence, with Ding Dong nibbling at his toast, until the waitress approached with my omelet. "Sorry," said the director, rising from his chair. "If I stay at the same table with that I'm going to be sick all over my shoes." He took his cup of coffee and walked out of the dining room, leaving me to wonder what an Ojibway exorcism ceremony would be like.

I was pondering this, hoping they'd let Al take pictures of the medicine man at work, when a small, curly-haired woman with a newspaper in one hand appeared in the doorway, looked around, spotted me, and approached at a stubby-legged trot.

Stage Fright

"Thanks a whole hell of a lot for not mentioning that last night's blackout wasn't the first time that something goofy happened with this show," said Heather Rondeau as she arrived at my table. She was holding the outstate edition of the morning *St. Paul Daily Dispatch*, with my story chronicling all the ongoing problems at the Glock Family Theatre prominently displayed on the regional front.

Chapter 13
A Doctor in the House?

At four-foot-eleven, Heather didn't exactly tower over me, even though I was sitting down. Her green eyes were roughly level with mine, and I could see the fires of prospective mayhem burning within them.

Assuming an air of wounded innocence, I said, "Where is it written that a reporter who has been on the scene, working a story for two weeks, is required to share background information with the most recent arrival on the block?"

"I didn't say you should give me your friggin' notes," she snapped. "I just think you might have had the decency to mention that there were a bunch of previous screw-ups so I could chase down the owner and find out for myself."

"The owner wouldn't have given you the time of day, or, in this case, night," I said. "All I got from dear old Herman was 'no comment.' I had to do a lot of legwork, and I'm not in the habit of sharing."

The flames in her eyes died down a bit and she plopped into a chair on the other side of the table. "You're right," she said, with a sigh. "I should have asked a hell of a lot more questions last night before I took off and started writing. I just got royally pissed when your paper came out this morning and made my story look like shit."

"Well, you can always do a follow for Sunday."

"That's what I'm here for," she said. "But if the owner won't talk, who will?"

It occurred to me that a reporter who worked in this town might be able to provide a morsel or two of helpful background information about some of the local dignitaries, such as the owner of a large auto sales agency and the president of the biggest bank in town. With this potential quid pro quo in mind, I generously offered to steer Heather toward some prime sources for her follow story.

"Among the actors, Alice Prewitt and Rhonda Lapierre can give you the juiciest quotes, if they're willing to talk, which they might be after last night's fiasco." Then, as an afterthought, I added, "Eric Laflamme can also give you an earful." I resisted the temptation to advise Heather to ask Angie Maguire about the earful Eric gave her and the mouthful she gave him. I had left those tender tidbits out of my story because they didn't pertain to the dirty doings of the so-called ghost.

"What about the director?" Heather asked. "Will he talk to me, do you think?"

Stage Fright

"Ding Dong has been under orders from Herman to keep his mouth shut about what's been going on here but he may be ready to spill his guts, especially after he sees everything laid out in my story this morning. Besides, he's going back to New York tomorrow, so it's worth a shot."

"He's leaving tomorrow?" Heather said.

"That's right," I said. "He says his job here is done, and he wants to get back to the comparative calm and quiet of New York City."

She bounced off the chair and said, "I'd better get after him right away."

"Good luck, or should I say 'break a leg?' Maybe we could get together and check each other's notes before you dash back to your office."

Heather pondered that for a minute before she agreed, and I figured she was trying to scope out the motive behind my sudden generosity. "Okay," she said at last, and with a wave of her hand she was off across the room to beard the mighty director at his table.

I sipped coffee, read my morning paper, and kept an eye on the interview. Heather introduced herself, and Ding Dong waved her away. She sat down across from him, notebook and ballpoint in hand, and started firing questions. Ding Dong stood up, and I was afraid he was going to walk away, but she said something that persuaded him to sit down again. His body language told me he would rather be in the seventh circle of Dante's hell, but he stayed there and talked, occasionally uttering a "son of a bitch" loud enough for me to hear.

Ten minutes later, Ding Dong rose again, turned and walked toward the door. To my surprise, Heather Rondeau stood up and followed him. The director nodded in my direction as he passed, and Heather hesitated long enough to whisper, "He's going to give me a cast list so I can phone some of the actors. See you tonight."

Well, shit, I thought, there goes my chance to pick her brain about Olson and Glanz. While I was wondering what to do next, my answer arrived in the form of Herman Glock. If Heather's eyes had been a bonfire, Herman's were a roaring inferno.

"How could you write that all that crap about my theater?" he asked. "You've ruined us. Absolutely ruined us!"

"I don't think so, Herman," I said, noting that his sledgehammer hands were clenched into white-knuckled fists. "After more than 300 people saw the lights go out last night, there was no way I could keep folks in the dark about all the shit that's been plaguing this show. And after tonight's ticket holders read this story, I'll bet you won't get one cancellation. They'll all want to see what's going to happen next."

79

Glenn Ickler

"Nothing's going to happen next," he said. "Except you're going to pack up your computer and get the hell out of my resort. And you can take your picture-taking buddy with you."

"Are you planning to refund our money for the portion of the week we don't get?" I really didn't think this would cancel the eviction notice, because we only had one night remaining, but I was stalling in hope that I could cool him down.

I was right about the futility of my refund request. "I'll give back the money for the whole goddamn week just to get you out of here," Herman said.

"Why don't you hold off on the refund until you see how many people cancel their reservations?" I suggested. "If I've really hurt your business, I'll leave before dinner, and you won't have to give me back a dime."

Herman's eyes continued to smolder like the rubble from a house fire while he considered that proposition.

"And as for my photographer buddy, he's got his family here, and he didn't shoot any pictures of the incidents," I said, hoping to pour still more coolant on the ashes. "Surely you don't want to cheat his little kids out of their last day of fishing just because of something I wrote."

"Check with me at five o'clock at the front desk," Herman said. He turned and stalked away, holding his back so rigid it looked like someone had rammed a broomstick up his butt.

If I was right about human nature, there would be few, if any, cancellations. The problem then would be getting a ticket for myself. There was no way in hell I was going to miss that night's performance, even if I had to stand for two hours way up in the lighting booth.

When I arrived at the front desk to meet Herman at the agreed-upon hour, he was on the phone, and had the flustered look of a puppy trying to decide whether to chase the squirrel prancing around in the yard or to take a run at the nearby family cat.

"We've had over fifty calls," Herman said as he put the receiver down.

Oh, shit, I thought. Time to pack my bags. Aloud, I said, "Fifty cancellations?"

"Two cancellations," he said. "The rest wanted tickets."

"Then you're still sold out for tonight?"

"We are. I guess I was wrong about people."

"There's an old saying about any publicity being good publicity," I said. "Does this mean I can stay here tonight?"

Stage Fright

"It does, with my apologies," Herman said. "And I saved you a complementary seat right next to Ding Dong for tonight's performance. You'll be disappointed, though, because nothing — I mean absolutely nothing — is going to happen that isn't in the script."

"I hope you're right," I said, even though I was certain that he was wrong. "And thanks." I wouldn't have to stand for two hours in the lighting booth, after all.

II

Alan Jeffrey did wind up in the cramped little booth that night because there were no other empty seats. Carol and Martha didn't even try to get in. Five minutes before curtain, Fred Sorenson, who was running the lights and sound, found a rusty metal folding chair so Al didn't have to stand.

However, there was one standee. I saw her slip in just as the lights were dimming for Act One. She stationed herself against the rear wall of the house, and because she was an inch less than five feet tall nobody else noticed that Heather Rondeau was there.

The curtain went up and I became aware of a string of tense muscles in my neck and shoulders. I made a conscious effort to relax these muscles and to breathe evenly every couple of minutes, but still I found myself expelling a long sigh of relief when the curtain rolled down to end the act, which actually had gone smoother than I had ever seen it. As the lights came up for intermission, I went out to the lobby where Al had promised to meet me if anyone was still in the theater.

"What do you think?" he asked, knowing damn well what I thought.

"I think we're in for a nasty surprise somewhere in Act Two," I said. "I just hope nobody gets hurt when the shit hits the fan."

The lobby lights blinked, and we returned to our seats. The curtain went up, no sandbags came down, and Act Two began as smoothly as its predecessor.

Maybe this really is the night that nothing goes wrong, I said to myself as Andy Anderson, playing Georgie, raced up the stairs shouting for Salome, who was played by Julie Christensen. Salome was behind one of the doors that opened onto the second-floor balcony. The script called for Georgie to rattle the knob, discover Salome's door was locked, and attempt to yank it open by pulling hard on the knob. Eventually he would give up in despair and run pell-mell down the stairs, shouting his undying love for the whore in hiding.

Glenn Ickler

Georgie arrived at the door and rattled the knob, all the while calling for Salome. Then he grabbed the knob and gave a mighty tug.

The knob came off in Andy Anderson's hand, sending him reeling backward against the railing of the balcony. This railing was constructed of fragile two-by-twos, nailed lightly into the floor of the balcony. The structure was not designed to hold any weight and the actors had been warned repeatedly not to lean so much as a hand on it. Consequently, when Andy's staggering, 200-pound body smashed into the railing, the structure disintegrated. Pieces of the railing — along with all of Andy Anderson — fell seven feet to the floor below.

Those in the audience who had never before seen this scene roared with laughter. Beside me, Ding Dong Bell simply roared. "Son of a bitch!" he yelled. "Son of a goddamn bitch!"

The laughter died immediately as it became apparent that Andy was not getting up. Ding Dong went running down the aisle, Julie Christensen emerged through the knobless door and stood dumfounded at the edge of the balcony looking down at Salome's ill-fated lover. Other people came popping onto the set from backstage, and everyone in the building could hear Andy yelling something about his leg. I got up and followed Ding Dong as far as the edge of the stage, where I almost collided head-on with a galloping Heather Rondeau.

"It's gotta be broken," she said, pointing at Andy. His right leg was twisted under him at a grotesque angle, and his agonized face was squinched up like a prune that had been left in the sun too long.

Ding Dong knelt beside Andy, looked at the leg and turned toward the audience, which had become as quiet as golf fans watching the deciding putt at the Masters tournament. "A doctor!" Ding Dong yelled. "Is there a doctor out there?"

From way at the back of the house, a baritone voice answered, "Here!" A moment later, a tall, broad-shouldered man walked past Heather and me and went up the stairs onto the stage. Under the stage lights, we could see that the man had copper-colored skin, high cheekbones, and a braid of coal black hair that fell halfway down his back. Heather's eyes met mine, and we shrugged in unison just as Al joined us and asked, "Do I really see an Indian on stage?"

That night's ticket buyers never saw the denouement of *Long Night's Journey Into Day*. They saw Heather Rondeau call 911 on her cell phone. They saw the director, cast, and crew try to comfort Andy Anderson while he alternately groaned and whimpered in pain. Those who waited the necessary fifteen minutes saw two briskly efficient EMTs trot in with a gurney, place the agonized and protesting actor

Stage Fright

on it, and trundle him off the set toward the scene shop door. It was déjà vu all over again.

After the exit of the emergency crew and their patient, Heather, Al, and I saw Ding Dong Bell and Herman Glock each take one of Julie Christensen's arms and almost drag her out of the theater. The director and the producer were so eager to get Julie into Herman's office and quiz her about the doorknob that they didn't even give her time to change out of the bright red teddy she was wearing for her next scene.

"God, would I like to have a mike planted in that office!" Heather said.

"Wish I'd thought of that," I said. "Or I wish we had a uniform from the costume shop," I added as we watched one of the Douglas County sheriff's deputies who had accompanied the ambulance pursue the trio.

"Do you think that actress loosened the knob?" Heather asked.

"It would seem too obvious, but anything is possible," I said.

"I think she's an innocent bystander," said Al.

"She might have done it by accident," Heather said. We both stared at her as if we were seeing a creature from some other planet. "Or not," she added in a small voice.

"This is it," Herman Glock said to a hushed gathering of cast and crew members and we three representatives of the news media in the lodge bar an hour later. He and Ding Dong and the cop had browbeaten poor Julie Christensen to tears before they were satisfied that she had nothing to do with the dicey doorknob. I had e-mailed my story to the Sunday Daily Dispatch and Heather had phoned a report to her city desk.

"This is the end of this production," Herman continued. "Andy's leg is obviously broken, and there's no way in hell we can replace him."

"Son of a bitch!" said Ding Dong Bell. "We worked so goddamn hard on this son-of-a-bitching show, and now it's down the shitter." He tossed down a scotch on the rocks in one gulp and slammed the glass down for a refill.

"Isn't there anyway you can get another actor to fill in, Mr. Glock?" asked Rhonda Lapierre. "We've all put so much into this show, you can't just call it off."

"Where would we get one?" Herman asked. "We've already cancelled tomorrow's matinee, and you can't expect some poor bastard to walk in here cold and learn the part in time for next Thursday night's show."

"Your only hope would be get somebody who is at least half familiar with the show," said Ding Dong.

83

"How about somebody who's been working backstage, like Jimmy Storrs?" asked Rhonda.

Jimmy almost fell off his barstool with a bottle of beer in his hand. "No way are you getting me on that stage," he yelled, teetering on his tiptoes as he struggled to remain standing. "Especially for this wacky show. It's jinxed. We're better off closing it down right now."

"I'm afraid you're right," said Herman. "I can't see anybody with either the talent or the desire to step into Andy's role."

My friend, Alan Jeffrey, nudged me and said, "You're going to hate me for this."

"For what?" I asked.

He turned toward the director, who was raising another glass filled with scotch and ice to his lips, and said, "Ding Dong, there is one person here who has been watching this show all week and who has community theater acting experience."

It wasn't hard to guess who Al meant. "Knock it off, you asshole!" I said.

"Think about it!" Al said. "You can save this theater and get a great story, all at the same time."

"Who are you talking about?" Ding Dong asked.

"My buddy, Mitch Mitchell," said Al, pushing me forward with a vocalized "ta-da!" fanfare. "He's familiar with the show and, in my humble opinion, he's a very capable performer."

"You've never said that before," I said.

"Agents stretch the truth all the time," said Al. "Now tell these nice folks you'll be proud and happy to appear as Georgie."

"Are you nuts? My vacation is over. I have to go back to work Monday."

"I'll bet you can talk Don into making next week's rehearsals and performances into an assignment. Just think — a first person account of the caring, benevolent reporter rushing to the rescue in a do-or-die battle with the ghost of the Glock Family Theatre."

"Bullshit!" was my caring, benevolent reply.

Ding Dong had slid off his barstool and was standing in front of me. "You think you could learn the lines?" he asked.

"That's the easy part," I said. "Who could teach me the blocking and coach me on characterization? You're going back to New York tomorrow."

"If you take Andy's part, I'll cancel my flight and stay another week," he said.

That changed the picture. How often does an amateur actor get to work with one of the world's premier professional directors?

"I'll have to talk my city editor into letting me do it," I said.

Stage Fright

"You can call him at home first thing in the morning," said Al. "I have great faith in your ability to con him into it, especially after he sees the story you sent in for the Sunday paper."

And so, as they say in the good book, it came to pass, with the grudging approval of city editor Don O'Rourke, that Warren Mitchell took over the role of Georgie, a character described in the script as a playboy with many more dollars than sense and a penis two sizes bigger than his brain. During the course of the show, Georgie makes it into the bedroom with all three prostitutes, which meant that I would be having intense rehearsal sessions with all three of the sexy young women in the cast. This fact was not lost on Martha Todd, who, after kissing me good-by late Sunday afternoon, said, "Have fun with the hookers, Mitch. But not too much fun!"

I assured Martha that any imaginary intimacies that occurred onstage would not become reality outside the confines of the proscenium.

"Call me once in a while with progress reports," Martha said. "And get me a ticket for Saturday night's performance." I promised that I would keep her up to date, both on my development as a rich and randy rake and the steadfast spook's efforts to ruin the production. I assured her that I would welcome her with open arms — and an empty cabin — on Saturday.

Minutes after Martha and the Jeffreys drove away, I learned of a plan to deal with the spook. During the private talks involving Herman Glock, his theater board members, and Ding Dong Bell, it had been decided to attempt an exorcism. An Ojibway medicine man had been persuaded to perform this rite on Sunday evening, before a rehearsal in which I would make my first attempt at portraying the playboy. The exorcism sounded like pure bullshit to me — and to Heather Rondeau — but we both vowed to witness the medicine man's machinations. The appointed hour was seven o'clock.

Chapter 14
Any True Believers?

Arriving at the theater at 6:37, I found Heather already there, with camera in hand. A few minutes later, Herman Glock and Ding Dong Bell arrived, followed by Oscar Olson and Gordon Glanz. Olson's first words were to Heather, telling her that the camera had to stay in her car. She replied, "The camera goes where I go."

"Then you'll go to the car, also," said Oscar. "This ceremony is not going to be turned into a media circus, with shutters clicking and flashes flashing." Heather decided he was serious and took the camera to the car, muttering mild obscenities all the way.

Taking Ding Dong aside, I asked, "Do you think there's any point in this?"

"It's nothing but a crock of superstitious bullshit," he replied. "Olson and Glanz dreamed this up and sold the idea to Herman. The poor son of a bitch is ready to try anything, no matter how screwy it sounds."

At 6:55, a black Lincoln drove up, and the medicine man emerged from the passenger side. He was decked out in full Plains Indian dress regalia, from the intricately beaded moccasins on his feet to the cluster of eagle feathers on his head. In between, he wore a buckskin jacket and loose-fitting trousers, both heavily decorated with beads and porcupine quills. The medicine man's face was inscribed with an assortment of symbols, but as he came closer, I had a feeling that something familiar lay beneath the paint.

Oscar Olson confirmed that feeling by announcing, "Allow me to introduce Doctor Henry Stone, otherwise known as Chief Running Deer, head medicine man of the Minnesota Ojibway tribe." Heather Rondeau and I exchanged quizzical looks. This was the doctor who had come forward to examine the injured Andy Anderson after the Saturday night fiasco.

We all trooped inside for the exorcism. Chief Running Deer, who was accompanied by a wizened, stoop-shouldered drummer aged somewhere between eighty and a hundred years, motioned for us to remain near the front door while he moved through the entire theater, chanting in his native tongue. He circled the foyer, went up and down the aisles in the auditorium, walked around the entire set, went through the door that had triggered the falling sandbag, and disappeared backstage. We heard the chanting and the solemn drumbeats move slowly from the scene shop to the area behind the flats and across to the other side, where he reappeared at stage left.

At center stage, the chief raised both hands high above his head and sang his final words loud enough for any spirit, no matter how long dead, to hear. When he lowered his arms, the drumming ceased.

"I'm sure you'll be safe from the ghost now," Heather whispered to me.

"Care to cover my back during rehearsals?" I asked.

"No, but I'll damn well be hanging around here to see what they do to you."

Oscar Olson and Gordon Glanz were shaking hands with the chief and thanking him for his efforts. I switched on my pocket tape recorder, walked over to them and asked for their comments on the ceremony.

The chief looked at me the way a picnicker eyes an approaching column of piss ants and left without even saying good-by. Glanz said, "I have no comment," and went out the door. This left Oscar Olson. I blocked his path to the door by moving into a position squarely in his face and, while Oscar was trying to decide whether or not to attempt an end run, Heather appeared at my left elbow.

Oscar decided to stand pat. "Well, it looks like I'm the spokesman," he said, flashing his car salesman smile. "All I can say is that Chief Running Deer is the most knowledgeable medicine man in this part of the country and if our problems were, in fact, being caused by a restless Ojibway spirit, they should now be at an end."

"How firmly do you believe that your problems were, in fact, being caused by a restless Ojibway spirit?" I asked.

"Firmly enough that I encouraged Herman to use this method in an effort to save his theater."

"Is the theater itself in danger, or just this production?"

"That's a matter for the board of directors to decide," Oscar said. "Now, if you'll excuse me, I have a wife keeping dinner warm for me at home. Good evening, lady and gentleman of the press."

"Bite me!" growled Heather under her breath. Oscar's step slowed just long enough to indicate that he might have heard her, but he went out the door without confirming my suspicion.

Soon the actors involved in my scenes as Georgie arrived, and Ding Dong walked me through the blocking. After two hours of drill, I had a feel for where I should be most of the time. I would begin to get a feel for, and of, the women with whom Georgie cavorted at the next rehearsal, Monday afternoon. My assignment for Monday morning was to memorize as many lines as my mind could absorb in one sitting.

Angela Maguire volunteered to take time off from her day job and come to my cabin to help with the learning process. Figuring that Angie would be more of a distraction than a learning aid, I resisted the temptation to share the morning with her, telling her that I needed to work alone at this stage of study. Actually, this was true. In addition, sidestepping Angie would enable me to brag about the preservation of my virtue when I checked in with Martha Todd Monday night.

I also had some other plans for the daylight hours on Monday. Heather Rondeau had promised to call me after doing some snooping into the background of Dr. Henry Stone aka Chief Running Deer. While she was doing that, I intended to study the program's thumbnail sketches of the actors and the crew in search of possible hints as to who might be responsible for the activities blamed on the ghost.

At eleven o'clock, after two hours of concentrated memory work, I decided to take a break and look over the cast list. I skipped quickly past the first two names, figuring that the wounded Andy Anderson wasn't a suspect, and the woman behind the door, Julie Christensen, had been grilled to the breaking point with negative results.

Next came Eric Laflamme, whose mutual sharing of Angie's charms gave him an obvious reason to hate Andy. Eric had the opportunity to loosen the doorknob, and he was strong enough to have handled the rabbit cage and hoisted the sandbag. The program notes said he was a woodshop teacher and football coach at the high school. I marked him as a possible suspect.

Then came Norman "Frenchy" Lapierre. Certainly he had both motive and opportunity to operate on his ex-wife's chair, but I asked myself if such a shrimp was strong enough to manipulate a wooden crate full of rabbits. Frenchy was an accountant in real life, and his hobbies, in addition to acting, were fishing and hunting. I decided he was a weak prospect, at best.

I immediately dismissed Rhonda Lapierre, figuring she wouldn't risk bodily injury by sabotaging her own chair.

Angela Maguire was a puzzle to me. Anyone who could sneak into the theater and pour piss into her erstwhile lover's whisky bottle was capable of any imaginable dirty trick. However, despite her prodigious chest measurement, I didn't think Angie had the upper body strength to hoist a sandbag or push that big box of bunnies into place. Still, I didn't dismiss her completely — she could be part of a team.

Stage Fright

I wrote off Alice Prewitt for the same reason I had passed on Rhonda Lapierre. I couldn't imagine Alice sandbagging herself. I did take time to read her bio and noted that she worked as a medical receptionist and her hobby was weightlifting, which confirmed my suspicion after observing her shoulders and biceps.

Next on the cast list was Randy Rhodes, the homophobe. It occurred to me that Randy might have other sexual hang-ups as well, hang-ups that could lead him to take destructive measures against a show about limitless lust and lasciviousness. Randy's bio said he worked in construction and was a deacon in his church. I decided to watch Randy a little closer.

The final cast member was Norman Rogers, the flaming gay who had managed to almost eliminate his swish while playing the role of a hell-raising heterosexual hunk. Norman was big — six-foot-one and at least 200 pounds — and certainly strong enough to be the theater ghost. The bio said he was a computer programmer and an amateur poet. Norman was not a likely suspect, but he was not a complete write-off, either.

Next came the crew. I couldn't imagine five-foot, two-inch Margie Hansen, who had been the stage manager for dozens of Glock Family Theatre productions, wrestling with the rabbit cage or pulling a forty-pound sandbag into the rigging. And Fred Sorenson, in the lighting booth, couldn't possibly have gotten backstage at the carefully timed moments when some of the traps were set.

Jimmy Storrs, the technical director, was another matter. He had access to all parts of the theater, he had knowledge of the script, and he had sufficient physical strength. I read his bio, looking for a possible motive, and saw he worked as an auto mechanic. I wondered if his employer was a competitor of Oscar Olson Motors. Jimmy needed to be checked out.

Clearing my mind as best I could, I returned to my line-learning chores until 12:30. At the lodge, I demolished a Reuben sandwich, a pile of potato chips, and a tall tumbler of iced tea in preparation for a rehearsal of Georgie's scenes in Act One. As customary, I arrived at the theater five minutes before the 1:30 call and was not surprised to see Heather Rondeau waiting for me.

Heather latched onto my left arm and dragged me into a corner at the rear of the auditorium. "I went through our files on Doctor Henry Stone and asked some people some questions about Chief Running Deer," she said. "I found out that he is a legitimate M.D., with a diploma from the U of M Medical School, and that his tribal activities seem to be pretty straight forward except for one item."

"And what is that item?" I asked.

"Two people who should know about such things told me that they think the chief is involved in some secret plans to build an Indian casino in Alexandria."

"Why secret?" I asked. "Indian casinos are legal in Minnesota."

"The big secret is in the financial backing," said Heather. "The local Ojibway don't have the money to start a casino, and the word is that the chief has been looking for someone — and not necessarily a Native American — to bankroll the project."

"That's interesting, but I don't see anything there that would be relevant to the Glock Family Theatre."

"Me, neither. The chief's only previous connection with the theater before the big exorcism performance seems to be that he bought a season ticket."

"Only one ticket?"

"He's not married, and nobody has ever seen him with a girl friend."

Just then, I heard the voice of Margie Hansen calling, "Places for Georgie's first entrance in Act One, please."

"That would be me," I said. "Let me know if you dig up anything that might lead to our nasty old ghost."

"Okay. And normally I'd say 'break a leg,' but that's kind of a touchy subject in this case."

I must confess that I spent a lot of time worrying about my leg — and every other part of my anatomy. I couldn't keep from looking over my shoulder and glancing up at the rigging every time I entered during the scenes we rehearsed that afternoon. The ghost might very well be pissed off about my emergence as an understudy for the fallen lothario. If so, I could be the next person targeted for a nasty surprise.

Despite my anxiety, the rehearsal was completed without any unscheduled events. Georgie had scenes with Sheba and Tania during the first act, and Margie Hansen got to stand-in for both roles because Angie Maguire and Alice Prewitt were back on duty at their day jobs. They were slated to join us for the evening rehearsal. Margie and I walked through the blocking, and I did a pretty good job of remembering the lines I had studied all morning. Ding Dong was favorably impressed.

The plan was to spend Tuesday afternoon and evening rehearsing my scenes in Act Two and to run me through all my scenes twice on Wednesday. My debut in front of a paying audience would come on Thursday night, if I hadn't been disabled by a ghostly act of violence before then.

Alan Jeffrey and his family had been offered free lodging for the weekend by an apologetic Herman Glock. They were planning to return in time to see the Friday evening performance. Martha Todd was due to join the party on Saturday, when we were scheduled to do both an afternoon and an evening performance. A Sunday matinee would complete the weekend's activities.

I planned to go back to St. Paul after the curtain fell Sunday, and resume my regular chores at the *Daily Dispatch* until the following Thursday, when the performance cycle would be repeated one more time at the Glock Family Theatre. After that, *Long Night's Journey Into Day* would be history. My sincere hope was that Warren Mitchell would not be history, as well.

The Monday night rehearsal also was accomplished without the interference of the so-called ghost. The highlights of my evening were clinches and some scripted grab-ass with Angie and Alice. These moments of intimacy had to be worked and reworked in order to overcome my unexpected reticence about feeling up a woman I hardly knew.

My shy, seventh-grade fumbling finally brought forth an explosion from Ding Dong Bell. "For Christ's sake, schmuck, just wrap your hands around her tits and enjoy yourself!" he yelled.

The scene went much better after that. After all, a guy has to do exactly as the director says. Well, doesn't he?

After the rehearsal, Ding Dong and the entire cast and crew adjourned to the bar in the Glock Family Resort lodge to unwind before going home. I was pleased to see everyone, from Julie Christensen to Jimmy Storrs, on hand because I intended to describe a little scheme that Al and I had cooked up to defrock the ghost. It was important that everybody on my list of suspects hear what I was going to say.

Chapter 15
Baiting the Trap

The assembly grew quiet when I announced that Alan Jeffrey and I had thought of a possible way to identify the theater ghost. I explained that our newspaper work brought us into contact with a wide variety of useful people. There were some audible "oohs" from my listeners when I said that one of these useful contacts was a St. Paul Police Department fingerprint expert.

"Al has persuaded the fingerprint man to follow him up here from St. Paul Friday afternoon," I said. "The guy can dust both the crate that held the rabbits, which is still sitting out behind the theater, and the main electric switch. Then he can take a set of prints from each of you."

"What if none of our prints match what he gets off the box and the switch?" asked Eric Laflamme.

"Then you will all be eliminated as suspects, which is what I hope is true," I said.

"Wait a minute," said Jimmy Storrs. "My prints are all over that goddamn rabbit box because I hauled it out of the theater."

"Are they also on the main switch?" I asked.

"No, I've never touched that switch."

"Then you shouldn't have a problem," I said, but I was pleased to see the worry clouds forming as Jimmy squinched up his eyes and forehead.

"When is this guy going to take our prints?" Frenchy Lapierre asked.

"Friday night, right after the performance," I said. "That's the best time because everybody connected with the show will be there."

"That's going to cut into our drinking time," Frenchy said.

"Maybe Herman will keep the bar open a little later. Anyway, it shouldn't take all that long. This guy has fingerprinted thousands of people, and he's very efficient."

Frenchy muttered something unintelligible, and I went back to my ginger ale, satisfied that the bait was firmly in the trap.

Before delivering my spiel about the fingerprint expert, I had arranged with Ding Dong Bell and Fred Sorenson to take turns with me hiding in the theater base-

Stage Fright

ment to see who might sneak in to wipe evidence off the main switch. I had volunteered to take the first watch, which would begin as soon as our party in the bar broke up. The director would relieve me at 5:00 A.M. and our man in the lighting booth would cover the hours between 9:00 A.M. and the 1:30 P.M. rehearsal.

At about quarter to one, the bartender announced last call, which caused a great commotion as everyone shouted out an order for his or her final libation. When that round of drinks had been served, I slipped out of the bar and, armed with a flashlight and Ding Dong's ring of keys, made my way to the theater.

Opting to enter through the scene shop, I unlocked the door, slid in, and flipped the bolt to lock the door from the inside. Turning on the flashlight, I found my way to the foyer, where the stairs to the basement were located. I was somewhat surprised to find the door to the stairway standing open, but I figured that the cleaning crew left it that way. It wasn't until I reached the bottom of the stairs that I began to think otherwise.

My mind started to change when I heard a faint scraping sound behind me. I stopped in mid-stride and tried to identify the source. Was it, I wondered, the creaking of the building, or was it caused by something more animated than wood and bricks. A second later, my question was answered.

My information came in the form of a smack on the back of the head that produced a gorgeous stellar display that included Polaris, Arcturus, and a vast expanse of the Milky Way. The blow sent me free-falling, but I felt someone's arms encircle me and slow my momentum just as my personal star shower faded and all my lights went out.

When I opened my eyes, I was lying on my left side, with my flashlight glowing a couple of feet away. My head felt like someone was playing The Anvil Chorus on it as I gingerly explored the back of my skull with my right hand. The lump I found there felt as big as a grapefruit, but later examination showed it to be closer in size to a walnut. It's funny how our senses can lie to us at critical moments like that.

As soon as I had collected my scattered wits, retrieved the flashlight, and hauled myself to a standing position, I walked through the basement to where the main switch was attached to the wall. I was not surprised to find the door of the box hanging open. The ghost had wiped the switch clean before bopping me on the head and thoughtfully catching me and lowering me gently to the floor. I'd have to thank the ghost for saving my facial features from damage, if I ever caught the bastard.

Ding Dong Bell was still awake when I went to his room to inform him that it wouldn't be necessary to get out of bed for the five o'clock watch.

"Son of a bitch!" he said. "Son of a goddamn bitch!"

When I got to my cabin, I pulled a handful of ice cubes out of the freezer compartment, wrapped them in a wet washcloth, and applied the makeshift cold compress to the lump on the back of my head. Holding the ice in place with my right hand, I dug through my shaving kit with the left, found the small bottle of aspirin I carry there, washed down two tablets with a glass of water, and laid down on the bed wearing everything but my shoes.

Eventually I slept, and in the morning I awoke with my head resting on a pillow soaked by the flow from melted ice cubes. A dull ache had replaced the rhythmic hammering in my skull, and the knob behind my right ear felt like it had been reduced by half. After a shower, a shave, and two more aspirin, I felt well enough to walk to the lodge for breakfast. Within minutes of being seated, I was joined by Ding Dong Bell.

"Any idea who whacked you?" he asked after inquiring about the current condition of my cranium.

"I wish I did," I said.

"It sure messed up your fingerprint idea. The son of a bitch probably went out back and wiped the rabbit box clean while you were conked out on the basement floor."

"You can bet on it. I'm calling Al right after breakfast to tell him the guy can cancel his trip unless he wants to see the Friday night show."

"If we still have a show by Friday night," the director said. "God knows what the son of a bitch will do to us next."

After breakfast, I called the *Daily Dispatch* and caught Al just as he was going out on an assignment.

"Welcome to the club," he said after I told him about getting flattened. "And I'm using both definitions of the word. I've still got a knob where that stage manager smacked me on the back of the head."

"I'm not sure the lump on my head is courtesy of Jimmy," I said.

"How about the out-of-the-closet gay guy? He might have a crush on you."

"Oh, shit, I hope not," I said. "But Norman is big enough to kayo me and strong enough to break my fall."

"You could have him put his arms around you and see if it feels familiar."

"Better yet, I could ask him to club you from behind Friday night and see if your lump matches mine."

Stage Fright

"I don't want any gay guys sneaking up behind me," Al said. "I got to go, now. Don't let the ghost get your spirit down."

Said ghost chose not to assault either my spirit or my body at the Tuesday afternoon and evening rehearsals. The word of my basement encounter spread through the cast and crew, making me the object of numerous comforting expressions of sympathy. I reluctantly declined an offer by Angie Maguire to perform an act with her head that would take my mind off the pain in my head. I involuntarily winced when Alice Prewitt caressed my lump with two long, cool fingers and said, "Ooh, nasty!" And I obligingly bent down when five-foot-four Julie Christensen said, "Oh, poor Mitch; let me kiss it and make it well."

Among the sympathizers was Herman Glock, who had heard the news from Ding Dong Bell. Words of sympathy gushed forth from the usually taciturn resort owner. These were followed by a profuse apology and an offer to pay for any treatment my wound might require. I allowed as how no medical ministrations would be necessary because I didn't seem to have a concussion and wasn't losing any blood.

"This is terribly embarrassing," Herman said. "We've never had a guest assaulted before in all the years we've owned this place."

If I had mentioned the words "lawyer" or "lawsuit," poor Herman probably would have offered me a half-interest in the resort. However, I resisted the temptation to make him squirm, figuring he already had enough trouble.

The bar was not as heavily populated Tuesday night as it had been after the Monday night rehearsal. Ding Dong was there, of course, but only a few cast members wandered in. Those who showed up expressed their happiness at having completed two consecutive days of incident-free rehearsals, but everyone was apprehensive about Wednesday night's run-through and the Thursday night performance.

"The lump on your head proves that the exorcism thing was nothing but a crock of shit," Rhonda Lapierre said to me.

"Like we didn't already know that!" said Ding Dong Bell.

When I got back to my cabin, the little yellow light on my phone was blinking. Having been burned once because I missed a message, I wasted no time in picking up this one. The voice was that of Martha Todd, who had learned about the crack on my cranium from Alan Jeffrey.

"Al says there isn't anything to worry about because the blow was to your head," said Martha. "But please call me and tell me that your brain isn't any more scrambled than usual." With friends like that, a guy needs no enemies.

It was almost midnight, but I called Martha anyway. It was obvious from the fuzziness of her mumbled "hello" that the telephone had awakened her.

"Who am I and with whom am I speaking?" I asked.

Martha groaned and replied, "You are the hotshot reporter who doesn't watch his backside, you're speaking with a person who was in the middle of a beautiful dream and it's almost midnight, you idiot."

"Is that any way to talk to an invalid? The beautiful young women here at the Glock Family Theatre have been much more sympathetic."

"Oh, really. And have any of those beautiful young women expressed their sympathy while visiting you in your bedroom?"

"I'm in far too much pain to have visitors. Not that I didn't get offers."

"I can imagine what kind of an offer you got from that big blonde bimbo with the bombshell boobs. But, as long as you're alone, tell me what happened."

After hearing my story, Martha's tone grew much softer, and she promised to apply some soothing ministrations to the wound when she arrived to watch the Saturday performance. "That's providing there is a Saturday performance," she added.

Chapter 16
Connected and Tuned In

A jangling telephone shattered my beautiful dream of being cuddled and comforted simultaneously by Angie, Alice, and Julie, all dressed in see-through shorty nighties. The digital dial on the bedside table clock was glowing 9:05.

"You sound like you're still in bed," said the voice of Heather Rondeau.

"Where else would a weary, wounded warrior be?" I said.

"What do you mean wounded?" she asked. I told her of my Monday night encounter with a blunt object, and she said, "I told you to watch your back. Do I have to come over there and watch if for you?"

"Not necessary. But why are you calling me at this ungodly hour?"

"Some of us still have to haul our asses out of bed in the morning and go to work for a living, you know. I'm calling because I verified that what our dear Indian chief is running after is some white man's money to finance a casino somewhere near this city."

"Okay, that's very interesting to your readers in Alexandria. What would interest me is a connection with the Glock Family Theatre."

"There may be a connection. Rumor has it that Herman Glock was asked to contribute to the casino and refused. If true, this might have pissed off the chief."

"Are you suggesting that Chief Running Deer is the man behind the ghost?"

"It might be the chief's revenge. Or an attempt to make Herman reconsider."

"How much faith have you got in this rumor?"

"Enough to pass it on to you. Why don't you ask Herman about his dealings with the chief?"

"I know damn well what the two-word answer would be."

"Do they start with the letters n and c?"

"No comment," I said.

"I thought that by now you and Herman would be pretty good buddies."

"He never forgets that I'm the reporter who wrote about all the bad shit that was happening in his theater. He does seem to have forgotten that I also wrote the puff piece about Ding Dong Bell that preceded it."

"People in the news have selective memories. Anyway, it's too bad you can't get cozy with Herman."

If I had been a character in a comic strip, a glowing 100-watt bulb would have been drawn above my head at that moment. "I know somebody who is cozy with Herman," I said. "Ding Dong Bell is here directing this fiasco because they were best buddies in college. Maybe I can persuade Ding Dong to ask Herman if he knows anything about Chief Running Deer's casino."

"It's worth a gamble," Heather said.

This sounded so much like an Alan Jeffrey remark that I replied, "It's a crap shoot, but I've got nothing to lose."

"Don't bet on it," she said. "Your jackpot might be another lump on the head."

My extended snooze caused me to miss connecting with Ding Dong Bell at breakfast. After consuming an order of syrup-drenched French toast and sausage, I spent the morning dutifully reviewing my lines and blocking. At noon, I took a table in the dining room. Minutes later, the director appeared, and I waved him to my table.

"Schmuck, how's your head?" he asked. "Still hurt like a son of a bitch?"

"It's pretty much okay unless I bump it," I said. "The girls did a lot to soothe the pain last night."

"What? Did they come to your cabin?"

"Only in my dreams. But they all petted me and fussed over me at the rehearsal. That's the best kind of therapy there is for a bachelor."

We put in our orders, exchanged some small talk about the weather, the boat-loads of fishermen we could see leaving from the dock, and eventually, the upcoming rehearsal and performance. Trying to sound casual, I asked Ding Dong if Herman Glock had ever said anything to him about being asked to contribute to an Ojibway gambling casino.

"What the hell would he contribute?" Ding Dong asked. "The guy's barely breaking even on the resort and the theater looks like it's going down the shitter."

"Just a rumor I heard, " I said. "I thought maybe he might have talked about it with his friends."

"Herm doesn't talk about financial stuff with anybody. I've heard more about the tough time they're having from Ingeborg than I have from Herm."

"Could you, as a longtime friend, ask Herman about a contribution to a casino?"

Ding Dong stared into my eyes until I blinked before he replied. "Why would I?"

I decided that casual wasn't going to work with a man who had spent his life dealing with the New York City media. "Because it might lead us to the ghost who

Stage Fright

drops sandbags, unleashes rabbits, loosens doorknobs, and whacks people on the head," I said. I went on to explain Heather's theory about Chief Running Deer possibly having a motive to make trouble for Herman Glock.

"Son of a bitch!" said Ding Dong when I finished. "Ain't that a pisser! But there's no Indians in the cast."

"The chief could be paying someone in the cast," I said. "Or in the crew," I added, thinking of Jimmy Storrs.

Ding Dong cupped his chin in his right hand while the wheels turned in his head. Finally, he said, "Okay, schmuck, I'll look for a chance to bring up the casino question. But I'll have to be careful as hell. Herm ain't the type to spill his guts to anybody, no matter how long we've been friends."

"Give it your best shot. If there's bad blood between Herman and the chief, the connection is worth exploring. Remember, the play you save may be your own."

"Likewise, the ass I get kicked if Herm thinks I'm too nosy may be my own."

"Good luck. I just wish I could come up with an excuse to interview Chief Running Deer."

"He's a doctor. Couldn't you have him look at the bump on your head?"

"Wrong end," I said. "I looked him up in the Alexandria yellow pages and Doctor Henry Stone is listed as a urologist."

"So ask him to check your prostate."

"No thanks," I said. "There's no way that the guy who may have caused my headache is going to get his finger up my ass."

Sometimes our wishes are granted in the most unexpected way. The yellow phone light was flashing when I returned to my cabin, and the voice was that of city editor Don O'Rourke, instructing me to call him as soon as I got back from lollygagging (his word) on the beach.

Loyal servant that I am, I called immediately.

"I hear you got bonked on the head," Don said. "Are you okay?"

"I may have to take several weeks of paid medical leave to recover from the debilitating blow and the ensuing shock to my nervous system," I said.

"Bullshit! Next I suppose you'll tell me that you're suing the paper for sending you out there to do the theater story."

"I'm suing both the paper and the city editor personally," I said. Knowing that Don wouldn't call merely to inquire about my health, I asked, "What's on your mind — besides what's left of your hair?"

"There's some kind of an anniversary of the discovery of the Kensington Runestone coming up," Don said. "I thought as long as you're out there within spitting distance of the museum you could interview the director and do a story for Sunday."

"I don't have a lot of free time. I'm busy learning lines and going to rehearsals."

"How long can it take to drive a few miles and talk to a couple of people? You don't have to write a goddamn novel."

"Okay, okay! I suppose you want it yesterday?"

"I'm a patient man," Don said. "Friday noon will do."

"I'll get to work on it," I said, wishing I could kick Don's skinny ass.

A few minutes later I was ready to kiss those bony buns. I fired up my laptop and went online to look for information on the Kensington Runestone. The fourth item listed under available resources was a paper entitled "The Kensington Runestone — as Seen Through the Eyes of a Native American." The author was Henry Stone, M.D.

By phoning the Kensington Runestone Museum, I learned what the occasion was. Officials there were preparing to honor the translator of the stone, Hjalmer R. Holand, on the centennial celebration of his work. I interviewed the director on the phone and he volunteered to have a messenger deliver some pictures and some additional printed material. This cut my legwork in half.

Another phone call, this one to the office of Henry Stone/Chief Running Deer, M.D., got me a late afternoon "we'll slip you in between appointments" date with the urologist/medicine man after I explained my mission and my need for quick access. The voice of the woman who took my call sounded surprisingly familiar, but I could think of no reason why I would know anyone in the doctor's office. I even thought I heard the woman giggle when she said, "Glad to hear that it's not a medical emergency."

After spending a couple more hours reviewing Georgie's lines, I drove into downtown Alexandria and found the doctor's office just half a block off Main Street. The small, white-walled waiting room contained eight beige upholstered chairs, four of which were occupied by men in their sixties and seventies. Behind the desk were two women, one of whom had her back turned, thumbing through some charts.

As soon as I introduced myself to the plump, fortyish woman who greeted me at the desk, the other woman turned and said, "Are you sure I can't slip you a catheter?" The voice was the strangely familiar one I had heard on the phone. The speaker was Alice Prewitt.

Overcoming the temptation to tell Alice what I would rather have her do with the organ in question, I expressed my surprise at seeing her smiling face in Doctor Stone's office. She said she had been working behind the desk there for about a year and, with the same giggle I had heard on the phone, added that she really couldn't treat me to a penile catheterization because she wasn't qualified "to handle the patients."

It was hard to resist giving an appropriately smutty response, but this was, after all, a doctor's office and the older receptionist was not looking amused. So, I simply smiled, expressed my regret that Alice wouldn't be serving me, and seated myself next to a white-haired man in bib overalls.

An hour dragged by as patients shuttled in and out of the examining rooms. Finally, with a wink, Alice said, "Doctor will see you now, Mister Mitchell."

She ushered me into an eight-by-ten examining room, waved me to the only chair and pulled one of those backless johnnies from a drawer.

"I don't need that," I said.

"It's not for you, silly," said Alice. "There's a real patient in the next room waiting for this."

"Lucky him," I said. At my tender age, I hadn't yet been subjected to a prostate examination during my annual physicals, but while I was in the Navy I had heard plenty of stories about the unpleasant procedure from fellow officers who were in their forties.

"Sorry I won't have a chance to see you wearing this," Alice said, waving the flimsy piece of cloth as she went out. "Doctor will be with you in a few minutes."

The promised few minutes plodded along until they equaled half an hour. I was beginning to wonder if I had been tucked away and forgotten when the doctor/medicine man opened the door and said, "Good afternoon, Mr. Mitchell."

Without the face decorations, I could see that the Ojibway medicine man was in his mid-forties. His height was equal to mine, his coal black hair hung down his back in a single braid knotted with a rubber band, and he was wearing glasses with mottled brown plastic frames that almost blended into his coppery complexion.

"Thank you for seeing me on such short notice," I said. "Did Alice — Miss Prewitt — explain why I'm here?"

"She said you are interested in a paper I wrote about the runestone," he said. "Whatever called your attention to that?"

I explained my runestone assignment, told him about the tight deadline and said I thought that a Native American's viewpoint on the stone would be a valuable addition to my story. This wasn't a complete fabrication — I did plan to use some quotes from the doctor. He looked skeptical and said he didn't have any copies in the office.

With notebook and ballpoint in hand, I asked him to summarize his comments about the runestone as best he could remember them. He frowned, paused to gather his thoughts before diving into the subject and plunged headlong into a five-minute monologue. When he finished, I put the pen in my shirt pocket, closed my notebook and thanked him for his comments and his time. Then I began the more important segment of my interview.

"On another subject, and off the record, your exorcism of the theater ghost seems to have been successful," I said. I was gambling that he had not yet heard about my painful basement encounter with said ghost.

"This week's rehearsals have been conducted without incident?" the medicine man said. He had risen from his chair, and I stood to face him, eye-to-eye.

"The rehearsals have been just great," I said. "Of course, we still have an important run-through tonight. By the way, I'm in the show now. I took the place of the poor guy who broke his leg last weekend."

"Really? I hope you have a more pleasant experience than he did."

"So far, it has been fun," I said. "And speaking of fun, some of my friends are coming up from St. Paul for the show this weekend, and they asked me to find out if there's a handy gambling casino anywhere nearby. Maybe you can tell me."

He looked into my eyes, obviously trying to ascertain the pureness of my motive, before he replied. "I'm afraid there's no casino near enough that one would call it 'handy,' Mr. Mitchell."

"That's too bad. There seem to be casinos all over the eastern and central parts of the state where the descendants of the original settlers are reclaiming the riches from the descendants of the white invaders, but there are very few in the west. Are there any plans to build one out in this area?"

Chief Running Deer shrugged and said, "I wouldn't know anything about that, Mr. Mitchell. My tribal duties are that of a medicine man; I am not a financier or a developer. Now, I must see my next patient." As he went out the door, I wanted to shout "liar, liar," but again I placed discretion ahead of valor. The chief's straight-faced lie made me even more eager to hear what Ding Dong Bell would have to say on the subject of casinos after his conversation with Herman Glock.

Stage Fright

It also made me eager to ask Alice Prewitt whether she had told her employer about my post-exorcism head-cracking confrontation with the ghost. Unfortunately, she had left for the day when I emerged from the examining room. Ah, well, I could console myself with the knowledge that I'd be seeing her at the theater in a couple of hours.

When I got back to my cabin, I phoned the Alexandria paper, hoping to catch Heather Rondeau at her desk and fill her in on my conversation with the disingenuous doctor. However, she also had left for the day and, true to form, the guy on the city desk refused to give out her home phone number. As a reporter who values his privacy, I both quietly cursed and openly applauded him for that.

At six o'clock, I went to the dining room to stoke up for the 7:30 run-through, which would be my last chance to mess up my scenes as Georgie without an audience watching. I was hoping to catch Ding Dong Bell at dinner, but the director never showed up. I put away a cornucopia of garden salad, a sizzling slab of deep-fried walleye, a baked potato the size of a softball, and a wide wedge of apple pie topped with a scoop of cinnamon ice cream. If nothing else, Herman and Ingeborg Glock were feeding me well.

There was no opportunity to quiz Alice Prewitt before the rehearsal got under way. However, during our big clinch scene, where I pulled her tight against me, reached under the teddy and groped her red panty-clad buns, she again caressed the bump on the back of my head and, with her lips brushing my ear, whispered, "It's going down." The effect of her hot breath in my ear forced me to break the clinch and create some space between our bodies because something else was going up.

At that point, she dragged me into one of the bedrooms, and with a grand flourish, I kicked the door shut behind us. As soon as the door was closed, Alice whispered a paraphrase of the old Mae West line. "Have you got a gun in your pocket or did Doctor Stone give you a prescription for Viagra?"

"When you blow in my ear like that, I don't need Viagra," I said. "Don't do it tomorrow night or the audience will be treated to an X-rated scene."

"Well, you know the old saying: A hard man is good to find." With that, she kissed my ear, turned and retreated to the dressing room. There was just enough light for me to see that she was putting a bit of extra action into her butt as she strutted away.

This stimulating encounter was the high point of a rehearsal that finished without interference from the ghost. I messed up a few lines but other actors saved the scenes with their adlibs and I promised to review the script at least twice before the curtain rose on the morrow. After some brief notes, mostly complimentary, Ding Dong Bell told us he was staying for the Thursday performance and flying home to New York on Friday. We gave him a standing ovation, he thanked us for our devotion to the production in the face of enormous obstacles, and most of us adjourned with him to the bar.

With a glass of ginger ale in my hand, I circulated, waiting for a chance to corner Ding Dong. This chance was a long time coming because the announcement of his imminent departure had made him the center of attention, and he was constantly surrounded by three or four well-wishers.

When I grew tired of circulating, I perched my butt on a barstool and was soon joined by Alice Prewitt, who perched her butt on the stool to my left and let the full length of her thigh rest against mine. She was wearing skintight blue jeans and an aqua T-shirt just snug enough to show me that she hadn't put on a bra.

Alice set her drink — it looked like white wine — on the bar, reached around behind my head, touched the remnant of the lump, put her lips against my ear and whispered, "Does this still turn you on?"

"Like flipping a switch," I said. Her right breast was snug against the back of my shoulder, our legs were pressed together from hip to knee, and I could feel my face and my groin growing warm in unison.

"Good," she said, with her lips still brushing my ear. "A girl likes to check the effectiveness of her assets every now and then."

"I think your asset is very effective, especially when I get to grab it."

"Be careful how you talk, Mitch. You know the old saying: flattery will get you everywhere."

"For a young woman, you know a lot of old sayings."

"One of my less-visible assets is a very good memory."

"I notice you've never blown a line onstage, except when the sandbag almost beaned you," I said. She was gently fingering the lump on my head. Her nipple had become a firm little knob against my back and I was aware of an increasing firmness of my own as an organ that had been neglected for several months rose to the occasion. As pleasant as this was, Herman Glock's busy barroom didn't seem like the place to consummate such an intimate moment.

Alice seemed to read my mind. "You have a cabin here, don't you?" she asked.

"Just a few yards away," I said. "Would you like to see it?"

"I thought you'd never ask."

Stage Fright

I started to get off the stool and then thought better of it. "I need to cool off a minute before I stand up," I said. "If you know what I mean."

Alice giggled. "I'll take a trip to the ladies room and powder my nose while you, uh, relax a little. Why don't I meet you out front in a couple of minutes?"

I agreed and watched the rhythmic swaying of her ass as she walked away toward the restrooms. I wondered if the muscles in her belly were as fine and firm as those I had felt in her butt. Damn, I said to myself, if I keep thinking about Alice's assets I'll never be able to get off this barstool.

A couple of sips of ginger ale and a look around the room helped to relieve the tension in my trousers, and a couple of minutes later I said "good night" to the bartender and walked out the door. Alice was waiting in the light of an almost-full moon and greeted me by pulling my head down, without touching the tender spot, and kissing me long and lasciviously on the lips. When her quick little tongue retreated and I was able to breathe again, I took her hand and led her to my cabin. While we walked through the shadowy pines in the moonlight, I thought of noncommittal Martha Todd, but not for long. How fickle we imperfect men can be when temptation rears its gorgeous red head.

Chapter 17
Another Opening

"Got anything for a girl to drink?" asked Alice. She had flopped into the armchair, kicked off her sandals, stretched her legs straight out in front and leaned back so that her nipples poked up like two round buttons under the thin cotton T-shirt.

"Nothing with alcohol," I said. "I can't handle it."

"You don't drink?"

"I'm an alcoholic."

"No shit? I've never met a guy who'd admit that before."

"Sometimes it's a social handicap," I said. "But it's a lot easier to work when you're sober."

"I suppose," Alice said. "I've never tried working when I was drunk."

"Before I went into treatment, I was drunk all the time, even when I was trying to write." I wondered why in the hell I was chattering away like this when all I really wanted to do was get Alice undressed and into my bed.

"Lots of famous guys wrote when they were drunk, didn't they?" she said.

"Yeah. Drunk, stoned, what have you. But it didn't work for me."

"What are you writing that you needed to talk to Doctor Stone?"

"Like I told you on the phone, it's a feature about the Kensington Runestone. The doctor wrote a piece about the runestone from the Indians' perspective a few years ago, and I wanted to get some quotes from him."

"Did you get everything you wanted?"

Not everything, I thought. To Alice, I said, "Pretty much. And after that we talked some about the theater ghost. Does he know I got whacked on the head after the exorcism ceremony?"

Alice sat up straight in the chair. "How would he know that?"

"I just wondered if maybe you had talked to him about it."

"Did he say anything about it?" She was sitting stiffly, with her feet drawn up as if she planned to rise. This was not getting us to the bedroom.

"No, he didn't say anything about it," I said.

Alice stood up and said, "Then why are you accusing me of telling him about it?"

"I'm not accusing you of anything. I just wondered if he knew about my getting whacked." I took a step toward her, intending to put my arms around her and get us back to our original agenda.

She pushed me away with both hands. "I don't know why you think I'd be blabbing to the doctor."

"Well, he did do the exorcism. I thought maybe he'd want to know what happened in the theater afterwards."

"You thought? And what do you think I am? I don't talk about the shit that goes in that theater with anybody, least of all with Doctor Stone." She was fumbling with her sandals, trying to slip her feet into them without the use of her hands.

"I'm sorry," I said. "I didn't mean to imply anything or to insult you or whatever the hell I've done. Let's forget about Doctor Stone and just go back to where you're whispering sweet nothings into my ear."

"I'll whisper nothing sweet into your ear, all right. I shouldn't have come here in the first place." She marched past me, opened the door, said "good night," and walked out, giving the door a solid slam behind her.

"Son of a bitch," I said, quoting Ding Dong Bell. "What in the hell brought that on?" Oh, well, Alice's inexplicable snit meant I'd have nothing to hide from Martha Todd. Damn it!

"Hey, schmuck, come over and sit down," said Ding Dong Bell in a booming voice when I entered the dining room Thursday morning. The director's basso profundo greeting caused every head in the room to turn so that at least a dozen pairs of eyes watched me shuffle sleepily to his table.

I had lain awake for a couple of hours trying to figure out what touched off Alice Prewitt's fuse, and I desperately needed a jolt of caffeine to get my engine started. My eyes were only half open, and I was barely able to mutter the word "morning."

"Good morning. And congratulations," said Ding Dong at a less lusty volume.

"Congratulations for what?"

"I hear you got laid last night."

"Where'd you hear that?" I said as I filled my coffee cup from the pot sitting in front of Ding Dong.

"People said you were snuggling up with Alice Prewitt at the bar and then you both disappeared. We all figured that meant you got lucky."

"I'm sorry to say you all figured wrong. My luck ran out when I said something that pissed her off and she put on her shoes and went home."

"She went home with nothing on but her shoes?"

"Her shoes were all she ever took off."

"Son of a bitch, that's too bad," Ding Dong said. "That Alice has got one hell of a body. Ten years ago, I'd have taken a shot at laying her myself."

"I can't figure out what happened," I said. "First she came onto me like gangbusters and then, out of nowhere, she stopped pouring on the honey and started spitting vinegar."

"What the hell did you say to her?"

I described the afternoon and evening events and related the cataclysmic conversation with Alice, as best I could recall it. My story inspired Ding Dong to repeat his favorite phrase. "Son of a bitch!" he said. "I didn't know Alice worked for that phony-baloney medicine man."

"Speaking of the medicine man, he flat out denied having any knowledge of plans for a casino in the Alexandria area," I said. "Did you find out anything from Herman about the doctor asking the Glock family for a casino donation?"

"I had dinner with Herman and Ingeborg in their kitchen last night, but when I kind of casually mentioned casino they both changed the subject quicker than your dick went up when Alice blew in your ear."

"Son of a bitch!" I said, mimicking Ding Dong again.

"I gave it a couple of tries, but it was obvious that casinos are a topic they ain't going to talk about."

The waitress set a three-egg, ham and mushroom omelet in front of me and I refilled my coffee cup from a fresh pot. Ding Dong had finished his morning bagel with cream cheese and lox, so he excused himself and left me to wallow alone in my breakfast.

Back at the cabin, I called Heather Rondeau's office and caught her at her desk. I told her about my interview with Chief Running Deer and mentioned my surprise at finding Alice Prewitt working in the doctor's office, but said nothing about our subsequent encounters. After all, a gentleman does not discuss his romantic trysts, successful or otherwise, with another woman.

Nor did I discuss striking out with Alice when I called Alan Jeffrey and filled him in on the medicine man's denial of what reliable sources had revealed to Heather.

Heather promised to ask those sources some additional questions about "the lying son of a bitch," and Al said he would like to nail "the son of a bitch" if he's behind the crap going on in the theater. Even they were starting to sound like Ding Dong Bell.

Stage Fright

My third call of the morning was to Martha Todd, who was babysitting Sherlock Holmes again while I played thespian for the week. I got her answering machine and left a message saying I had been thinking of her last night. I did not elaborate on the context or longevity of those thoughts.

After these calls, I went outside with my script and settled into a lawn chair parked in the shade of a century-old oak tree. A few fluffy white clouds decorated the blue denim sky and, as I reviewed Georgie's lines, a soft summer breeze whispered its brand of sweet nothings along the back of my neck. Halfway through the first act, the script fell into my lap and I fell sound asleep.

The dinner bell, which Ingeborg rang to proclaim the beginning of the lunch hour precisely at noon every day, snapped me out of my slumber. Son of a bitch, I said to myself, I've pissed away the whole morning. Now I have to study my lines and write the runestone story between lunch and dinner. This thought upset me so much that I almost ordered nothing but a salad for lunch. Fortunately, my appetite returned in time for me to consume a bacon cheeseburger with an order of fries.

The condemned man ate a hearty meal, I thought as I nibbled the last of the fries. I wondered how Alice Prewitt would twist that old saying. Probably she'd turn it into something about the condemned man eating a hearty woman. A dirty mind is a terrible thing to waste.

Thursday afternoon flew by. First I typed madly on my laptop and e-mailed the runestone story to the *Daily Dispatch*. Next, I sat myself down in a straight-backed wooden kitchen chair and made a final study of Georgie's lines. When the dinner bell rang at six o'clock, I was confident that I wouldn't stop the show either by spouting an off-the-wall line or by going totally blank.

Although the production was in its second week, this was opening night for me. Consequently, a small flock of opening-night butterflies had begun to inhabit my stomach by the time I ordered dinner, so I confined my consumption to the usual mound of salad greens, a small rib-eye steak cooked medium rare and a serving of roasted potatoes. No dessert tonight, I said when the waitress brought my coffee. The damn butterflies would have to do without anything sweet.

While getting into my costume, the butterflies were jolted by a slap on the back from Randy Rhodes, who gave me a smile and a wink when I turned to see who had pummeled me from behind. At first, I took Randy's greeting to be a good-luck salute. Then I found myself on the end of a long, cold stare from Eric Laflamme, and

I realized that these guys thought I had spent the previous night screwing Alice Prewitt.

Obviously Angie Maguire thought I had taken Alice to bed also. As she passed me backstage on the way to her first entrance, Angie gave me a jiggle of her bulging bodice and said, "So, like, what's tight-ass Alice got that I ain't got?" Before I could reply, she spun and walked away, putting more action than a windmill in a williwaw into the old derriere.

As they always do, the butterflies fluttered away the minute I walked onstage and delivered my first line. I was slow picking up a couple of cues, but I got through the first act without a single fluff. Margie Hansen's eyes were glowing like hundred-watt light bulbs when she approached me during the intermission.

"I'd swear you've been with us since the first rehearsal, Mitch," the exuberant stage manager said. "You're better than Andy, already."

"Thanks," I said. "Just be damn sure the doorknob is on tight when I yank it."

"Believe me, between myself and Jimmy Storrs, we're checking everything that moves or shouldn't move," she said.

Margie's mention of Jimmy Storrs did not exactly raise the level of my confidence, so I decided to check the knob myself before the curtain went up for Act Two. I went onstage, climbed the stairs, tugged on the knob, and found it firmly attached. I examined the railing, which had been repaired and strengthened so that it would offer more support if struck by an off-balance body, and found no problems there. Then I went back down the stairs and exited through the bedroom door at downstage right.

In the dim light backstage, I saw someone walking away from the prop table. I started to follow the shadowy figure in order to identify the person, but I hadn't taken more than a couple of steps when Margie called places for Act Two. This meant I had to walk around behind the set and station myself at the up-center door, through which I would be entering the brothel a couple of minutes after the second act began.

This entrance would lead to my steamy scene with Alice Prewitt, who had stayed out of speaking range after a deadpan initial greeting when I arrived at the theater.

Wondering how convincing our foreplay as Tania and Georgie would be, I made my entrance, exchanged some banter and went into the clinch with Alice. Mechanically, our grasping and groping went like clockwork. Alice threw herself recklessly into my arms and kissed me. I reached under the teddy and squeezed her ass with the usual gusto. What was missing was the heat we normally generat-

Stage Fright

ed, and I was relieved when she spoke our exit line and dragged me off through the door.

As I kicked the door shut, she released my hand and started to walk away. I followed, caught her by the shoulder and whispered, "We need to talk."

"I can't imagine what about," she replied.

"Some people think we spent last night in the sack together."

"Can I help it if some people have dirty minds?"

"We should either correct their thinking or make it come true tonight."

"Have you ever heard this old saying? Go take a flying fuck at a rolling doughnut." With that, Alice Prewitt rolled away.

Throughout the second act of *Long Night's Journey Into Day*, Pimpernel, the madam's husband, played by Frenchy Lapierre, carried a gun tucked in his belt in front of his right hip. When not in use, the weapon, a .22 revolver, was kept in a locked cabinet until minutes before Act Two began. This weapon was the only prop that the prop mistress, Johanna Engquist, did not handle. The routine established by the director and the stage manager was that, shortly before she called places, Margie Hansen would take the gun out of the cabinet, load it with blanks and place it on the prop table. Frenchy would pick up the weapon and stick it in his belt while walking to his place.

As soon as the show ended, Frenchy would hand the gun directly to Margie, who would remove the blanks and lock the gun and the ammunition in the cabinet.

The script called for some of the brothel's customers, including Georgie, to get rowdy near the end of the show. In order to restore order, Pimpernel would pull the gun from his belt to fire a warning shot. Naturally, this being a farce, the gun would go off prematurely and Pimpernel would shoot himself in the foot. Frenchy had developed a really funny routine of hopping about the stage on one foot while waving the pistol so wildly that the rest of us were obliged to dive behind every available piece of furniture for cover. Unfortunately, hardly anyone outside the cast had ever seen this moment of high hilarity because the antics of the Glock Family Theatre ghost had chased nearly all the customers away from the previous performances before Frenchy fired his shot.

But on this night, every one of the theater's 311 seats was still occupied as the brawl between brothel customers and brothel service providers broke out onstage and Pimpernel went for his gun. I was engaged in a three-cornered wrestling match on the floor with Norman Rogers (Cliff) and Julie Christensen (Salome) when the

Glenn Ickler

shot rang out, and we all looked up expecting to see Frenchy doing his one-legged dance.

Instead, Frenchy was standing motionless, smoking gun in hand, staring at his foot with a look on his face that conveyed a state of mental shock combined with raw physical anguish. Following Frenchy's gaze downward, I saw the source of his pain and dismay. Blood was oozing up through a hole in the top of his shoe.

Frenchy's lips began to move but no words came out. Finally, he squeaked, "I shot my goddamn foot." The audience roared with laughter.

Somebody ad-libbed, "Poor Pimpernel, let's get him to a doctor!" Randy Rhodes managed to stay in character as he put an arm around Frenchy and led him out the front door while the audience, unaware of what had really occurred, continued to howl. When the door closed, 622 hands came together, applauding Frenchy's foot-dragging exit.

This left the rest of us onstage with the task of putting the scene back together and staggering through the closing minutes of *Long Night's Journey Into Day*. Somehow we made it to the end and the cast even managed to take a curtain call — minus Frenchy, who had been half carried by Randy to the dressing room. There Margie Hansen removed Frenchy's shoe, wrapped his bleeding foot in a towel and called 911 on her cell phone, all the while babbling that she had loaded nothing but blanks into the chambers of the gun.

"I believe you, I believe you," Frenchy was saying over and over to the blubbering stage manager as a dozen of us from the cast and crew pushed and elbowed our way into the six-by-ten dressing room. In less than a minute, we were joined by Ding Dong Bell, Herman Glock, and Gordon Glanz. Ding Dong was shouting, "Son of a bitch, what the hell happened?" Herman was asking the same question without the profanity. Gordon Glanz was glowering at everyone without saying a word.

Close behind this troubled trio came Heather Rondeau, who was several inches too short to see what was going on. Undaunted, Heather wormed her way through the mob until she stood beside me. She looked down at the blood-stained towel encasing Frenchy's foot and said, "Did he really frickin' shoot himself?"

"Casper the theater ghost put live ammunition in the gun," I said. "He really did shoot himself."

"Jesus Christ, that's a felony — messing around with guns," Heather said. "Did anyone call the cops?"

"Margie called for an ambulance, and they always send a cruiser or two along. We could all be in for a very long night of playing questions and answers."

Stage Fright

The EMTs arrived, loaded Frenchy onto a gurney, and wheeled him out along the oft-traveled path through the scene shop to the ambulance while Heather continued to quiz me on the procedures for storing, loading and handling the gun.

Suddenly, she yelled, "Thanks! I gotta go talk to the cops." With that she raced off to squeeze a quote out of one of the two sheriff's deputies engaged in a six-way conversation with Ding Dong Bell, Herman Glock, Gordon Glanz, and a nearly hysterical Margie Hansen. I followed Heather to the circle of inquisitors, put an arm around Margie, and tried to help Ding Dong calm her down.

It took several minutes to get Margie seated in a dressing room chair and sedated with a tranquilizer provide by the director. Realizing that, like Heather, I had a story to turn in, I listened as long as I could and then headed for the door. A strong hand grabbed my shoulder and stopped me in my tracks.

"You can't leave," said the tall, 220-pound deputy attached to the hand.

"I'm a reporter," I said. "I have to file my story."

"Nobody in the play can leave the theater until the sheriff gets here."

"Can I run quickly to my cabin, write my story, and come right back?"

"It don't work that way, buddy. Nobody in the play can leave until the sheriff says so. Period."

"How about a phone call? Can I make a phone call?"

He had to think about that for a minute before he could answer. Finally, he said, "I guess a phone call is okay as long as you don't leave the theater."

Naturally, my cell phone was back in the cabin. However, I borrowed Margie's, which she had flung onto the dressing room counter after calling 911. I called the *Daily Dispatch* city desk and dictated the story to a rewrite man.

"That's a hell of a story," said the guy on the desk.

"Stay tuned," I said. "There are more and better stories yet to come."

Chapter 18
Long Night's Journey

My forecast of a long night playing questions and answers was 100 percent accurate. Because the resort was outside the city limits of Alexandria, the investigation was conducted by the Douglas County Sheriff's office. Sheriff Einar Andersen and a homicide detective named Bergquist interrogated each of us individually in the Green Room. They asked me what I knew about the procedure for storing and loading the gun, where I was during the intermission, whether I saw or heard anything suspicious, and where I was at the moment the gun was fired. I told them about the unidentified figure I had seen leaving the prop table in the semi-darkness just before the stage manager called "places." When I said I wasn't certain whether the person was male or female, I heard Bergquist mutter, "Some hell of a reporter."

The curtain had come down on the stage version of *Long Night's Journey Into Day* at approximately 10:45 P.M. The long night's journey offstage went on until after 1:00 A.M., but the word was passed that Herman was keeping the bar open so we could gather to compare notes and let off steam after the inquisition. State law said he couldn't sell booze after one o'clock, so Herman announced that liquor sales had ended and he was hosting a private party as of that moment.

Eventually, everyone involved in the production wandered in, except Margie Hansen, who was an emotional wreck, and Rhonda Lapierre, who volunteered to drive Margie home. Well, almost everyone else was there. When I looked around the room for Alice Prewitt's free-flowing red hair, I couldn't spot it in the crowd.

"Anybody seen Alice?" I asked Jimmy Storrs.

"Maybe she went straight to your cabin," Jimmy said, giving me one of those smart-ass "I know what you've been doing with her" looks.

"Not likely," I said. "She's pissed at me about something."

"What's the matter? Couldn't you get it up last night?"

"Not after the fourth time." Let Jimmy pass that little tidbit around, I thought. It would be good for my reputation, and it might bring me some additional late-night companions. I would have to maintain tight control of the traffic, however, with Martha Todd due to arrive on Saturday afternoon.

Stage Fright

The atmosphere had been almost funereal when I wandered in at one o'clock, but an hour later the barroom babble had risen to a decibel level above and beyond that of a normal party. People finally were unwinding and letting go after the shock of seeing Frenchy's foot leaking blood and the trauma of being sizzled on the sheriff's grill.

The hubbub came to a halt when Herman Glock banged on the bar with his fist and called for silence. The dark cloud on Herman's face did not inspire levity.

"I want to thank all of you for hanging in there and finishing the show," Herman said. "I also want to say that it's pretty obvious we won't have a show tomorrow because there's no way we could replace Frenchy that quick, even if we wanted to."

"Are you saying we don't want to go on with the show?" asked Norman Rogers.

"I'm saying that the board of directors is meeting tomorrow afternoon to decide whether to cancel the rest of the run, which I'm sure we will do, and, after that, whether to call off the rest of the season."

Herman couldn't have gotten a bigger reaction if he had dropped his drawers and mooned us. Everyone started yelling in opposition to both proposals, and Herman was forced to bang on the bar so hard I thought he would break his hand.

When he again could be heard, the resort owner said, "I'm sorry, but it looks like tonight's performance will be the last one given at the Glock Family Theatre this year, and maybe the last one ever."

"You can't like just shut everything down," shouted Angie Maguire. "We been like rehearsing for the next show for the last couple weeks." Angie had been typecast as a ditzy blonde in the upcoming musical comedy.

"I apologize to all of you who have worked so hard on this show and the next one, but I can't see the board voting to go on with the season," Herman said. "The kind of publicity a crime like this will generate can pretty much kill this theater."

"Or bring more people in," I suggested.

"That worked one time, Mr. Mitchell, but I can't see it happening again. People aren't going to come to a theater where guns are going off and live ammunition is flying around the stage."

Ignoring Herman's slightly exaggerated description of what had taken place, I asked, "What time is your meeting? I'd like to be there as a reporter."

"The meeting is private. We are not a public corporation, and we don't have to let anybody into our meetings."

"How about members of the cast and crew?" asked Randy Rhodes. "Don't we got anything to say about it?"

"I'm sorry, but you don't," said Herman. "The only people who can make these decisions are Mr. Olson, Mr. Glanz, and myself. We already know what the situation is, so I don't see what anybody else could tell us."

"We could tell you we want to replace Frenchy and do this show again," said Julie Christensen. "He doesn't really have that many lines to learn. You could probably do it yourself if you set your mind to it."

"Not a chance," said Herman. "You can come in tomorrow and pick up any personal belongings you have in the theater, but Mr. Glanz was here tonight, and I know he will vote to cancel the run and the season when we meet tomorrow."

"How will you vote on those questions?" I asked.

"That's between me and my wife and the other board members," he said. "Now I think it's time for all of us to go home and get some rest. It's been a long night."

The funereal atmosphere returned as we filed out, heads drooping and voices muted. "Well, I guess we're finished with this show," I said to Ding Dong Bell.

"Yeah, son of a bitch," he said. "But what ever happens here, I'm getting on that plane tomorrow morning and heading back to New York, where all the shootings happen outside the theater."

"What time's your flight?"

"Early. Something like seven o'clock."

"I guess I'll say good-by now, then," I said, holding out my right hand. "Working with you has been a wonderful experience, despite all the other crap."

Ding Dong grasped my outstretched hand, then dropped it and wrapped me up in a bear hug that sent my breath whooshing out into the early morning air. "Hey, schmuck, you did a hell of a job as a stand-in. And that piece you wrote is one of the best I've ever had printed about me. Give me a call next time you're in New York and I'll get you tickets to anything you want to see. Okay?"

He released me and I gasped out the word "Okay." On the way back to the cabin I took inventory of my ribs and was pleased to discover they were all still in their usual places. Here in Minnesota, people don't even hug their children with that much force.

I was up early Friday morning because I wanted to catch Heather Rondeau before she went out. I was determined to report on the Glock Family Theatre board meeting, and I needed help. Forging an alliance with Heather would make it doubly difficult for Herman and his pals to keep their meeting "private." Maybe the theater wasn't a publicly owned corporation, but last night's shooting was a matter of pub-

Stage Fright

lic record and the future of this once popular operation was a matter of public concern.

"Those assholes!" Heather said when I told her what was happening. "What time is that meeting?"

"I don't know yet, but I'll find out and let you know."

"If I'm not here when you call, leave word with the desk. I'm going to be at that meeting if I have to shoot my way in."

"Bad choice of words, considering last night's little prank."

"Bite me," she said. I started to ask where, but the line was already dead.

Next, I called the *Daily Dispatch* and said I would be filing a story about the upcoming Glock Family Theatre board meeting for the afternoon edition and would have the results of the meeting in time to do a piece for the Saturday morning run. I had my call transferred to the photo desk and asked for Alan Jeffrey so I could tell him that the performance he and Carol had been planning to see was about to be canceled. I was told that Al was out shooting pix of a morning traffic accident, so I left word for him to call me on my cell phone and went to the lodge dining room for breakfast.

Sniffing out the when and where of the board meeting was going to be a challenge. The woman at the front desk of the lodge said she had no idea where theater board meetings were held. I took this to be a lie she was telling to protect her job security. Since I had no recourse to instruments of torture, I was forced to accept this as gospel. The young woman hostess in the dining room also denied knowledge of the meeting place, and I was inclined to believe she was telling the truth.

Having little appetite, I settled for a couple of fried eggs, four slices of wheat toast covered with blueberry jam, and a pot of coffee to start my day. I was just pushing back my chair when the cell phone clipped to my belt gave a jingle.

"I read your bang-up story this morning," Alan Jeffrey said after exchanging hellos. "The way Frenchy waves that gun around, it's lucky that all he shot was his foot."

"The audience thought it was a barrel of fun," I said.

"Well, the shot was meant to trigger a laugh."

After some discussion, Al decided that he and Carol would come up to Alexandria anyway. Herman Glock had promised them a free cabin, and they had persuaded Carol's parents to take Kevin and Kristin for the weekend. "The four of us can do a little fishing in the daytime and go to our separate cabins to indulge in our favorite indoor sport at night," Al said. "It'll be sort of like a quickie second honeymoon for Carol and me."

His mention of "the four of us" reminded me that I should call Martha Todd and tell her that the show had been canceled. I was clicking through the cell phone directory for her number when it occurred to me that this might not be a smart thing to do. If she knew there was no performance, Martha might decide not to make the long drive to Alexandria and there would be no indoor sport for us. I turned off the phone.

Back in my cabin, I called the hospital in Alexandria for a condition report on Frenchy and learned that Norman Lapierre had been treated and released. I looked up Frenchy's home number and punched it in. My call was answered by a woman, whose throaty voice I recognized instantly as belonging to Frenchy's ex-wife.

"Hi, Rhonda," I said. "This is Mitch, calling to check on Frenchy. I didn't expect to find you there." I had heard some of their dressing room squabbles and couldn't imagine them living under the same roof again.

"Oh, somebody has to take care the little shit-head," Rhonda said. "Our only daughter lives way out in California, so I'm the only one around to wait on him."

"So, how's he doing? I was surprised when the hospital said he'd been released."

"Oh, he's lucky, as usual. The bullet missed all the big bones and the main artery, so they patched up the hole, wrapped up his foot and shipped him out for me to take care of. He needs to keep it elevated for a couple of days, and then he can start walking around with a crutch."

"He is lucky," I said. "Both because of where the bullet went and to have you around to take care of him."

"I'll tell him you said that the next time he bitches about the service he's getting."

"Do that. And have a good day."

"Yeah, right," Rhonda said. "A good day with Frenchy is like a bad day in hell."

Wondering if I would have a domestic murder to report before the weekend was over, I dashed off a quick story about the impending theater board meeting and Frenchy's medical condition, e-mailed it to the desk, and waited for Don O'Rourke to respond. "Keep your head down and go to that meeting," he replied. "Just remember that your medical plan doesn't cover gunshot wounds."

"I'm buying a bulletproof vest and charging it to the *Daily Dispatch*," I typed back. This time I didn't wait for Don's reply. I shut down the computer and called Oscar Olson Motors in Alexandria. I asked the woman who answered if it would be possible to see Mr. Olson in the early afternoon, and she transferred me to his secretary.

Stage Fright

"I'm sorry," said the secretary. "Mr. Olson has a meeting right after lunch and expects to be out of the office most of the afternoon. Perhaps I can get you in to see him sometime tomorrow."

I thanked her and said I would check my schedule and call back. Then I called the president's office at the Douglas State Bank and asked if it would be possible to see Mr. Glanz right after the lunch hour. This woman's response was more specific. It would be impossible to see Mr. Glanz because he had an out-of-town meeting scheduled for 1:30, and he was expecting to be away from his office for most of the afternoon.

Okay, now I knew the when. And apparently the where was here at the resort. My remaining challenge was to narrow this acreage down to a specific square footage.

Herman had promised to leave the theater unlocked so people could collect their personal property. I decided to station myself there in hope that someone in the cast or crew would know where board meetings were held. I walked in the front entrance and was perusing some pictures of past productions in the lobby when the janitor, a man known only as Sven, came in carrying a vacuum cleaner.

"Cleaning up the mess after last night?" I asked.

"Oh, no, I do dat later," said Sven. "Right now I got to get da Green Room ready. Dere's a big meetin' in dere today, you know."

I nodded knowingly and said, "Oh, that's right. The 1:30 board meeting."

"Yah. Da room got to be wacuumed and dusted and you got to have note pads and pitchers of ice water and glasses and all dat stuff set up yust exactly right ven dose guys get togedder."

"Well, I'd better let you get at it then," I said. "Nice seeing you, Sven."

"Yah," he said. "Haf a good day."

Well, it was looking surprisingly good, so far.

"One-thirty in the theater's Green Room" I said to Heather Rondeau a couple of minutes later. "Can you make it?"

"You can bet your bippy I'll be there," she said.

"Better come a little early so we can talk ourselves in. Last night, Herman let me know that reporters are as welcome in his board room as cockroaches are in his kitchen."

"Yeah? Well, today he's going to have to deal with both. See ya." She was gone before I could even say have a good day.

119

It was almost time for Ingeborg Glock to ring the lunchtime bell, but I decided to make one more phone call while I waited for this welcome sound. Alice Prewitt's absence at the post-interrogation party had been preying on my mind all morning. I punched in Doctor Henry Stone's office number, and when the other woman answered I asked to speak to Alice.

"Ms. Prewitt isn't in today," said the woman.

"Oh, is she ill?" I asked.

"We don't know. She just didn't show up today."

"She didn't call in?" I asked.

"That's what we said," she replied in a tone that indicated the conversation was about to end abruptly.

"Do you have her home number?"

"Of course we do, but we're not allowed to give it out."

"How about Doctor Stone?" I said, grasping at the only available straw. "May I speak to him?"

"Doctor Stone is not in the office today," she said. "Would you like to leave a message for Ms. Prewitt?"

"No, that's okay." We can just stick it up our ass, I thought as I clipped the phone back onto my belt. The lunch bell was clanging and I responded like Pavlov's dog. However, the taste of my Reuben and fries barely registered on my consciousness as I replayed the conversation with Doctor Stone's royal receptionist and wondered where in the hell Alice Prewitt had gone.

At quarter after one, I pushed the question of Alice Prewitt's whereabouts out of my mind and concentrated on the more immediate problem of staying in the Green Room during the Glock Family Theatre board of directors meeting. Heather met me at the door, and our butts were parked in a couple of chairs near the meeting table when Herman Glock walked in.

"What the hell is this?" Herman asked.

"We're here to cover the board meeting," I said. "Have you met Heather Rondeau from the Alexandria paper?"

"Yes, I've had the pleasure," he said. "Mr. Mitchell, I told you last night that this isn't a public corporation, and this isn't a public meeting. Now both of you please remove yourselves."

Calmly, with Socratic logic, we presented the arguments that the previous night's shooting was a matter of public record and that it was the public who supported the theater by purchasing tickets. First Oscar Olson and then Gordon Glanz entered while the discussion was going on, and they adopted Herman's position that the meeting was not open to anyone but board members. For a minute, it even looked like Oscar might convert his vocal objection into physical action, but Herman held up his hands like a bank robber surrendering to an armed posse and offered us a compromise.

"You two wait outside, and I'll give you a full rundown on our meeting as soon as it's over," Herman said.

"What if we decide to stay in here?" asked Heather.

"Then I'll phone the sheriff and ask him to remove two trespassers from my theater," Herman said. "And when the meeting's over, I'll give my exclusive report to the local TV station."

"Okay, Herman you got yourself a deal," I said, motioning my companion toward the door. "Come hither, Heather, and let us wait without."

"Without news, probably," Heather grumbled as the door slammed behind us. "They'll only tell us what they want us to know. We won't get any of the good stuff."

"Fear not," I said. "I always carry a mini tape recorder in my shirt pocket."

"A hell of a lot of good it's doing in there!"

"It's not in there. I took the liberty of duct taping it under the meeting table while you were standing there getting in Herman's face. I switched it on right after Herman said he'd call the sheriff if we didn't go quietly. The first sixty minutes of the meeting will be recorded for posterity and, if you treat me with proper respect and reverence, I'll let you listen to the tape free of charge."

With her palms together and her fingers pointing upward in an attitude of prayer, Heather bowed and in a solemn tone of great respect said, "Bite me." Then we settled down in the theater's little office just off the lobby to wait for Herman Glock.

Chapter 19
Board Stiffs

Thursday night's events caught up with me, and I was dozing in the swivel chair behind Herman Glock's desk when Heather said, "Here they come!" in a voice that lifted me two inches off the seat with my eyes wide open and my hands in a defensive position.

"Good god, you'd wake up the dead," I said.

"Good god, I thought you were the dead," she said. "Let's get our butts out there." A glance at my watch told me it was a couple of minutes before 3:00.

We scooted into the lobby to meet the three approaching board members, each of whom looked like he was marching to his own respective funeral. I was willing to bet that they were mourning the death of the Glock Family Theatre. Unfortunately, I would have won that bet.

"As chairman of the board, I have a statement to make," said Oscar Olson as the mumpish trio came to a halt. Heather and I both had our pads open and our ballpoints poised. "It is my sad duty to inform you that the Glock Family Theatre board of directors has, this day, made three extremely difficult but vitally necessary decisions. First, the board of directors has voted to cancel the remaining performances of *Long Night's Journey Into Day*, and, second, the board of directors has voted to cancel the remainder of the summer season. Third and last, because the Glock Family Theatre is deep in debt, the board of directors has voted to close this facility permanently, effective immediately." He turned as if to walk away and, I stopped him in mid-stride by asking whether the votes were unanimous.

"The details of the votes are not a matter of public record," Olson said.

I turned to Herman Glock and said, "Herman, you promised to give us a rundown on the meeting. How did the voting go?"

"I'm sorry, Mr. Mitchell," Herman said. "The board also voted to announce only the results of the vote to the press, not the breakdown of the voting."

"Does that mean you're backing out of your promise to give us the details of the meeting?" asked Heather.

Herman winced, as if he had been skewered in the gut with a sharp instrument, and said, "I'm afraid that I spoke out of place when I made that statement,

Ms. Rondeau. I apologize for promising more than I am able to give you at this time."

I felt doubly sorry for Herman, first for the demise of his theater and second for the drubbing he must have taken from the two corporate stiffs on the board. Herman was an honorable man, and I was sure he meant it when he promised to give us a detailed report in return for our peaceable exit from the meeting room. I could hardly wait to retrieve my tape recorder and listen to the conversation it had preserved.

"How will you inform the people in this show and those rehearsing for the next show?" I asked. "Will you call them all together for a meeting, or what?"

"I will telephone everybody on the list personally," Herman said. "And of course we'll look to your newspapers to spread the word."

"What about the season ticket holders?" Heather asked. "Will they get all their money back?"

"Every ticket holder will receive a full refund," said Oscar Olson. "You can print that information, also."

I wanted to say you can kiss my ass, also, but instead I asked, "Where will the money come from to make the refunds? You just said the theater is deep in debt."

"The theater and all its contents will be sold in order to raise the necessary cash and balance the books," said Olson.

I looked at Herman Glock and saw tears in the corners of his eyes.

"Mr. Olson, who do you think will buy a money-losing theater?" Heather asked.

"The answer to that is easy, Miss Rondeau," he said, giving her a smarmy little half-smile. "We already have a buyer."

"Who?" Heather and I asked in unison.

"The theater is being purchased by a firm known as OCC, Incorporated. I'm not at liberty to disclose any other details about the buyer at this time," Olson said. "The new owner is another privately held corporation, and the future use of the property will be announced by the new owner in due time. Now, if you'll be kind enough to excuse us, Mr. Glanz and I have to get back to our respective day jobs."

Like twin martinets, Olson and Glanz marched away.

"They're actually in step," I said to Heather as we watched them retreat.

"They ought to be goose-stepping," she replied.

"Herman, can you tell us anything more now that they're gone?" I said, turning back to where the theater owner had been standing. There was no answer because no one was there.

"Where'd he go?" asked Heather.

"God knows," I said. "Let's leave him alone for awhile and go listen to my tape."

"Oh, shit, yes!" she yelled. "Go get that tape and let's hear what's on it."

We took the tape recorder back to my cabin, letting it rewind as we walked. I dug a couple of bottles of root beer out of my fridge, popped off the tops, gave one to Heather, and we sat down at the little wooden dining table to listen.

"The meeting started a few minutes late and ended a little before three," I said. "That means we've got about two-thirds of it on this 60-minute tape."

The first couple of minutes gave us a garble of scraping chairs, clinking ice cubes, and mumbled nothings as the three board members took their places and poured themselves glasses of water. We heard Gordon Glanz complain about the nosiness of "goddamn newspaper reporters" and Herman Glock say, "Well, they've got a job to do, just like us."

"Thank you, Herman," I said.

Finally, Oscar Olson called the meeting to order and said there were three items on the agenda: One, the cancellation of the current production due to disastrous and criminal activities in the theater; two, the proposed cancellation of the remainder of the summer season due to substantial financial losses, and three, the future disposition of the Glock Family Theatre, which was "mired" (Oscar's word) deep in debt.

The disposition of item one didn't take very long. Even Herman didn't argue against the cancellation of *Long Night's Journey Into Day*. He said that a number of ticket holders had called this morning to cancel their reservations, and even if he wanted to continue, there was no way to do it without Frenchy Lapierre. The vote was 3-0.

The second agenda item resulted in a longer and more intense discussion, with Herman Glock arguing doggedly against Gordon Glanz's motion to cancel the rest of the summer season.

"How can we ever get out of the hole if we don't produce plays?" Herman asked.

"Producing more plays will just put us deeper in the red," said Glanz. "You said yourself that people are calling in to cancel their reservations. They won't even be making reservations for the next one after last night's fiasco."

"We'd be starting over, with a clean slate," Herman said.

"Bullshit!" said Oscar Olson. "All people are going to think about is Frenchy Lapierre getting shot and that other guy, what's his name, falling off the set and

Stage Fright

breaking his goddamn leg. And you can bet that there will be more stories about the Glock Theater ghost in all the goddamn newspapers."

"Damn right there will be," Heather interjected.

"If we cancel, we'll have to refund all the season ticket money," Herman said. "That will wipe us out completely!"

"That's to be discussed in the next item on the agenda," said Olson. A few minutes later, they voted to cancel the season, with Herman standing alone in vocal and heartfelt opposition.

Herman's objections to item two paled in comparison to his impassioned battle against item three, which was a motion by Gordon Glanz to close the theater permanently and sell it immediately to pay off the company's "burgeoning" (Glanz's word) debts.

"I know the theater can make money if we hang in there and reopen with a fresh start this winter," Herman said. For years, the Glock Family Theatre had produced a low-budget, three-play winter season that drew substantial crowds because it provided relief for area residents suffering from cabin fever and an evening diversion for some of the ice fishermen who occupied shacks on the frozen lake in December, January, and February.

"Face it, Herman, your theater's going down the toilet," Glanz said. "You might as well flush it now before pissing more money away down the hole."

"That Indian ghost that put the hex on *Long Night's Journey Into Day* will do the same thing to the next show and the next show and the next," Olson said. "If Chief Running Deer couldn't get rid of the spook, nobody can. In plain language, Herman, you're fucked!"

"I don't believe that," Herman said. "That ghost is a living somebody who was connected with this production. If we start over with a complete new cast and crew, the ghost will be gone."

"In your dreams!" said Glanz.

"That ghost is a permanent resident, Herman," Olson said. "You ain't going to get rid of him that easy."

"The ghost may have gone too far, putting real bullets in Frenchy's gun," Herman said. "The sheriff is in the act now, and he might find out who the ghost really is."

"That nitwit?" Olson said. "He couldn't find his ass with both hands."

The debate raged on through the remainder of the tape, with the voices growing louder and shriller. The tape ran out before the vote was taken, but there was no doubt in our minds about who voted yes and who voted no.

Glenn Ickler

"Poor Herman," Heather said when the machine shut down.

"Poor Herman is right," I said. "He loves that theater, and so does Ingeborg. It's too bad those two stiffs won't let him try to recover."

"I wonder how deep in debt the theater really is. We never heard any figures."

"Maybe I can coax some numbers out of Herman after he cools off. I'd also like to find out if Herman knows anything about OCC, Inc., and why they want to buy the theater. I'll use my 'deepest sympathy' approach and see if it softens him up."

"Good luck," Heather said. "Now I'd better go write my story. Won't board members Olson and Glanz shit their britches when they read our stories in the morning?"

"Let's hope. Do you need to borrow the tape?"

"No, I took pretty good notes while we were listening. I'm also going to call the secretary of state's office and see if I can find out who incorporated OCC, Inc."

"Let me know if you get anything."

"I will. And you call me if you get any real numbers from Herman."

When she was gone, I fired up my laptop and tapped out my story for the morning *Daily Dispatch*. I used an assortment of direct quotes off the tape, which I knew would send Olson and Glanz up the wall when they read the story, and of course I included the 2-1 vote counts. I hoped they wouldn't blame Herman for supplying those.

My words had just taken flight to St. Paul via the wonderful world of e-mail, and I was sitting back with what I'm sure was a self-satisfied smirk on my face when the dinner bell sent out its happy six o'clock summons. The day's events had left me without much appetite, but I considered it my duty to keep my body strong, so I traipsed obediently to the dining room. While I ate a delectable helping of deep-fried walleye, I tried to think of a way to cook the goose of the Glock Family Theatre's ghost. Unfortunately, not even Julia Child provided a recipe for that.

When I left the lodge to return to my cabin, the wind had picked up considerably. It was blowing from the northwest, which meant it was sweeping across the cooling waters of the lake. I was wearing a short-sleeve shirt, and my arms immediately developed a severe case of goose bumps. This would be a fine night to hole up in my cabin and finish the mystery novel I had started way back before I agreed to take on the role of Georgie. My next visit with Herman Glock could wait until morning. I hoped the chilly night would help him cool down enough to realize that Heather Rondeau and I were his best allies.

Stage Fright

Before settling down with the book, I phoned Martha Todd, figuring she would read my stories in the paper and wonder why I wasn't calling to discuss her weekend visit to the Glock Family Resort. Again I got her answering machine.

"Hi, it's your friend the practicing thespian," I said. "I suppose you're doing your restaurant server thing tonight. I'll be in my cabin all night if you want to call me back."

Martha normally arrived home from the restaurant job a little after nine, but the phone did not ring. I finished the book, yawned a couple of times, and looked at my watch. It was almost ten o'clock. I could either hike to the lodge and watch the local news on the big TV set in the lounge or I could stay in the cabin and go to bed. Poking my head out the door, I discovered that the wind was blowing even harder and colder than it had been after dinner. That made the decision easy. I closed the door from the inside and threw the locking bolt.

I had been asleep for a couple of hours and was dreaming about shooting Oscar Olson in the foot. The dream gun in my hand was going bang, bang, bang, and Oscar was dancing like a bear at a Russian sideshow. Suddenly, I realized that I was no longer dreaming but the bang, bang, bang was continuing. It was coming from my front door.

Waking up is never easy for me, and it is doubly difficult at a few minutes after midnight after only two hours of sleep. Slowly, it registered on my brain that if the banging sound was coming from my front door, something other than the wind might be creating the noise. With a groan, I rolled out of bed and started toward the door.

Something else registered on my brain when I was halfway across the living room. Unless I have visitors, I do not wear pajamas or any other item of apparel when I sleep. Perhaps, I thought, it would be prudent to wrap something around my naked body before opening the door. No need to shock whoever is out there, I said to myself as I pulled the blanket off the bed, draped it over my shoulders and pulled it together in front at a strategic level.

I was the one who was shocked when I pushed the door open a crack. Standing there, with her long red tresses blowing straight out in the wind, was Alice Prewitt.

"You've got to let me in," Alice said. "They're going to kill me!"

Chapter 20
Getting to Know Who

Who could reject a plea like that? I opened the door wide and backed out of the way. Alice darted into the room yelling, "Lock the door! Don't let them find me!"

I slid the bolt back into place, turned toward Alice, who had collapsed into the armchair, and asked the obvious question: "Who are you hiding from?"

Graciously ignoring my faulty grammar and sentence construction, Alice said, "Them."

"And who is them?"

"I don't know who they are. I heard one of them say they had to get rid of me, so I took off and ran to my car and drove here."

"And where is your car now?"

"I kind of hid it behind the lodge on the grass where you're not supposed to park."

Won't Herman love that, I thought. I also thought it was time to throw some light on the subject, so I turned on the small lamp on the wall above the kitchen table. In the candlepower generated by a 40-watt bulb, I saw that Alice was still wearing the pink T-shirt and blue jeans she had put on while awaiting her turn to be interrogated by the sheriff and his surly deputy. The hair that usually fell softly about her shoulders in brushed coppery waves was a tangled, wind-whipped mass. Her lips were blue with cold and her eyes were locked on my face with the proverbial deer-in-the-headlights stare.

"Okay," I said. "Why would 'they' want to kill you?"

"Because I told the Norwegian guy I was quitting," Alice said.

"Quitting what?"

"Quitting doing their dirty work. He told me it would just be scary pranks — that nobody would get hurt. Then Andy broke his leg and I had to hit you on the head and Frenchy shot his foot and ..."

"Wait a minute," I interrupted. "Did I hear you say that you hit me on the head?"

"Yes, I'm the one who hit you. That's why I came onto you in the bar the next night. I wanted to make sure you weren't hurt. Then you scared me away when you

Stage Fright

said you'd been talking to Doctor Stone about the ghost because I thought maybe you suspected me."

"Well, that's a let down. I thought it was my masculine charm and handsome features that turned you on."

"Maybe it was a little," she said. "You are kind of attractive for an older guy."

Ooh! That hurt. "What do you mean older guy!" I said. "I'm only thirty-six. Well, thirty-seven next month."

"That's what I mean. I just turned twenty-one."

"Lucky you. But let's go back to that whack on the head. If you knocked me out in the basement, then you must be the one who turned out all the lights."

"That's right. I'm the one who turned the lights out. And I'm the one who brought in the rabbits and the one who loosened up the doorknob and the one who put the real bullets in Frenchy's gun."

"You're the one who has been doing all that shit?"

"Yes, Mitch, I'm the mysterious theater ghost!"

With that, Alice buried her face in her hands and broke into hysterical sobs. I wanted to wrap her up in my arms and comfort her, but because one hand was needed to hold shut the blanket I was wearing the best I could do was put my right arm around her shaking shoulders and mutter soothing words.

"He said nobody would get hurt," she said between sobs. "I believed him when he said nobody would get hurt."

"It's okay," I told her over and over. "It's okay."

It took a good ten minutes for Alice to stem the salty flow. When the tremors rocking her body dropped to a mere two on the Richter Scale, she turned her teardrop-drenched face up to me, looked soulfully into my eyes and said, "I gotta pee!"

I pointed her toward the bathroom and while she was there I dashed into the bedroom and slipped on my khakis and the shirt I had dropped on the floor at bedtime. More comfortably attired, I waited for her to come out of the bathroom and pondered her amazing confession.

Was she telling the truth? Certainly she was strong enough to be the ghost. I had been impressed by her unusually muscular shoulders and biceps the first time I saw her. Later, onstage, I had been surprised at how firm and muscular her buns were when I gave her ass a squeeze.

"Okay," I said when she emerged from the bathroom with her face rinsed clean and her hair combed into straggly strands. "Sit down and start over from the beginning. You claim you're the theater ghost?"

Alice walked meekly across the room, fell into the chair, and curled into a fetal ball. "Yes," she said, staring at her knees. "I'm the one who did all those things to mess up the rehearsals and performances. Well, most of them anyway. Somebody else put the shit on the phone and poured the piss in the whisky bottle."

"I know about those. But what about the sandbag? That almost beaned you."

"That was my diversionary tactic. I did that so nobody would suspect me."

"I could have sworn you were really scared when that thing fell."

She uncurled enough to look up at me and half smiled as she said, "That's the best piece of acting I did in the whole show. Actually, I was kind of scared. That idiot Norman opened the door a little too soon and the bag came closer than I'd planned on."

She bowed her head again, and I realized I was towering above her like a police interrogator. I lowered myself closer to her level by dragging a chair over from the kitchen table and sitting down beside her.

"Want to tell me how you became the ghost?" I asked in the most soothing voice I could summon.

"Are you going to turn me in to the cops?" she asked.

"Maybe. Maybe not. But if you want to stay here and hide from whoever is chasing you, you have to tell me everything. Otherwise I'm tossing you out that door."

Alice sighed, uncurled to a sitting position, and looked at me to see if I meant what I had said. I gave her a look that would freeze a bottle of 100-proof gin and she sighed again. "Okay," she said. "They paid me to do it."

"Who paid you?" I asked.

"I don't know who it was. One night after one of the first rehearsals I got a phone call from this guy with a really heavy Norwegian accent. In fact, it's so heavy I think it's fake. He goes, 'Vould you like to make some easy money and haf some fun at da same time.' I can't do the accent very well."

She stopped, as if that was the entire story. "And you said yes?" I asked.

"Hey, I just finished two years of community college, and I'm trying to pay off my student loans. Of course I was interested in extra money, and the pranks he talked about that night were fun things, like moving furniture around the set when no one was looking or screwing up people's hand props. So I go, 'Okay, I'll do it.' It wasn't until later that he started ordering me to do the rough stuff."

"Ordering you?"

"By that time, he had me by the short hairs. Told me he'd call Herman Glock and tell him it was me being the ghost if I didn't keep doing what he wanted."

Stage Fright

The mental picture of having Alice Prewitt by the short hairs momentarily sidetracked my train of thought. However, I managed to get my mind back on the mainline rails after a fleeting moment of wondering if those curly little hairs were as red as the long flowing locks on her head.

"This guy with the Norwegian accent kept calling and giving orders?" I asked.

"That's right. And he gave me the number of an answering machine where I could call him and leave a message if I needed to talk to him."

Ah, here was a break! "Is the man's voice on the answering machine?" I asked.

"No," Alice said. "It's the canned message they put on at the factory." Okay, so much for that break.

"So how did this guy get your name and number in the first place?"

"Probably off the cast list. Why he picked me, I don't know."

"Maybe he knew you needed money. How did you get paid, by the way?"

"The guy told me never to lock my car. After every ghost trick I'd find an envelope with five twenty-dollar bills in the car. Sometimes it was put there at night, sometimes during the day when I was at work. I never ever saw who did it."

"Spooky," I said.

"No shit," said Alice.

"And you have no idea who the guy with the Norwegian accent is?"

"No. Like I said, I think it's fake but that doesn't help."

She was right, it didn't. What might help was more information about her flight from "them" this evening. I asked her what had happened.

"After the sheriff and his asshole buddy got done quizzing me about Frenchy's getting shot, I went home and called the answering machine and left a message saying I was quitting, whether he turned me in or not. Pretty soon I got a call from the Norwegian guy asking me to meet him in the parking lot where I work. He told me he wanted to work out some 'mutually satisfactory' separation agreement. I assumed that meant more money, so I went to meet him." She stopped, shivered and hugged herself around the chest, so I asked if she'd like to wrap up in the blanket. She said she would, and she pulled it up to her chin when I handed it to her.

"So what happened in the parking lot?" I asked when she looked snug.

"I pulled in and stopped and two guys wearing ski masks and black clothes yanked the doors open and jumped in — one next to me and one in the back," Alice said. "Scared the living shit out of me."

"Did they hurt you?"

"No, but the one next to me showed me what looked like a gun and said for me to drive where he told me to. We went to a boarded-up farmhouse somewhere north of town. They marched me in and pushed me into a bedroom and told me I was to stay there until their boss told them what to do. That's where I was all day today."

"You spent the whole day in that room?"

"Except for a couple of times when they let me out to go to the john."

"Didn't their boss ever come?" I asked.

"He didn't show up until after dark. It must have been about nine o'clock. I couldn't really see my watch because there weren't any lights in the room and the window was covered with plywood."

I asked if she had seen the boss and of course she had not. Alice said her two captors and the boss stayed in the kitchen and she heard what sounded like an argument. "I couldn't make out the words at first," she said. "Then, real loud, the boss goes, 'Look, you assholes, you've got to take her to the lake place and get rid of her.' That's when I got really scared."

"I'll bet you did," I said. "Is that when you took off?"

"Yeah. I snuck out of the bedroom and tiptoed to the front door and managed to slip out without anybody hearing me. My car was right where I'd left it so I ran to it."

"They left the key in the ignition?"

"No, but I'm forever locking my keys in the car so I carry a spare in one of those little magnetic boxes hooked to a metal part under the fender."

Sometimes it pays to be a klutz, I said to myself. To Alice, I said, "Didn't they follow you?"

"I didn't see anybody. I guess they didn't hear me drive out, and I kept the lights off until I was afraid I'd go in the ditch. But they're sure to come looking for me as soon as they see the car is gone."

I agreed. "Okay, you can hole up here for awhile until we decide what to do. It sounds like you're mixed up with some people in a business a lot more serious than playing pranks in the theater."

"Thanks," Alice said. "Have you got anything to eat? I'm hungry as hell."

Luckily for her, I had bought some crackers and cheese to snack on while I read my mystery. She polished off two-thirds of a box of Triscuit and more than a quarter pound of cheese, washed them down with my last can of root beer and curled up in the chair with her eyes closed.

"You don't have to spend the night in that chair," I said. "There are two beds in the next room."

Stage Fright

"I'm too tired to move," she said, sounding like she was already in dreamland. She was an armful, but I picked her up, carried her into the bedroom, laid her down, and pulled the blanket up to her chin. Without undressing, I crawled into my bed, where I lay awake for more than an hour wondering what the hell I was going to do with Alice Prewitt come daylight.

The first thing I heard Saturday morning was a flushing toilet. The first thing I saw was Alice Prewitt tiptoeing back into the bedroom. My digital watch read 8:12.

"You don't have to tippy-toe," I said. "I'm awake."

"Sorry," she said. "But as long as you're awake, do you mind if I take a shower?"

"Be my guest."

"It looks like I am your guest. Got any clean towels?"

I told her there were towels in the cabinet under the sink and laid my head back down on the pillow. Alice closed the bathroom door and soon I heard the shower running. Several minutes later I was still horizontal, wondering what to do with Alice, when I heard a knock at the door.

My first thought was that Alice's pursuers had found her car and were coming to get her. I peeked out the window cautiously to see if the knocker was the mysterious "them." What I saw was even more frightening than two men dressed in black. Standing on my doorstep, wearing blue jeans and a scoop-neck white blouse, was Martha Todd.

I realized I had to do two things very quickly. Number one, open the door. Number two, get Martha Todd the hell away from my cabin before Alice Prewitt walked out of the bathroom.

"Hi, sweetie, did I wake you?" asked Martha when I opened the door. She dropped the overnight bag that she had been holding in her right hand, stepped up, put her arms around my neck and gave me a quick peck on the lips. Before I could block her path, she bounced past me into the cabin.

"No, you didn't wake me," I said. "I was just getting dressed."

"Really? It looks like you slept in those clothes."

"Some of us are less sartorially adept than others. You're, uh, you're looking great. And you're earlier than I expected."

"I rode up with Al and Carol," Martha said. "I stayed over at their house last night so we could get an early start. Al wants to get in some fishing time this morning." That explained why Martha had not returned my phone call. In the brief silence that prevailed while I was fishing for a way to get Martha out the door, I was relieved to hear no sounds coming from the bathroom. A running shower surely would have kindled Martha's curiosity.

"That's great," I said. "Look, I was just going to walk over to the dining room for some breakfast. Want to join me?" Please, god, let her take the bait, I said to myself.

"We stopped for eggs and toast along the way, but I'll keep you company."

I wanted to shout, "Hallelujah!" Instead, I held the door open and gestured for Martha to precede me. She was one step away from the safety of the great outdoors when Alice Prewitt strode out of the bathroom wearing nothing but a towel.

Chapter 21
Matters of Timing

The unannounced appearance of Alice Prewitt wearing a band of white terry cloth would have been startling enough if the towel had been wrapped around her body, blocking the view of her torso from low cleavage to middle thigh. No such luck. Because there was no hair dryer in the bathroom, Alice had wound the towel around her head, obscuring only the area from her eyebrows up. Stunned as I was, I let my eyes drift downward from the towel, pause a moment to take in the sight of two up-tilted, pink-nippled young breasts, and journey swiftly past her muscle-ribbed tummy to the titian triangle between her thighs. Yes, Alice was a true redhead.

Alice also was, I suddenly realized, holding a pair of neon green panties aloft in her left hand. And Alice's lips were moving.

"Hey, Mitch, you wouldn't have some under shorts I can borrow, would you?" she was saying. "I've been wearing these panties since Thursday morning and they're getting kinda grungy." Then Alice saw Martha. The turbaned one sucked in her breath, said, "Oh, jeez, I'm sorry, I didn't know we had company," and dashed to the bedroom.

Martha's jaw had dropped to the vicinity of her belly button, but she recovered faster than I did. "Looks like I'm too early," she said. "Again!"

She zipped past me out the door and grabbed up her overnight bag, but I caught her by the shoulder. "Please listen to me," I said. "This isn't what it looks like."

"Is that a recorded message?" Martha asked. "I could swear I heard that one the last time I dropped in. As a writer, you should be more creative." She twisted out of my grasp and ran down the path toward the lodge.

I felt as if I was in a play where the timing was all fouled up. Instead of doors slamming just in time to conceal one character's actions from another, the doors were closing a second too late, and every character's foibles were revealed to those most damaged by the revelation.

"Shit!" I said, slamming the door with a bang louder than Frenchy's pistol. "Shit! Shit! Shit!"

Back in the bedroom, I found Alice sitting naked on her bed, drying her hair with the towel. Looking up at my red scowling face, she said, "Sorry, Mitch, I was just going to give you a quick look at what you missed the other night. Was that your girlfriend?"

"The closest thing I have to a girlfriend, or now I should say had," I said.

"She's the same one who caught you with Angie Maguire, ain't she?"

"How do you know somebody caught me with Angie Maguire?"

"Angie talks as fast as she drinks. In the bar the other night she goes, 'That goddamn Mitch is gay,' but you sure as hell didn't act gay around me."

"Angie's a goddamn blowhard!" When Alice giggled, I knew I'd chosen the wrong word.

"She told me that's what you wouldn't let her do," Alice said.

"Forget Angie, damn it!" I dug in my bedside dresser drawer for some underwear, pulled out two sets of low-risers and tossed the purple one to her. "Here. I'm sure my underpants will be thrilled to be next to your buns."

"Ooh, nice color," she said. "Thanks for the loan."

Alice declined my additional offer of a clean T-shirt and I started toward the bathroom to take my shower. Once again, there was a knock on the door.

"Busy place," Alice said.

"If I'm lucky, it's the assassins come to drown you in the lake," I said.

That snapped Alice out of her reverie. "Oh, shit, do you think so?" she asked.

"Tell you in a minute," I said, peeking out the window again. This time the knocker was Alan Jeffrey. "You're safe, Alice," I said, and I opened the door.

"What the hell did you do to Martha this time?" he said instead of "hello."

"More bad timing," I said. "Come on out, Alice, it's only my old pal, Al."

Out she came, wearing only a translucent pale pink bra and my purple underwear, and fluffing out her hair with the towel.

"Meet Alice, the Glock Family Theatre ghost," I said.

"Holy shit!" said Al. "No wonder Martha is pissed."

Alice said hello to Al and went back into the bedroom to finish dressing. I asked where Martha was, and Al said she had come running to the front desk, where he and Carol were registering. "You son of a bitch," Al said. "This was supposed to be a getaway weekend for Carol and me, and now, thanks to you, I could damn well wind up spending another night here in your cabin."

"That will make a cozy threesome," I said. "Unless we can find some other safe place for Alice."

Stage Fright

Naturally, Al asked why Alice needed a safe place, and I recited the story. He agreed with me that we couldn't hide her in my cabin much longer. We were discussing how to get Herman Glock and possibly the sheriff involved when Alice rejoined us, with her hair dry and her pants and T-shirt on.

"Herman will beat the shit out of me for ruining his play, and the sheriff will throw my ass in jail for loading Frenchy's gun with real bullets," Alice said. This woman really had a way with words.

"I'll keep Herman from strangling you, and I'll bail you out if the sheriff arrests you," I said. "You'll be a lot safer if the sheriff rounds up those two bastards who kidnapped you."

"The boss that came to the house and the guy with the Norwegian accent will still be looking for me. I got no family around here, Mitch. Where the hell can I go?"

"Maybe your boss, the medicine man, will protect you," Al said.

"Not a bad idea," I said. "What do you think, Alice? Would Doctor Stone help you hide until the sheriff nails those two?"

"Doctor Stone's a pretty good guy," she said. "He might find me a place to stay."

I pointed to the bedroom. "The phone is on the table between the beds. Do you know his home number?"

"He's probably in the office this morning. I'll give him a call."

"While you're doing that, we'll go talk to Herman."

"No, wait. Don't leave me here alone," Alice said. So we waited while she called the doctor. She came out of the bedroom with a smile on her face and said Doctor Stone had promised to come and get her in a couple of hours, as soon as he finished seeing the patients in his waiting room.

The three of us traipsed to the lodge to find Herman, and we were told by the woman at the registration desk that he had gone to the theater to clean out his office. We moved on to the theater and went in the unlocked front door. Alice decided to go backstage and pick up some make-up she had left in the dressing room while we talked to Herman. Al and I started toward the little office off the lobby, but we were halted in our tracks by a heart-stopping shriek from the auditorium.

A second later, Alice burst through the door, screaming, "Jesus H. Christ!" As she ran toward us, her eyes were as wide as they were the night the sandbag almost hit her, but this time it was not an act. "Look in there!" she shouted, waving toward the door from which she had just emerged.

Al and I almost knocked each other down as we raced to the door. Once inside, we were stopped cold for a second time.

Lit by a trio of spotlights, the limp form of Herman Glock dangled from a rope at center stage. He was dressed in the tuxedo he always wore on opening nights, but his first-night smile had been replaced by a slack-jawed look of wide-eyed wonder as he stared through dull, unblinking eyes across the rows of seats in the house he loved so much. The chair that once had broken under the weight of Rhonda Lapierre lay on its side near Herman's feet.

Al started running toward the stage, and I turned back to the lobby, where Alice had fallen to her knees and was upchucking the final remnants of last night's crackers and cheese onto the carpet. "Call 911!" I yelled at her. "Now! Get off your ass and call!" The force of my voice drove her to her feet, and she ran to the office while I turned back to the auditorium and the grotesque scene on the stage.

Al was standing beside Herman, pressing two fingers against the wrist of one limp arm in search of a pulse. Al looked at me and shook his head. "No use hauling him down," he said. "The poor bastard's already cold. It's too bad we didn't get here half an hour sooner."

"More bad timing," I said. "That's the story of my life these days."

"We'd better go out and calm Alice. There's nothing we can do in here."

I agreed and we went back to the lobby. Alice was not there. Nor was she in the office, although it was obvious that the phone had been moved hurriedly and roughly.

"Maybe she went back to your cabin," Al said.

"You stay here and I'll go look," I said, and I took off for the cabin at full speed. As I passed the end of the lodge, where Alice had parked her car, I saw that it was gone. Shit, I said to myself, where in the hell did that damn fool go?

I started walking back to the theater and was almost there when an ambulance and a Douglas County sheriff's patrol car came rolling into the parking lot with all lights flashing. They screeched to a stop on the blacktop in front of the theater, and their arrival was noted by everyone in the lodge and the dining room, including Ingeborg Glock, who went trotting toward the theater to see what was going on.

I intercepted her a couple of steps from the front door and said, "Ingeborg, please don't go in there."

"Why not?" she said, trying to step around me. "What happened?"

"There's been an accident," I said. "Please, trust me, you don't want to see it."

Ingeborg looked hard into my eyes and her face turned white. "It's Herman, isn't it?" she said.

"It is," I said. "Please don't go in."

Stage Fright

Her knees began to buckle and I wrapped my arms around her to keep her from falling. "He's dead, isn't he?" she said in a barely audible whisper.

"He's at peace," I said. "He's got no more worries."

Ingeborg threw back her head and let out an anguished moan that must have been heard on the far shore of the lake. Her body began to shake with sobs, and I didn't know what to do next.

"Mitch, let us take care of her," said a soft, female voice at my elbow. The speaker was Carol Jeffrey, and beside her I saw Martha Todd. I gently transferred Ingeborg, whose legs were now pure jelly, to those two angels of mercy. With one on each side, Carol and Martha walked their newly widowed hostess back to the lodge while I went into the theater to face another round of twenty questions.

After being quizzed at length about our bizarre discovery by the county medical examiner and a deputy sheriff, Al and I sat for a moment in Herman's office trying to make sense of the situation. Uppermost in my mind was Alice Prewitt's whereabouts. I wondered out loud if she had she run blindly away or if she had decided not to wait for Doctor Stone and had gone to him for protection.

"Why don't you call the doctor's office and see if she's there?" Al said.

"Yes, why don't I?" I said. "I think my thought processes have been totally wiped out." I dug out Herman Glock's phone book, found the number, and punched it in. Again the other receptionist answered, and I asked if Alice Prewitt was there.

"She was here," said the woman. "She come running in acting crazy, yelling something about somebody being dead and it being her fault."

"Oh, god!" I said. "Where is she now?"

"Doctor gave her a sedative, and then he took her to his house."

"So she's okay?"

"As far as we know," said the woman. I thanked her, hung up, and relayed the information to Al.

"At least Alice is safe," Al said. "Now we should go see how Carol and Martha are doing with Herman's wife — what's her name?" Before I could answer, another voice asked, "Was it you guys who found the body?" Standing in the office doorway was Heather Rondeau.

"It was," I said. "Did you just get here?"

"No, I've talked to the EMTs and the M.E. and the deputy, but they already had him in a body bag when I got here. What did it look like? Is it for sure a suicide?"

"Christ, it never occurred to me that it wasn't," I said. Al and I described the scene to Heather, leaving out Alice Prewitt's participation in the proceedings. We had agreed not to mention her confession and disappearance either to the authorities or the newspaper reading public until we had a better understanding of what was going on.

"It looked like he got into his opening-night costume, set up the spotlights, rigged the rope, stood on a chair, and kicked it away," I said. "I can't imagine the cops writing it up as anything but a suicide."

"What about a note?" Heather asked.

"Nothing on or near the body that we know of," Al said. "Maybe he left one in the lodge somewhere."

"Poor bastard," Heather said. "I suppose you never got to talk to him about the board meeting or how much money the theater had lost."

"That's what we came over here to do," I said. "How about you? Did you find out anything from the secretary of state's office?"

"Oh, shit!" she said. "Did I ever! You will be most interested to learn that there are three names on the OCC, Inc., incorporation papers. The first name is Gordon Glanz, and the second name is Oscar Olson."

"Oh, my god!" I said. "And who's the third?"

"That's even more interesting. The third name is Henry Stone, M.D."

It was time for Al and I to say, "Oh, shit!" in unison. For once, I was on cue.

"What's wrong?" Heather asked.

"He's got Alice," I said.

"Who the hell is Alice?" she asked. So we had to tell her about Alice Prewitt's role in the demise of the Glock Family Theatre, ending with her hysterical appearance in Doctor Stone's office and his supposedly providing her with safe haven.

"If the doctor is in business with Olson and Glanz, and if the two assholes who were supposed to get rid of Alice are working for Olson and Glanz, Alice could be in deep shit," Al said.

"We need to find her," I said. "Heather, do you know where the doctor lives?"

"No, but he might be in the phone book," she said. Al grabbed the phone book off Herman Glock's desk, flipped through the pages and discovered that Henry Stone's home number and address were not listed.

"There's a city directory in the newsroom," Heather said. "Everybody in Alexandria is listed in that."

"Take us to your newsroom," I said. Less than a minute later, the three of us were crammed together in Heather's two-seat Tracker racing toward Alexandria on a network of back roads that our chauffeur said would get us there quicker than Interstate 94.

Chapter 22
The Problem With Alice

Heather's driving was inspirational. I was inspired to shut my eyes several times, and Al was frequently inspired to yell, "For Christ's sake, slow down!" Somehow we arrived at the newspaper office unscathed, having covered the twenty miles separating it from the Glock Family Theatre in twenty minutes flat.

It was early afternoon on Saturday. The newsroom was deserted except for the city editor and a couple of copy editors putting the finishing touches on the Sunday paper. Heather alerted the city editor to the fact that she had a major story in the making, then grabbed the city directory and looked up Henry Stone, M.D.

"Nice neighborhood," she said as she copied the address into her notebook. "All big new houses."

"Let's get our asses over there," I said. "We'll see if it's big enough to hide a terrified theater ghost."

Back into the Tracker we went. After five minutes of weaving through Alexandria's streets and running a couple stop signs, Heather parked us in front of a sprawling, one-story rambler that actually had an eight-foot totem pole in the front yard. We piled out of the Tracker like circus clowns emerging from a midget car, trotted to the door, and rang the bell. There was no answer.

We rang again and waited. Then we knocked and waited. We went around the house, found a back door, and knocked. Still no answer.

Al jiggled the knob, but the door was locked. We peered in several windows and saw nobody inside. The front door was also locked. We went back to the street and stood beside the Tracker.

"I guess he took her somewhere else," said Heather.

"We'll never find her," said Al.

I started to agree, but suddenly, a light went on, just like in the comic strips. "The guy the kidnappers called the boss told them to take her to the lake place and get rid of her," I said. "Has the doctor or either of his business buddies got a lake place?"

Heather didn't know, so we scrunched ourselves back into the Tracker and returned to the newsroom for another perusal of the city directory. There was only the one listing for Henry Stone and there was no listing for Oscar Olson, which

Heather said meant that he lived outside the city limits. We found Oscar's address in the phone book and determined that his home could not be located on a lake. When we found the listing for Gordon Glanz, Heather assured us that his house in Alexandria wasn't anywhere near a lake either.

"That leaves us high and dry," Al said. "And your ghostly friend Alice is up shit's creek without a canoe."

"You're right," I said. Then another light, this one much lower in wattage, went on. "What if one of them has a place on our lake? I mean the lake we're staying on, twenty miles out of town."

"So what?" asked Al. "How would we ever find out?"

"Ingeborg Glock would know. She and Herman have been there so long that they know who owns every piece of property on that lake."

"I suppose it's worth a shot," Al said.

"Let's haul ass!" said Heather.

"But we don't have to haul ass quite so fast," I said.

"Bite me," she said, and off we went on another high-speed run. If I was Catholic, I'd have been clutching my rosary in white-knuckled fingers all the way.

About a dozen neighbors and resort guests were huddled in front of the big fireplace in the lodge as though they were seeking warmth, despite the fact that the temperature had climbed to seventy-six degrees. Within the circle, we spotted the blonde head of Carol Jeffrey and we quietly made our way to her side.

"Where have you guys been?" Carol asked. "The cops finished asking questions and left over an hour ago."

"You wouldn't believe where we've been in that hour, but we'll tell you all about it later," Al said. "Right now we need to talk to Herman's wife for a minute."

"I don't know if that's possible," Carol said. "We got her calmed down and we're trying to let her rest a while before her family starts arriving and everything gets nutty."

"We need to ask her a couple of questions," I said. "This sounds trite as hell, but it really could be a matter of life and death."

"Whose life and death?"

"The redhead who was in my cabin this morning. She could really be in danger."

"In more danger than when she was sleeping with you?"

Stage Fright

"Damn it, Carol, she did not sleep with me. She slept in the other bed, and she was taking a shower all by her lonesome when Martha made her surprise entrance and took center stage."

"Martha said the woman was naked from the hair down."

Al cut me off before I could reply. "Carol, please!" he said. "We don't have time to argue about what Mitch and Alice were doing last night or what she was or wasn't wearing in the shower. She came to Mitch's cabin because her life had been threatened, and now the same people probably have got her again. We need to talk to Mrs. Glock for a minute because Mrs. Glock might be able to help us find her."

"One of Ingeborg's best friends is with her in the bedroom," Carol said. "I'll go see if you can go in and ask questions."

"Be sure you tell her how important it is," Al said. Carol gave him a look that would have converted steam to ice crystals and headed off toward the Glocks' living quarters. The three of us sat in silence with the quiet assemblage in front of the fireplace until Carol returned.

"Ingeborg said she would help," Carol said. "But just one of you can go in." Since I knew Ingeborg better than either Al or Heather, I was elected.

Ingeborg was a fair-skinned Swede with hair so blonde that it was almost white. Because she spent most of her working day indoors, she always looked pale in comparison to her suntanned husband and their vacationing customers. The morning's tragedy had drained what little color she had, causing her hair and skin to blend together in a monotone of semitransparent yellowish gray. I approached the bed and opened the conversation by offering my sympathy for her loss. She responded in a half-whisper, thanking me for my help outside the theater.

"I wish I could have done more," I said. "Now another person's life is in danger and I need your expertise. Do you know if Oscar Olson, Gordon Glanz, or Doctor Stone have houses here on the lake?"

"Oscar Olson and Gordon Glanz killed my husband," Ingeborg said in a much stronger voice. "As sure as if they put the noose around his neck and pulled it tight, those two men killed my husband."

"I agree with you. Now I want to stop them from maybe killing somebody else. Do you know if either of them has a house on this lake?"

"That bastard Glanz has a summer place here." She turned her head away, and I was afraid she would start sobbing again.

"Where is it?" I asked quickly. "What does it look like?"

Ingeborg turned her face toward mine again. "It's on Merganser Bay," she said. "You go to the left after you pass the point with the sand bar, and it's the second big bay you come to."

"What does the house look like?"

"It's set back halfway up the hill. It's a one story place with all glass across the front and a big redwood deck facing the lake. His damn old dock sticks farther out into the water than anybody else's because he drives the biggest boat on the lake."

"Thank you," I said. "That will help us a lot. You take care of yourself, now." I waved good-by like a little child and backed out of the room on the tips of my toes.

The four of us — Al, Carol, Heather, and I — retreated to the Jeffreys' cabin to digest the information about Gordon Glanz's summer place and discuss what to do next. I was hoping to find Martha in the cabin, but Carol informed me that, after helping get Ingeborg to the lodge, Martha had put on her bikini and gone to sit on the beach.

"She was pretty shook up, and she said she needed to be alone," Carol said. "But you should see her in that bikini."

"I'd love to see her in anything right now," I said.

"Don't count on it," Carol said. "She's really pissed at you this time."

Heather brought the conversation back on track. "Your love life can wait, Mitch," she said. "Right now we have to find Gordon Glanz's house, remember?"

"Since the only description we have is from the lake side, the only way we'll find it is by boat," Al said. "I think Mitch and I need to go fishing in Merganser Bay."

"You're not going without me," said Heather. "I'll call the desk and tell them I've got some more legwork to do before I write my story about the suicide."

"You're too dressed up to go fishing," I said. She was properly clothed for her morning's work as a reporter, with a pale blue satiny blouse tucked into the elastic waistband of a pair of loose-fitting black slacks.

"So loan me some fishing clothes. You must have some old stuff I can wear."

It took a cooperative effort to get Heather properly outfitted. Carol found a pair of Al's jeans that looked like they were ready for the ragbag. Heather had to roll up ten inches at the bottom of each leg, but the waist was nearly the right size. I dug into the laundry bag in my cabin and pulled out a ten-year-old Mount Rushmore T-shirt I had worn to several rehearsals. If nothing else, Heather would smell like a fisherman.

We took three fishing rods, a tackle box, and a pair of binoculars and piled into the boat that came with the Jeffreys' cabin. As we putt-putted past the swimming beach, I saw the slender, hourglass figure of Martha Todd stretched full length on a blanket. The convex curves of the hourglass were accentuated by two wisps of blaze orange cloth. It took all my willpower to stay in the boat and watch this vision fade into the distance as Al revved up the motor.

Al steered well clear of the sandbar we had hit on our earlier excursion, which caused Heather to ask why he was taking the long way around, and cruised into the first large bay to the left. He aimed at the wooded point that marked the far side of this bay, took care not to get too close to shore, and turned into a wider expanse of water that had to be Merganser Bay. Al slowed to trolling speed, and we put our lines into the water so we would look like walleye fishermen to anyone watching from the shore.

Thanks to Ingeborg's description of the dock, Gordon Glanz's summer place was not hard to find. The dock did, indeed, protrude much farther than any of the others. Scanning the hillside behind the dock with our binoculars, I saw a long, low cabin with floor-to-ceiling windows and a deck running the full width of the side facing us.

"That's got to be it," I said. "Let's troll a little closer to shore and see if we can see anything moving." After we had cruised on past, Al turned us around and steered us in for a closer look. A large boat with what looked like twin 50-horsepower motors on the back was tied up at the dock, but we saw no signs of life in or around the house.

"One more time," I said after we had passed the dock. Al turned us around again, and as we slipped past the third time, we saw a man emerge from the front door, walk to the edge of the deck, and light a cigarette. Through the binoculars, I could see that he was wearing a black T-shirt and black jeans. All he needed to match Alice's description of her Friday morning kidnappers was the addition of a ski mask.

"Bingo!" I said. "Now let's go home and figure out what we're going to do."

"You're going to call the sheriff, aren't you?" said Carol Jeffrey when the three of us tromped into her cabin.

"There is a major problem with that," Al said. "Number one, we're not absolutely sure Alice is there. The sheriff would need a warrant, which might not be so easy to get without more concrete evidence of an actual abduction. Then, if we did get a warrant and Alice wasn't there, it would be very embarrassing to have the troops go storming into the house yelling and waving their guns."

"There's another problem with Alice," I said. "She has been involved in some criminal action but not by choice. First she was duped and then she was forced to follow orders. She should have a chance to talk to a lawyer before she's grilled by the sheriff again and the TV reporters come swarming around making her look like a freak."

"You're awfully generous to cover for somebody who confessed that she bopped you on the head and knocked you cold," Heather said.

"He's always happy to cover for his female friends," said another familiar voice. Martha Todd was standing in the door that led to the bedroom. Unfortunately, she had taken off her orange bikini, and the hourglass was lost inside a pair of baggy gray shorts and an extra-large Prairie Home Companion T-shirt. "In fact, he's happy to cover them with everything but clothes," she added.

That seemed like a cheap shot to me. "So how much clothing do you wear in the shower?" I asked.

"About the same," Martha said. "But I do put something on when I get out of the shower — unless I'm with somebody who's already seen everything I've got."

I was about to say that some women aren't so prim and proper about who sees everything, but Carol beat me to the draw with, "Please, you two, we can talk about this later. Right now we're worried about the missing woman."

"I'm sorry," said Martha. "I didn't know she was missing anything but a chest full of silicone." Another cheap shot, I said to myself.

"Why don't you sit down with us and listen to what's going on?" Carol said. "It might even help you and Mitch straighten out your problems."

To my surprise, Martha accepted the invitation and joined the circle while we planned an after-dark raid on the Gordon Glanz summerhouse. When the planning powwow was finished, Heather went back to Alexandria to write her story about Herman Glock's suicide. She agreed to keep Alice Prewitt's name out of the paper and made me promise, in turn, to take her along on our nocturnal search and rescue effort.

After Heather departed, I went to my cabin to write my suicide story for the Sunday morning *Daily Dispatch*. When I finished, I read it over and e-mailed it to the desk. The Sunday city editor e-mailed back a couple of questions, and I answered them. Then, for the first time since we discovered Herman Glock's dangling corpse, I stopped running, thinking and doing things.

This was my first opportunity to sit still and reflect on a day in which events had been tumbling endlessly in front of me, just beyond my reach. Martha Todd, whose trust I treasured, was convinced I was lying to her. Alice Prewitt, a friend who had come to me asking for protection, was missing and in danger. Herman Glock, who had been generous and friendly to me while he was dealing with deep person-

Stage Fright

al demons, was dead by his own hand. I felt the sting of tears boiling up behind my eyes. I put my face down into my hands and began bawling like newborn baby. I didn't look up again until I felt a soft hand pressing on each of my shoulders.

The touch startled me, because I hadn't heard the door open.

"It's nice to know that big boys can cry," said the owner of the hands. Through the blur of tears, I saw the face of Martha Todd.

"The day just kind of caught up with me," I said with a sniffle. Martha kissed me on the forehead, dug into the pocket of her shorts and pulled out a crumpled tissue.

"It hasn't been used," she said, handing me the soft folds of paper. I thanked her, wiped my eyes, and blew my nose. When I finished that routine, she said, "I didn't mean to embarrass you. I just came over to say that even though I'm jealous as hell of the redhead, I admire you for sticking your neck out and trying to rescue her."

"There's no reason to be jealous," I said. "There's nothing going on between Alice and me except that she came to my cabin late last night looking for a hiding place. We were in the show together, we had a couple of drinks together at an after-party, and she apparently thought she could trust me in a pinch. So far all I've done to help her is lend her a pair of underpants."

Martha laughed. "Now there's a picture — that little cutie's butt decked out in your boxer shorts."

"I do not wear boxers," I said. "Hang around awhile and I'll show you what I'm wearing today."

"I'll take a rain check — which I may or may not use — on that invitation. Right now all four of us have to find a place to eat dinner. The dining room in the lodge is closed until further notice."

We drove in Al's car toward Alexandria on I-94 and found a family-run pizza joint named Georgio's five miles from the resort. While we ate, Al told me he had talked to Sven, who helped Herman service the boats when he wasn't cleaning the theater, and obtained a larger, twenty-horsepower motor for the evening's fishing trip. "I wanted something that would get us home faster than that little six-horse job," he said. "The twenty is the biggest one they have. Old Sven said we must be 'goin' out for some really big vuns out dere in da dark.'"

"Yah, he should only know how big," I said. "If ve're lucky, ve'll come home vit' a trophy fish what tips the scales at about 120-pounds."

"Is that what this fish weighs when it's dressed?" asked Martha. I was relieved to see she was smiling.

147

Chapter 23
Away All Boats

Heather Rondeau, clad solidly in black, was waiting at the Jeffreys' cottage when we returned to the Glock Family Resort. We were just past the summer solstice, the longest day of the year, so we still had a couple of hours to wait until darkness enveloped the lake. Al and I changed into the least visible inky attire we could find, and then we all sat on the dock, fidgeting and slapping mosquitoes and urging the sun to go down.

It was almost ten o'clock when Al, Heather and I clambered into the aluminum boat. He was steering from the stern seat, Heather was settled amidships, and I was the bow watch. From the dock, Carol cast off the lines and said she would call the sheriff if we weren't home by four in the morning. We had agreed that six hours should be enough time for us to complete our mission and return to home base.

It took three pulls on the starter rope to get our new motor running. I held my breath, hoping this wasn't an omen, as Al cursed and yanked on the rope. Finally the damn thing sputtered to life, and we made for open water.

As night marauders, we were traveling light. We each had a flashlight, which we hoped not to use. In addition, Al was carrying his Swiss Army knife, with which he planned to cut the gas lines on the boat equipped with the twin 50s, and a nifty little lock picking tool he had acquired a few years earlier while working with a private detective. I was going ashore with a can of Mace, borrowed from Heather, hooked onto my belt. This was our only defensive — and offensive — weapon.

Al and I had minimal experience with a boat in the dark, having done some night fishing while staying within sight of the light at the end of the resort's main dock. We were amazed at how damn black the world became after we rounded the point with the sandbar and started across the first broad bay. The only light along the shoreline came from the windows of a couple of summer homes. The only light where we were cruising came from the twinkling stars above.

"I hope to hell you guys can see more than I can," Heather said.

"No problem," Al said. "I can still see my hand in front of my face. Of course, that's all I can see. How about you, Mitch?"

Stage Fright

I was trying to think of a smart-ass reply when a wall of deeper darkness loomed up in front of us. "I can see you need to turn or we're going to hit the woods!" I yelled. "Turn this son of a bitch right now!"

Al swung the bow hard right, and we spun 90 degrees to put us parallel to the shoreline, which wasn't more than ten yards away. He throttled back to medium speed and followed the darkened landmass around the point and into Merganser Bay.

Again the bank president's prodigious dock made it easy to find his house. Gordon Glanz had mounted a light on a tall pole at the end of his dock, and the beam beckoned us the way a flame summons a moth. Fifty yards from our target, Al cut the motor and the wind carried us silently toward the dock, with the aid of an occasional pull on the oars by Heather, who said she had rowed more than one fishing boat in her time.

The wind that helped us to drift shoreward so quietly double-crossed us when we got close to the dock. We were blown against the pilings with a clang of aluminum against wood that echoed off the hillside and reverberated across the water. We sat tense and silent, with Al and me gripping the dock to hold the boat in place, while we waited for some kind of reaction from the residents of the house.

Lights were glowing in the rear, but the front room and deck were dark. After several minutes passed with no additional lights flashing on, we all relaxed, and Heather whispered, "Jeeez, I almost peed in my pants."

"Keep your powder — and your panties — dry," I replied. Al and I lashed our respective ends of the boat to the dock and climbed out as quietly as we could. The plan was for Heather to stay in the boat, ready to cast off the stern line as soon as we got back to the dock, with or without Alice Prewitt. After Al cut the gas lines in the other boat, he and I intended to work our way stealthily up the hill. With me going to the left and Al to the right, we would circle the house, peeking in windows when possible, and meet in the back for a strategic conference.

The tall light that had helped us locate the dock was a hindrance to our next move, which was slashing the fuel lines. Al's figure was fully illuminated as he crawled on hands and knees to the big boat. Anyone looking out of the front windows would have spotted him at once. Our luck held out, and he slipped down into the hull to do his dirty work. A minute later he slid back onto the dock and crawled all the way to the sandy shore where I was waiting in the shadow of a tree.

"Got'em," he said, holding up two short lengths of rubber hose. "I took a chunk out of each one so they can't just duct tape them together."

"That ought to keep them at home," I said. "Let's circle the house and then circle the wagons when we meet in the back yard."

"Happy trails to you," he whispered. We parted and started moving cautiously up the hill, hoping we wouldn't fall into any holes — or encounter any living critter bigger than a mosquito — in the gloom. Twice I was sorely tempted to do a quick on-and-off with the flashlight, but I swallowed hard both times and stepped into shadows darker than the inside of a coal miner's hat with no consequences.

I had just stubbed my toe against an extremely solid obstacle when, without warning, I had light. The moon, full and round and bright as a set of headlights on high beam, was rising from behind me over the lake.

The moonlight illuminated the object before me, which was a wooden terrace retaining wall as high as two railroad ties. The moonlight also illuminated me, and I ducked instinctively behind the terrace. My instinct proved to be the salvation of my ass. Seconds after my belly hit the ground, I heard the front door open and footsteps clump to the edge of the deck, which was barely first-down yardage away.

"Hey, the fuckin' moon's up," the man on the deck yelled. "We oughtta be out gettin' us some fish to eat."

"Oh, fuck the fish!" came a man's voice from inside. "We'll be fuckin' outta here before noon tomorrow." Ah, yes, a rich vocabulary is a wonderful thing.

The ground felt colder than the air, which had dropped somewhere into the low sixties, and I began to shiver. I was doing my damnedest to quell my involuntary quakes when a new problem arose. Well, actually, it descended. With a whining hum, the biggest damn mosquito in Minnesota settled onto the back of my left hand and sank its proboscis into the soft flesh between the thumb and forefinger. I felt a slight sting at the moment of penetration and ground my teeth together hard as I fought to overcome the urge to smash the critter with my other hand.

I reminded myself that this man could be armed and the sound of the slap might lead to a wound that would drain a lot more blood from my body than a mosquito could siphon. My tormenter continued to feast from my veins while the man on the deck kept feasting his eyes on the moon. "You little pig," I thought, "maybe you'll suck up so much liquid you won't be able to take off and I'll get to smash your bloody little ass when this moonstruck clown goes back into the house, which should be any minute."

The next sound I heard was that of a match being struck. A moment later the fresh, late-night breeze carried the smell of cigarette smoke to my nostrils. The son of a bitch was taking a smoke break while I was being eaten alive.

Stage Fright

With the same whining hum that had announced her arrival, the fully gorged mosquito rose off the back of my hand and flew away into the darkness. I was sure that I would have a huge, itchy, red welt on her feeding place within minutes. Another mosquito buzzed my ear, and I asked myself why in the hell I was out here in the goddamn woods in the middle of the goddamn night.

When the cigarette finally was burned down and snubbed out, the smoker turned and went back into the house. When I heard the door slam shut, I breathed a silent "thank you," swatted a mosquito on the side of my face and pried myself off the ground.

I gave the smoker a couple of minutes to settle down inside before I moved closer to the house. My objective was the first lighted window, which turned out to be the dining room. Two swarthy men in their late twenties or early thirties were seated at the table with stacks of poker chips in front of them. One man was shuffling the deck. Both were wearing black T-shirts and black jeans and heavy five o'clock shadows.

The window was open, so I could hear their voices and the click of poker chips through the screen as they bet on their hands and raised each other several times. The one who finally called held the losing hand. He knocked over his stacks of chips and said, "I'm sick of playin' poker. When's that fucker comin', anyways?"

"He's comin' first thing in the morning," said the other player. "I told ya that a hundred times already."

"I can't wait to get the fuck out of here. And I still think we should all lay that broad before we dump her in the lake."

"You better fuckin' leave her alone, or it'll be your fuckin' ass that's on the line."

"Okay, okay! I won't touch her. Anyways, it's your turn to stand the fuckin' midnight watch. I'm goin' to bed."

The poker loser left the room, and I saw him turn toward the rear of the house before he went out of sight. The poker winner sat at the table for a couple of minutes before he also left the room. I was just about to abandon the window when he returned with a can of beer and a bag of pretzels. Leaving him slurping and munching contentedly, I ducked under the window and moved quickly around the back corner, hoping to discover where the other man had gone.

Lights shone through two high, narrow windows in the rear of the house. One light went out just as I was sticking my head up to peek in, so I concluded this must be where the losing poker player had gone for his night's repose.

I was slinking along the wall toward the other lighted window when I saw the silhouette of a man glide around the corner at the far end of the house. With my hand on the can of Mace, I froze, waiting to see if it was friend or foe. When the shadow was within ten feet, I heard him whisper, "Circle the wagons."

"Happy trails," I replied, letting go of the Mace.

We held a brief whispered conference in which I reported what I had learned and Al said he had seen the watch stander come into the kitchen on the other side of the house and gather up the beer and pretzels. Al had located a side door that led into the kitchen. "It's locked but it looks pickable if we need to get in that way," he said.

The lighted window we were about to peep through was less than three feet wide and only eighteen inches high and the opening was at least four feet off the ground. It was the style of window that swings upward when it's cranked open, and the bottom was sticking out about a foot. As a possible entrance, it rated very low on a scale of ten.

However, what we saw inside the room went off the top of the scale. Alice Prewitt's copper curls were resting on a pillow in a bed to our left. In defense against the chill night air, she had pulled the gray army blanket that covered her all the way up to her chin. She appeared to be comfortably asleep.

The lamp providing the light stood on the other end of the room behind an overstuffed armchair. This chair was occupied by a heavyset, middle-aged woman, whose eyes were focused on a paperback book she was holding low, near her lap. As we watched, the woman's head slowly drooped forward, and her eyelids closed. When her chin touched her substantial bosom, her eyes popped open, and her head snapped upward. We watched this cycle repeat itself three times.

"Probably a trashy romance," Al whispered.

"If we're lucky, it's dull enough to put her completely to sleep," I replied. "Let's get away from the house and figure out what we're going to do." As we moved to a hiding place behind a row of backyard shrubs, I looked at my watch and saw that it was twenty minutes after midnight. We still had plenty of time.

Because the window was so small, we decided that our best route to Alice's room was through the side door. After Al picked the lock, we could slip through the kitchen and into the hallway that led to the bedrooms. Before launching this invasion, we would give the drowsy paperback reader time to reach a deeper level of relaxation in her comfy chair. When she woke up while we were rousing Alice, she'd be staring at a can of Mace held inches from her nose.

Stage Fright

As we sat on the ground waiting for sufficient time to pass, we could feel the temperature sliding downward. When my watch dial glowed 01:00, we rose and found our bodies stiff from the dampness and the cold. Our joints almost creaked out loud as we crept back to the bedroom window and peeked in. Alice was still asleep, with the blanket pulled down far enough to reveal her muscular upper arms and the straps of her pink bra. The woman in the chair had fallen deep into the arms of Morpheus, with her chin resting serenely on her forty-six-inch chest and the book lying loose in her lap.

Again we backed off behind the bushes to discuss our next move.

"Nice of the old gal to cooperate by going to sleep," Al said. "But it looks like your redhead is sleeping in her undies. She's going to have to get dressed, or she'll freeze her buns off out there on the lake."

"Search and rescue operations never go as smooth as they look in the book, but I'm sure we can deal with Alice's state of undress," I said. "We'll hustle her into her clothes and get the hell out of the house."

"What about the warden? If she wakes up, she'll scream the second we leave."

"If she wakes up, we make her come with us and we leave her on the dock."

"You mean kidnap a kidnapper?"

"We'll handle her with kid gloves," I said.

"No kidding," said Al.

We walked quietly through the moonlight to the side door. Al was selecting a pick with which to open the lock when we heard a most disturbing sound from the lake. It was the purr of a boat motor. As we crouched in the darkness and watched, we saw a boat slightly larger than our little fishing craft cruise into the dock and stop opposite the one that Al had neutralized. The light at the end of the dock was no longer glowing, but in the moonlight we saw a man jump out onto the dock and make fast the lines. A second, less limber man got out and both came hiking up the hill.

The sight of the new arrivals was scary. But, even scarier, was the fact that we could not see our boat tied up at the dock behind the big one. Well, as I said, search and rescue missions never go as smooth as they look in the book.

Chapter 24
Carrying On

"Now what do we do?" Al said as we hid behind the shrubs for the third time.

"We check out the house again and try to figure out what's going on inside. One of the new arrivals is probably the asshole in charge of getting rid of Alice."

"So now we have five people to wade through on the way to the rescue."

"Only five of them against two of us — that's about the right odds for a couple of old Navy bombardiers, don't you think?"

"Sky anchors aweigh," Al said, and we tiptoed back to Alice's bedroom window.

The noise made by the arriving twosome and the man greeting them had awakened both Alice and her female guardian. Alice was sitting in the middle of the bed with the blanket pulled up around her shoulders. The heavyset woman was hauling herself out of the chair. She went to the door, opened it, and stuck her head out into the hallway in an effort to hear what was being said in the dining room.

We could hear nothing, so I whispered to Al that I was going to sneak around to the dining room window. He said he would keep an eye on the redhead and her warden.

Peeking through the dining room window, I saw the poker hand winner, who was holding a bottle of beer, and the driver of the other boat, who was of similar age and dress. A short, baldheaded man with a forty-eight inch belly, who was wearing a dark pinstripe suit, a pale blue shirt, and a yellow necktie with some kind of little red figures on it was with them. Three empty beer bottles stood on the table where Poker Winner had been sitting, and I could hear enough to understand that the fashion plate with the bulging belly was chewing out the drinker for his excessive consumption of the brew.

The fat fellow's harangue was interrupted by the entrance of the poker hand loser, who shuffled in wearing only a pair of white skivvies. "What's goin'on?" he asked.

"That's what I was wonderin'," the fat fellow said. "Your buddy here is suckin' up a six pack while he's supposed to be makin' sure the broad don't get away."

"How can she get away?" said Poker Winner. "You got Maggie in there practically sittin' on her fuckin' bed while she sleeps."

Stage Fright

"The reason I got Maggie sittin' in there is to make sure you two animals don't do nothin' you ain't supposed to do," Fatso said.

"Like what?" yelled Poker Winner. "You already told us we ain't allowed to stick it into that redhead like we should."

"Hey, I wouldn't mind a piece of that ass myself," Fatso said. "But I get my orders from higher up."

"So who's to know if we all knock off a piece before we dump her?" said Poker Loser. "Let's go in there and chase Maggie out and have us a party!"

Fatso, who was four inches shorter than Poker Loser, rammed his rotund belly against the taller man's groin, looked up into his face and said, "Listen, you asshole, the people payin' us don't want no signs of sex abuse on the bitch's body when it's found, so get that stupid idea outta your goddamn head!"

A new voice, this one deep but female, cut through the general ruckus. "Did I hear somebody say something about chasing Maggie out?" The stout woman who had been in Alice's room was standing in the dining room doorway.

I decided it was time to move. Not bothering to be quiet, I scurried around the back and told Al to forget the kitchen door. Instead, we each grabbed one corner of the partially open window and yanked, forcing it all the way up with a screeching sound that caused Alice Prewitt to look our way. She watched in wide-eyed wonder as Al sliced through the screen with the Swiss Army knife and helped me get my butt up over the sill and dive headfirst into the bedroom.

"Get your clothes on, kid, we're getting out of here," I said.

"I don't have any," Alice said. "They took away my clothes and my shoes. All I've got is my bra and your underpants." She unwrapped the blanket and showed me.

My purple low riders had never looked so good, but this was not the time to enjoy the view. "Bring the blanket and let's go," I said.

"But I'm barefoot! How can I walk in the woods?"

"I'll carry you," I said. "It will be a pleasure. Now get your ass in gear."

Alice ran to the window and tossed out the blanket. With me hoisting her buns from the rear and Al catching her on the outside, she sort of swam through the narrow opening. I followed with a headfirst dive into a cradle formed by four waiting arms.

"Let's get away from the house," Al said.

"Unhh!" I said, hoisting 120 pounds of muscular woman in my arms. Alice wrapped her arms around my neck and, with Al carrying the blanket, we trotted toward our spot behind the bushes. I was beginning to enjoy the sensation of cradling a nearly-naked woman when we reached our hiding place, where I set

Alice's feet down on a patch of short grass. She was shaking, both from cold and excitement, so she hastily wrapped herself up in the blanket.

"Now what?" Al asked.

"They left my car up on top of the hill," Alice said, pointing to a set of wooden stairs that led farther up the hillside.

"We've got a boat," I said. "At least, we had a boat. If ours isn't there we can take the one the fat guy came in."

"Yeah, we can't leave Heather sitting out there high and dry," Al said.

"Or, in this case, low and wet," I said. "The first thing we should do is get farther away from the house before they find out Alice is gone." I picked her up again and we took off at an angle down the hill, distancing ourselves from the house while we moved toward the lake. The angle also took us farther from the dock laterally, but we decided to cross that bridge — or, in this case, beach — when we came to it.

After a few minutes, I was beginning to suck wind loud enough for Al to hear me huffing and he suggested a rest stop. We found a soft spot where Alice could stand and I set her down. The wind off the lake had increased in velocity and decreased in temperature and the moon was dodging in an out of passing banks of clouds.

"It could be blowing up a storm," Al said.

"Into each life some rain must fall," I said.

We were looking back through the trees toward the house, preparing to resume our trek to the lake, when lights began popping on in every room.

"They know you're gone," I said to Alice. "Let's get moving." I lifted her again and she brushed my cheek with her lips as she snuggled into place.

"If we make it, I'll return the ride," she whispered against my ear.

Before I had time to fantasize about this delightful prospect, men started pouring out of the house. Firing off expletives as they ran, the three young thugs in black went charging up the stairs to where Alice said they had left her car. Fatso stood at the kitchen door shouting instructions. Big Maggie was nowhere in sight.

The periods of total darkness when clouds obscured the moon grew longer, slowing our progress as we struggled toward the water through increasingly thick underbrush. Alice's blanket caught on something with thorns, and we had to stop and rip the rough wool away from the branch. Behind us we heard more shouts and the sounds of men moving through the trees and brush. They had seen that Alice had not escaped on wheels and they were searching the woods.

Stage Fright

"Let's get farther away," Al said. We set a course parallel to the shore, which increased the distance to the house. It also meant we would have a longer stretch of lakefront to cover when we made our final move toward the dock.

Beams from flashlights arced through the underbrush between our position and the house, and the shouts of the hunters grew closer as they expanded their search area. Despite the chill wind, I was sweating like a Kentucky Derby winner and puffing like the Little Engine That Could when we finally hit the shoreline.

"Let's cool it for awhile," Al said. "It looks like they've got us blocked off from the dock right now anyway."

I put Alice's bare tootsies down on the sand and flopped on my butt beside them.

Alice knelt beside me and asked, "Are you okay?"

"I'll live long enough to take that ride you promised," I said. She put a cool hand on the back of my neck and kissed my earlobe, sending a shiver down my sweaty spine.

We sat in the sand for what seemed like hours, listening to the hunters and watching the flashlight beams crisscross in the night. The moon disappeared completely and I could feel the cold dampness of the air replacing the warm sweat in my soggy shirt.

A voice close by yelled, "I'd like to kill that goddamn Maggie. She never should have left that fuckin' broad alone." It sounded like Poker Loser.

"Just find the fuckin' redhead," said a voice I recognized as Poker Winner. "Let Fatso deal with that stupid Maggie."

Beside me, Alice shivered and snuggled close.

The voices and flashlight beams slowly moved away, uphill toward the house. Apparently the foul-mouthed hunters had reached the perimeter of their search area and were now closing in on their prey — they hoped.

"Time to get to the boat," I said, hoping it would be there. My watch was glowing 03:53 when I again pulled Alice up into my arms. She gave my earlobe a flick of her tongue and I said, "If you do that again I won't be able to walk as fast."

With Al leading, we hugged the tree line at the water's edge and plodded toward the dock. Our footing kept changing from sand to gravel to mud — and sometimes shallow water. Once Al went in over his knees trying to work his way around a fallen branch, so we backtracked and went around the other side of the tree.

We were about thirty feet from the dock when the clouds parted and the moon shone through, revealing a narrow strip of sand at water's edge. I was sucking wind again, and Alice volunteered to walk the rest of the way. "I'm still enjoying the ride, but I don't want to lose you after coming this far," she said.

"Whoof!" I said, lowering her toes to the sand. Alice's hot little tongue flicked my earlobe again as she unwrapped her arms and stepped away.

With the moon lighting our way across the soft, smooth sand, we found our way to the dock. Once we were on the planking, the moonlight showed us an even more appealing sight. Our boat was now tied up in front of the big power craft, and Heather was unwinding the stern line from the piling to which it was secured.

We all slid down into the boat and I cast off the bow line while Heather and Alice settled side-by-side on the middle seat. Al jumped in and pushed us away from the dock.

"Where the hell were you when the other boat came in?" Al asked Heather as he gave the starter rope a pull.

"I heard it coming and rowed over behind that big willow," Heather said, pointing to the silhouette of a tree leaning so far out over the water it looked poised to fall in.

Al gave another pull, but the motor still didn't start. We heard a shout from the house and looked up the hill to see a man standing on the front porch pointing in our direction. This time the friendly moon had betrayed us.

We heard Poker Winner shout, "She's gettin' away in a fuckin' boat!" Then the motor roared to life on Al's third pull, and he swung us out into water that had become choppy in the northwest wind. Looking back, I saw the three men in black run down to the dock and clamber into the big power boat.

"Your friends are about to experience extreme disappointment," I yelled to Alice, who was also watching the trio. "We cut the gas lines on that boat."

A couple of minutes later, the three men reappeared on the dock. They ran to the smaller boat, jumped in, and cast off the lines.

"That boat's more our size," I said as I folded my arms across my chest and sat back as smug and snug as possible with the icy spray from the waves beginning to penetrate my shirt.

"Maybe the boat is our size but the motor's not," Heather said. "I checked that sucker out and it's got sixty horses on it."

So much for feeling smug. "Two-block that goddamn throttle," I yelled to Al.

"It won't go any faster," Al yelled back. "What you see is what you got. We can run but I don't know where we're going to hide."

Stage Fright

Behind us, I could see the other boat swing away from the dock and turn in our direction. As I watched them slowly begin to close the distance between us, the water was turning to a lighter shade of blue and the moon was fading in a brightening sky. My watch read 04:48, and I realized the sun would poke its crown over the horizon in about fifteen minutes. I also realized that Carol had phoned the Douglas County sheriff forty-eight minutes ago. Either he or a deputy probably would be at the Glock Family Resort to help us if we could get there without being caught.

I looked again at the boat growing larger behind us and realized that this was a damn big "if."

Chapter 25
Crossing the Bar

As our pursuers chased us across the choppy waters of Merganser Bay, the man kneeling in the bow kept crossing and uncrossing his arms above his head, signaling us to stop. After several minutes, he picked up and waved something else. I didn't need binoculars to determine that the object was a rifle. The man moved the object to his shoulder, and I saw something splash into the water about twenty yards behind us and slightly off to the right. The roar of our boat's motor drowned out the sound of the shot.

"Keep your heads down," I shouted. "The son of a bitch is shooting at us."

That warning sent Heather off the seat and into the bottom of the boat at Al's feet. Alice followed suit, huddling in her blanket on the cold aluminum in front of me.

I saw another splash behind us, this one a little closer. I wasn't sure if the shots were missing because they were meant to be a warning or if the range was too great and the ride too rough for accuracy. This was not the time to stop and ask.

We reached the expanse of water between Merganser Bay and the Glock Family Resort inlet, but at the rate our pursuers' sixty horses were overhauling our twenty, the gunner would be within range before we could gain the safety of Herman Glock's dock. Until we got within sight of the sheriff, we had, as Al said, no place to hide. Or did we?

"Al, take us around the point as close to shore as possible," I yelled.

"We'll hit the damn sandbar on the other side," he said.

"You're right. That's just what we want to do."

"Are you nuts? We'll be stuck there."

"Not if you pull up the motor and Heather works like hell with the oars."

"What if they see us?"

"We've got to get our ass off the sandbar before they get around the point to where they can."

Another bullet landed in the wake just off our stern and the bow of the other boat was beginning to look amazingly large to me.

We rounded the tree-studded point of land only a few yards from shore, taking us out of sight of our pursuers. With me leaning over the bow to watch the

Stage Fright

water, Al steered straight for the sandbar. The other boat still was not in sight when I saw the shadow ahead and yelled, "Cut it!"

Al killed the motor and hoisted the propeller out of the water just as the bow struck the sandbar, and the boat shuddered to a halt, nearly pitching me overboard. Heather was already in the middle seat and holding tight in anticipation of a quick stop. She was on the oars in an instant, pulling with all her strength to get us across the sandbar. The added weight of the two women caused the boat to ride lower in the water than it had on our previous encounter with the obstacle and Heather was having a tough time moving us. Al jumped over the side and started pushing from the stern. His efforts, plus Heather's determined work on the oars, finally propelled us back into deep water. Al hauled himself into the boat just as the stern was clearing the edge of the bar.

At this moment, a stinging rain began to fall. Water was running down Al's face when he pulled the starter rope and the motor sputtered and quit. He gave a second pull with the same result just as our pursuers rounded the point and came roaring toward us with their sixty horses running at top speed. The distance separating us from disaster was diminishing rapidly as our powerless boat continued to drift only a few yards beyond the sandbar. As it had twice earlier, the third pull on the starter rope brought the balky motor to life. Al quickly two-blocked the throttle and steered toward the resort dock.

The man with the rifle, still kneeling in the bow of the faster boat, rose to his feet and brought the weapon to his shoulder. Seeing this, Heather again slid off the middle seat and curled in a ball in front of Al.

Looking backward, I found myself staring into the gun barrel. They were so close that I could see the face of the rifleman, whom I recognized as Poker Winner, when I yelled at Al to duck. I dropped off the seat and sprawled on top of Alice Prewitt's blanket-covered body. I twisted my neck and looked up at the rifle, waiting to hear a shot — or feel the smashing impact of a bullet.

The rifle barrel was leveled at the back of Alan Jeffrey's head when the fast-moving boat behind us slammed onto the sandbar and stopped like a sports car smashing into a tree. The bullet intended for Al went skyward as Poker Winner was propelled forward and upward and out of the boat. He hit the two-foot-deep water headfirst at an angle of approximately 150 degrees and, like a careless swimmer diving into shallow water, his head struck bottom. When he resurfaced, he lay face down, motionless, while the rain poured down on his back in torrential sheets, and we continued on our way to the safety of the late Herman Glock's resort.

Peering back through the downpour, I could see one man lying half over the bow from which Poker Winner had been flung and the other stretched face down across the middle seat. The prop was dug deep into the sandbar, and the boat was going nowhere.

"You can get up," I said. "The race is over and the best crew won."

"Where are they?" asked Alice, looking back. "I don't see any of the bastards."

"What looks like a log floating in front of the boat is the guy who was about to shoot," I said. "The other two are in the boat but out of the battle."

Minutes later, we cruised into the Glock family dock, happy to feel the rainwater streaming down our necks. The dawn's early light revealed the simultaneous arrival of a blue and gray sedan, which came to a halt next to the lodge. The car had a set of lights on top and a Douglas County sheriff's logo on the front door.

Alice spotted the cruiser and asked, "Are you going to turn me in to the cops?"

"Not if we can help it," I said. "At least not until you find a damn good lawyer."

"Time to execute Plan Bravo," said Al.

"Okay," I said. "What is Plan Bravo?"

"Damned if I know," he said. "But we need it quick."

Heather had the answer for Al. "You and I can go up to the lodge and report a boating accident to the sheriff while Mitch hustles Alice over to his cabin and hides her."

What a great plan, I thought. While the sheriff was cleaning up the mess out on the lake, Alice could be taking a nice hot shower and getting all pink and warm. I would be out with Al and Heather monitoring the rescue operation and talking to the deputies for half an hour or so. Then we would all be eager to adjourn to our respective shelters to get out of the rain. I would revive myself with a steamy shower and join Alice in an even steamier bed to take that ride she had been promising.

"Let's hustle up to my cabin and get you out of those wet things," I said to Alice. With one hand holding the blanket shut around her waist and the other hand clasped in mine, the bedraggled and barefoot redhead walked gingerly beside me up the pine-bark path to my cabin. I could hardly wait for the golden moment when we would both be both cozy and dry and I would be saddling up for the promised ride.

I was fantasizing about mounting Alice's saddle when I opened the cabin door.

"It's about time you got here!" said a voice from the living room chair. Martha Todd uncurled her limbs from the fetal position, stood up and walked over to greet us. "God, you both look like death warmed over. Must have been a hell of a night."

Stage Fright

I struggled to bring my mind back to reality from a vision of red pubic hair and form a coherent reply. Finally I came up with, "Were you waiting up for us?"

"All night," Martha said. "Carol finally called the sheriff at four o'clock, like she said she would." She looked at Alice, who stood shivering in the wet army blanket, and said, "Honey, you're going to come down with pneumonia. Let's get you into a hot shower and find you something dry to put on."

I watched my riding partner disappear into the bathroom on the arm of Martha Todd and wondered if I'd ever have a chance to collect on the debt.

Chapter 26
Tale of the Tape

After Alice had showered and snuggled herself into a lavender, terrycloth robe that Martha produced from an overnight bag in my bedroom, I decided to take a quick shower and put on dry clothes before going out to watch the rescue operation. The sight of Martha's bag parked near my bed was encouraging, but now we were three, and three was definitely a crowd.

"Are you going out to talk to the sheriff?" Martha asked as I walked into the living room feeling comfortable for the first time since I hit the shore at Gordon Glanz's summerhouse. "Alice tells me they were planning to drown her."

"They were setting up a phony boat accident," I said. "It was their bad luck to have a real boat accident themselves."

"While you find out how bad their accident was, Alice and I are going to take a nap in your beds," Martha said. "Hope you don't mind."

"Why should I?" I asked, knowing damn well why I did mind.

"Good," said Martha. "See you later."

"Alligator," added Alice. She had the audacity to look back over her shoulder and wink as she followed Martha into the bedroom — my bedroom. As I said, three definitely was a crowd.

Muttering expletives to myself, I put on a hooded plastic rain slicker and returned to Minnesota's great outdoors to see what had transpired at the lake while my libido was being crushed indoors. The rain had not let up while I was being let down.

A pickup truck with a boat trailer was parked at the Glock Family Resort launching ramp. Three slicker-clad men in a fast-moving powerboat decorated with a sheriff's department logo were returning to the dock from an inspection of the craft stalled out on the sandbar. Three waterlogged people — Sheriff Einar Anderson, photographer Alan Jeffrey and reporter Heather Rondeau — stood waiting on the dock.

I trotted down in time to hear one of the deputies say, "We got two guys hurt pretty bad and one who ain't going to make it. Where's that goddamned ambulance?"

Stage Fright

As if in reply, the ambulance came rolling in with all lights flashing and stopped with a scrabble of flying gravel a yard in front of the sheriff's pickup. Two familiar looking EMTs jumped out and ran toward us. I had seen these men so often that I knew their first names.

"What have we got?" asked the EMT named John.

"Two that need backboards and one that needs a body bag," said the sheriff.

"Holy shit!" said the EMT named Ernie. "What happened?"

"Looks like they hit a sandbar with the throttle wide open," said a deputy in the boat. "Go grab your stuff and I'll give you a ride out."

"I'll get on the horn to the medical examiner and send for another ambulance," Sheriff Anderson said. He turned to Al, Heather, and me and said, "After we get this mess cleaned up, I want to talk to you people someplace where it's dry."

"We'll meet you in the lodge," I said, as the sheriff turned away. "Come on, kids," I said to Al and Heather. "It's time for people with brains to get in out of the rain."

"I have to get some shots of them bringing in the wounded," Al said.

"We can watch from the lodge, and you can run out and shoot when the EMTs get to the dock. Right now the three of us — and your wife — all need to talk about what we're going to tell the sheriff."

"Okay," he said. "Let's go to my place and dry off while we talk." We followed him to his cabin and marched in, dripping water with every step. When I peeled off my slicker, Al did a double take and asked, "How the hell did you get so nice and dry?"

"The two co-occupants of my cabin permitted me to make a quick change while you were pointing out bodies to the sheriff," I said.

"Two co-occupants?" asked Heather.

After giving her a brief summary of the situation and the new sleeping arrangements, I said that we needed to coordinate our answers to the sheriff. "We need to decide just how much of this morning's fun and games we're going to share with Mr. Anderson at this time," I explained.

"He might nail the fat guy and the female gorilla if we tell him to send a squad to Glanz's house right now," Al said.

"Vince and Maggie," I said. "Maybe, but chances are that by now they've called for somebody with wheels to come and get them the hell out of there."

"So, do we send the sheriff after Gordon Glanz?" Heather asked.

"I'd rather have us go after Gordon Glanz," I said.

"Carol, what did you tell the sheriff when you called?" Al asked.

165

"I told him what we had agreed on," she said. "That you guys went out late last night and I woke up at four o'clock and was worried because you weren't back."

"He took his sweet time getting here," Heather said.

"I guess I didn't sound panicky enough," said Carol. "Maybe I should take acting lessons from Mitch."

"Actually it's good that he took his time or he would have seen that the boat was chasing us when it hit the sandbar," I said. "Now we can construct our own version of what happened until after we make our move on Glanz."

"You sure like playing with fire," Heather said. "How many times do you want to get shot at?"

"I doubt that the distinguished Mr. Glanz will be so crude as to shoot at us," I said. "I want to get as much of the story as I can before we blow the whistle on him and Olson and the big Ojibway medicine man. Once the cops grab them, all we'll get is 'no comment' until the trial."

"Yeah, you're right," she said. "I'd sure as hell like to find out why those birds are doing all this before they're put in a cage."

We agreed to tell the sheriff that the three of us had gone fishing at midnight, planning to return by dawn, and that Carol had become worried when she woke up and saw the storm clouds coming in. We lost track of the time, but started for home when the rain began falling. We saw the other boat behind us, heading balls-to-the-wall toward the Glock resort dock, apparently trying to outrun the rain, and saw them hit the sandbar. We thought the injured men were lucky to have the sheriff already on hand to summon help.

"Think he'll buy it?" Carol asked.

"I think he will unless those two bozos tell him they were chasing us and planned to kill us," I said. "What are the odds on them doing that?"

"About as good as me winning fifty million big ones in the lottery," said Al, whose clothes had finally stopped dripping on the cabin floor. "Oh, shit, here they come now, riding on backboards." He grabbed his camera and dashed out into the rain.

"We hotshot reporters should try to get their names from the sheriff," said Heather, following Al out the door. I put my slicker on before I went out to join the party, where we were told that none of the three men carried any identification.

"Why am I not surprised?" Heather whispered to me.

"Try to pretend you are," I replied.

"Why don't we all go into the lodge and you tell me everything you know about this?" said Sheriff Einar Anderson. Since this was not really a question, we followed him into the lobby, like a row of ducklings trailing their mama.

It was obvious that Einar was skeptical, but we stuck with our story. Eventually he was forced to accept our version of the morning's events. We quizzed him as to the conditions of the two anonymous casualties and learned that one was unconscious from a head injury and the other was awake but incoherent because of intense pain in his back and ribs.

Sheriff Anderson finally departed, after warning us that he would "be in touch," and Heather Rondeau went home to get dry, after promising that she would return. Al and I decided to listen to the tape of the Glock Family Theatre board meeting again to see if we had missed anything that would provide a motive for hiring Alice to sabotage *Long Night's Journey Into Day*.

The sissy insisted upon showering and changing to dry duds before reviewing the tape, so I returned to my cabin, where my two alluring but aloof roommates were still snoozing in my twin beds. I plopped into the overstuffed chair to wait for Al and picked up a magazine to read. I barely got the cover turned before my eyelids rolled down like the curtain on the Glock Family Theatre stage.

Al's persistent pounding on the door dragged me out of a dream about dashing after a boatload of naked women with rifles, who stayed just a few yards ahead and kept shooting at me. In a semi-conscious state, I rose and wobbled to the door. The knocking had also roused the sleeping beauties in the bedroom and they emerged. Unfortunately, Martha had loaned Alice a jogging suit and both were fully clothed.

We postponed listening to the tape long enough to question Alice about how she got to Gordon Glanz's summer home. She said Doctor Stone gave her a sedative because she was nearly hysterical over Herman Glock's suicide, and when she calmed down, he drove her to the house at the lake, telling her she would be safe there. They were greeted by Maggie, the housekeeper, who told the doctor that she would take good care of Alice.

"Right after the doctor leaves, Maggie makes a phone call," Alice said. "She gives me a cup of tea that must have something in it because I get really woozy. She helps me into the bedroom and undresses me down to my undies — Mitch's and mine — and tells me to lie down and take it easy. I doze off and when I wake up, the two assholes who kidnapped me the first time are standing there looking me over like I'm a plate of spaghetti and meatballs."

"You're lucky they were just looking," Al said. "It sounded like they had some other ideas."

"They sure as hell did. But Maggie goes, 'You know you ain't supposed to touch that girl.' She treated me like shit, but she did keep those two animals from raping me."

"So your wonderful boss — the healer of men, the Ojibway medicine man — set you up to be drowned," I said.

"I have a hard time believing he would do that to me, but it looks like that's what happened," said Alice.

"Seems like you can't trust anybody any more," Martha said. She was not looking my way, but I assumed this remark was meant for me as well as Alice.

"Time to listen to the tape," said Al before I could say something stupid.

I swallowed my retort, started the machine, and fast-forwarded to the point where Oscar Olson called the meeting to order. Alice Prewitt actually leaped out of her chair.

"That's his voice!" she screamed.

"Whose voice?" I asked.

"The guy who hired me to play tricks in the theater. Put a Norwegian accent on that voice and that's him."

"That's the voice of Oscar Olson, the chairman of the Glock theater board."

"It's the fake Norwegian guy's voice. I know it is."

We kept listening and Alice became more agitated. "That absolutely is the son of a bitch who set me up the first time those bastards grabbed me," she said.

"Okay," I said. "Now we have the two board members and the doctor together in a corporation that bought the theater; we have Oscar hiring Alice to mess up what should have been a big money maker for Herman Glock; and we have all three of them risking their professional lives by planning to murder Alice. These are all successful, wealthy men. Why would they gamble like that?"

Al's eyebrows went up a good half-inch and he said, "I think you might have just given us a clue what OCC, Inc. stands for." Three heads turned toward him in unison. "Could it possibly be something like Ojibway Casino Corporation?"

"Bingo!" I said. "You hit the jackpot! I'll bet those bastards wanted the land the theater is on to build a casino and Herman wouldn't sell it. It's an ideal location, so they came up with a sneak attack to wreck the theater."

"And they wrecked poor Herman in the process," Al said.

"And they decided to wreck Alice when she said she was quitting. They're scared to death that she can wreck their whole money-grubbing scheme."

"Don't you think maybe it's time to get the sheriff involved?" said Martha. "Alice won't be safe until those three greedy bastards are put away."

All four of us jumped at the sound of loud, persistent knocking on the cabin door.

Chapter 27
The Heat of the Night

Cautiously, I peeked out the window to see who was hammering on the door. What I saw was the bespectacled face of Heather Rondeau peering out from under the hood of a yellow raincoat that went all the way down to her shoe tops.

"You don't have to break the damn door down," I said as I opened it.

"Sorry," she said. "I thought you might be sleeping. I almost went to sleep a couple of times driving out here." She saw the group sitting around the table and asked, "What the hell's going on? Are you having a party?"

"Yes, it's a pajama party," I said. "We've been listening to my tape in our sleep and learning things subliminally." We got Heather caught up on the knowledge we had acquired in this manner and were beginning to discuss our next move when we were interrupted by another knock on the door. This time it was Carol Jeffrey, wondering why we were all sitting around talking when we should be catching up on our sleep.

I replied that we could all grab forty winks as soon as we had devised Plan Charlie. Carol asked why we needed a Plan Charlie, so we brought her up to date.

"Plan Charlie should be simple," Carol said. "You call the sheriff, the sheriff puts Alice somewhere safe, and then the sheriff goes after the three big bad guys while Heather and Mitch write their stories. After that, the four of us all go home to St. Paul."

"That sounds very clean and efficient, but we're trying to keep Alice out of it until we get her some good legal advice, which is hard to come by on a Sunday," I said. "The lawyer I want to get for her is in St. Paul, and she does not take calls at home on weekends. What we need to do is hide Alice from both the sheriff and the three big bad guys at least until tomorrow."

"Are you volunteering to keep her here in your cabin?" Carol asked. Martha shot me a look that would have sliced a stone in half when I replied that, yes, I was.

"That's not safe," said Heather Rondeau. "Those guys know that you're staying at the resort, and when they don't find Alice at her apartment they'll come looking for her here. Alice will be much safer if I take her home with me."

"You're right, Heather," Al said. "This would be the first place they'd come looking for her."

So it was decided that Heather would take Alice to her house. I would call the desk at the *Daily Dispatch* and tell them I had to stay over at the resort one more night to nail down a major story. Carol then announced that she and Martha were going back to St. Paul in the Jeffreys' car today after taking a quick nap.

"You can ride home with Mitch whenever you're done with this god-awful mess," Carol said to Al.

"I thought you and Al were here for a romantic, three-day getaway weekend," I said, hoping to keep Martha in my cabin until morning. With the redhead gone, we were no longer a crowd of three.

"I'm afraid the romance got away," Carol said. "After everything that's happened this weekend, we're all too tired and upset to have any fun. I, for one, can't wait to get away from this place." Martha nodded her head in vigorous agreement, so I gave up all hope of salvaging anything from the weekend and matched her gesture with a kindly nod of understanding.

After Heather left with Alice in tow, Al and I decided that my cabin might not be the safest place for me to spend the night if Olson and Company sent out some more goons to find Alice. So, while Carol and Martha went off to the Jeffreys' cabin for a catnap, he and I went to the registration desk to see if I could move into a room in the main lodge for the night. Mercifully, the rain had stopped and the clouds were beginning to separate into cottony white clumps, leaving patches of blue in the spaces between.

"I'm sorry, but we're pretty much closed because of Mr. Glock's death," said the woman at the desk. "If you've got a reservation, you can stay, but we're not renting any rooms or cabins to anyone but family members until after the funeral Tuesday."

"Well, I've got a reservation that's good through tomorrow," Al said. "I guess we move you into my place for the night as soon as my wife and your girlfriend move out."

"Damn, there goes my reputation," I said.

"I'm more concerned about mine," he said. "After all, I'm a married man."

☨

The four of us had another round of pizza at Georgio's about five o'clock, after which the women left for St. Paul, and Al and I drove back to the Glock Family Resort in my Honda. As we were parking the car, we spotted a familiar figure getting out of a taxi at the front door of the lodge.

"Welcome back, Ding Dong," I said as we walked up behind him. He spun around as if he had heard a gunshot, but he relaxed when he saw who had spoken.

"Son of a bitch, you scared me," said Ding Dong Bell. "This place makes me jumpy as a kangaroo on a hot sidewalk."

"That goes for all of us," I said. "Bet you never thought you'd be back so soon."

"I sure as hell never thought I'd be back for Herm's funeral. Son of a bitch, if I'd had any idea he was thinking about killing himself I never would have left."

"I don't think those thoughts began until after you left. Come over to cabin number five after you get settled in and we'll tell you all the gory details."

"Okay, I'll be there as soon as I finish giving my regards to Ingeborg."

"Don't ask Ingeborg too many questions. There's a lot that she doesn't know," I said. "We've identified the ghost and figured out who was behind wrecking your show and the theater."

"Son of a bitch!" said Ding Dong. "If you've got any ice, I'll be there with a brand new bottle of scotch."

"Plenty of ice," said Al. "And I'll even help you with the scotch."

"I'm about ready to join you," I said.

"Over my dead body," Al said. "And we've already got one too many of those."

We talked until almost midnight, while Ding Dong and Al made a dead soldier out of a fifth of scotch and I killed most of a two-liter bottle of ginger ale.

After a wobbly trip to the bathroom, Ding Dong said, "Son of a bitch, I'd better go find my room while I can still stand up."

"Need any help?" I asked.

"Schmuck, just point me the right way." We put him outside on the path, aimed him at the lights of the lodge, and watched him weave his way toward his night's repose.

"Didn't the woman at the desk tell you they weren't giving rooms to anyone but family members?" Al said.

"Apparently Ding Dong is a family member," I said.

The famous director had barely faded from our sight in the darkness of the night when Al and I raced each other to the bathroom and the beds.

The sky was still ebony, but an eerie orange light was flickering outside the window when the sounds of sirens awoke us. Stumbling to the front door, we looked out and saw flames leaping upward a good twenty feet against the sky. Those flames were rapidly consuming the cabin in which a less cautious Warren Mitchell would have been sleeping his last sleep.

Stage Fright

We had both hit the sack in our underwear, so Al and I threw on sweatshirts and jeans and joined the ring of resort guests and employees and Glock family members who were watching a crew of volunteer firefighters preparing to tackle the blaze. It looked as if they were planning to send a crew into the blazing building, so I hurried to the chief and identified myself as the sole occupant of the cabin.

"You're sure there's nobody in there?" he asked.

"I was spending the night in another cabin with a friend, and I locked the door of this one when I left."

"You're lucky you found yourself a friend," he said, and from his expression I knew he was thinking "female."

My appearance caused the chief to abandon all efforts to save any part of the fast-disappearing cabin and the firefighters turned their hoses onto the surrounding woodland, wetting the rain-soaked area even more thoroughly to keep the flames from spreading.

I felt a strong tug on my left sleeve and turned to find Heather Rondeau at my side. "You got out of there okay?" she said.

"I was never in there," I said. "I had the foresight to move in with Al tonight, just in case I had visitors."

"So you didn't lose anything?"

"The tape of the meeting is safe, if that's what you're worried about."

"It is, now that I know you're okay."

"Christ, Heather, don't you ever sleep?" Al asked. "What the hell time is it?"

"It's a little after three," said Heather. "I do sleep but I've got a scanner by the bed that picks up everything in Alexandria and Douglas County. I heard the call for firefighters out here and I had a gut feeling it was your cabin that was burning."

"Where's Alice?" I asked. "Did she come, too?"

"No way in hell," said Heather. "I told her to stay in my bedroom and I would call her as soon as I knew what was happening. I'm going to do that right now." She punched in the number, talked briefly to Alice, clicked off, and turned to me. "She said thank god you're okay. Said she couldn't live with herself if she caused another death."

"Is she still blaming herself for Herman's suicide?" I asked.

"Yes, she is — and not without reason."

"She was just a pawn. She's got to understand that it wasn't her fault."

"Maybe you and the hotshot St. Paul lawyer can convince both her and the cops of that. I gotta go talk to the fire chief. See you in the morning." Off she went, to get some quotes for her story.

173

"Any bets on the cause of the fire?" Al asked.

"You don't think it was spontaneous combustion?" I said.

"More likely an overheated casino contract."

We managed to get a couple of hours of toss-and-turn sleep before the sunlight streaming in the bedroom window persuaded us to drag our butts out of bed. After a breakfast of Al's industrial strength coffee and a two-day-old bagel he found in the fridge, I put in a call to the St. Paul law office of Linda L. Lansing, P.C. Linda was the smartest, hardest-working defense attorney I had ever encountered while covering Ramsey County District Court. I reported on a couple of her toughest trials and my attempts to be fair and accurate were rewarded with an invitation to join her for lunch. One lunch led to another, and we tried to get together occasionally when Linda was not tied up in court. Our friendship never got beyond the soup and sandwich stage, even though Linda was tall, dark, and very sexy, because Linda's middle initial could have stood for "lesbian." Not only had Linda L. Lansing marched proudly out of the closet, but she also strode firmly into the forefront of the local gay rights movement.

Linda's secretary took my number and promised that Ms. Lansing would call me back within the hour.

My second call was to the fire chief to inquire about the cause of our early morning house warming.

"My preliminary report will say the probable cause was arson," he said. "Me and the captain will be over there later today with the fire marshal to begin our investigation, but we all noticed a strong smell of an accelerant when we arrived at the scene."

"Gasoline?" I asked.

"Absolutely. The fire seems to have started at the rear of the structure, in the bedroom, which often indicates that an occupant was smoking in bed. However, since you were, uh, engaged elsewhere last night, and the cabin was unoccupied, we can eliminate that as a possibility."

There was nothing to be gained from a discussion of the gender of the person with whom I had spent the night, so I thanked the chief and said I would call again to check on the results of his investigation.

Al, of course, expressed tongue-in-cheek surprise when I told him the chief suspected arson. "He also thinks you're a woman," I said.

"Must have been the way my hair looked in the dancing firelight," said Al.

Stage Fright

Linda L. Lansing called back a few minutes later and I gave her the briefest possible explanation of our problem. "Jesus, Mitch, those people play rough up there," she said when I stopped to take a breath after a five-minute monolog.

"There's a lot of money to màde from a casino," I said. "And they don't seem to care who gets hurt as long as they get their chance to make it." I hadn't even reached the part about last night's would-be Mitchell roast.

"Okay, tell your lady friend that I'll represent her. Keep her under wraps until I get up there tonight. I've got a full day of appointments on my calendar but I'll hop in the car about 5:30 and head up your way."

"Thanks, Triple-L. You are the soul of generosity."

"You only say that because you hope I'll work pro bono."

"Now that you mention it, I don't think Alice has got much money stashed away."

"Tell her that I'll charge her the total of her earnings as the ghost."

"That sounds fair. I'll pass the word and sit tight until you get here."

"Good. Keep your head down and your ass covered. Ciao!"

I relayed Linda's closing advice to Al, who observed that this would be an improvement over my usual posture.

"You mean straight, tall, and easily targeted?"

"No, I mean with your head up your ass." With friends like him, etc.

I decided to turn silently away from this crude assessment and walk to the lodge, where I could buy a morning paper. I was halfway there when a gleaming black Lexus rolled into the parking lot and stopped near the front door. The man who got out was tall and slender. He wore a dark suit and carried himself with majestic dignity. His skin was the color of copper. His braided, black hair hung down his back almost to his waist, and it was tied with a scarlet ribbon near the end. Doctor Henry Stone was coming to call on the grieving widow.

Chapter 28
Stonewalling

What incredible balls the man has, I thought, as I watched him stride into the lodge. Well, let the son of a bitch give his regards to Ingeborg; I would wait by his car and greet him with my regards when he came out. I was sure the medicine man would be especially glad to see me after our early morning campfire.

When Chief Running Deer emerged ten minutes later, he found me lounging against the glistening side of his Lexus. He registered no sign of surprise when I greeted him with, "Good morning, doctor."

"Good morning," he said. "Mr. Mitchell, is it?"

"Excellent memory, doctor. Although I'm not surprised, since some of your associates seem to know all about who I am and where I live."

"I beg your pardon. What associates do you mean?"

"I mean the associates who tried to toast me with something hotter than a glass of champagne last night."

The man looked genuinely puzzled and said, "I'm afraid I don't understand your meaning, Mr. Mitchell."

"I mean the guys who burned down my cabin, thinking I was in it," I said.

"I heard there was a fire here last night. It was your cabin that burned?"

"Don't play games with me doctor. Of course it was my cabin."

The quizzical look grew more intense. "Games? Again, I don't understand you, Mr. Mitchell."

"Oh, please!" I said. "This is getting us nowhere, doctor."

"I quite agree, Mr. Mitchell."

"We need some straight talk, doctor."

"About what, Mr. Mitchell?"

"About the fact that you and Oscar Olson and Gordon Glanz conspired to steal the theater from Herman Glock in order to build a casino and then arranged to kill a young woman when she tried to quit working for your rotten organization."

This got a reaction. The stoic Ojibway's copper complexion turned a deeper red, and he took a step toward me. "It sounds like we do need to talk," he said. "But this parking lot is hardly an appropriate place."

"Come with me to the cabin where I'm now staying with my photographer friend," I said. "The three of us can wash your dirty linen in privacy."

Doctor Stone looked at his wristwatch. "I have patients who will be waiting for me in the office."

"You'll also have the sheriff waiting for you if walk away." I took my cell phone from my pocket. "I can either call Sheriff Anderson right now or I can talk to you."

The doctor sighed, withdrew a cell phone from his coat pocket, and said, "Let me call my office." Two minutes later we were sitting in Al's cabin, and our host was pouring us a round of his corrosive coffee.

Neither Al nor I knew exactly where to start. Finally, Chief Running Deer broke the ice by saying, "Mr. Mitchell, it sounds like you are accusing me of taking part in some dirty — and even criminal — activities. I wish you would explain exactly what you think I have done."

"You are one of the three incorporators of a business known as OCC, Inc., are you not?" I asked. The doctor nodded. "Now, tell us the purpose of that corporation?"

"Are you asking this for a newspaper article?" he asked.

"No, sir, I'm asking this as a man who has almost lost his life twice because of OCC. For now, your answers are off the record."

"Again, Mr. Mitchell, I am at a loss to understand how OCC could have threatened your life. Anyway, off the record, the corporation was organized to arrange funding for the construction of an Ojibway casino in this part of the state and, if possible, locate an appropriate site for the building."

"But last week you denied knowing anything about a casino when I talked to you in your office."

"Yes, I did. And I will continue to deny it publicly. OCC is a privately owned company, and our policy is to remain confidential until the proper time arrives. There are people here who would oppose us if they were aware of our goal, Mr. Mitchell."

"And one of those people was Herman Glock?"

The medicine man shook his head. "Good god, no. Mr. Glock declined to contribute any funds when I asked him for a donation, but I hardly considered him to be an opponent. In fact, he wished us well, but he said that his theater was losing money and his resort was barely breaking even. I accepted this explanation and didn't solicit Mr. Glock again."

"You are aware that your two partners in OCC, acting as board members of the Glock Family Theatre, voted to close the theater and sell it to OCC despite Herman's strong objections?" I asked.

"I am aware that the theater has been closed and that the OCC board has voted to make an offer on the property."

"You don't know that the offer was accepted by a 2-1 vote the day before Herman Glock hung himself at center stage?"

"The OCC board has not met since that tragedy, Mr. Mitchell. If this transaction had anything to do with Herman Glock's suicide I am truly sorry."

"Give me a break!" said Al. "I suppose the next thing you tell us is that you didn't know that Alice Prewitt was the so-called ghost who wrecked the last production."

"My god!" Chief Running Deer said. "It was Alice who did that?"

"Oh, please!" I said. "Cut the innocence act, doctor. Next you'll want us to believe that you don't know anything about your partners, Olson and Glanz, arranging to have Alice drowned in a fake boating accident on the lake."

The medicine man turned as pale as possible for a man with his coloring. "That can't be true," he said. "When Alice came to me she was babbling incoherently and crying hysterically, and I took her to Gordon Glanz's lake house to rest. She didn't show up for work this morning, so I assume she's still there."

"Well, assume otherwise," Al said. "We put her where your next set of goons won't find her."

"Please," said the doctor. "Tell me what you're talking about. Drowning and goons — you've lost me."

"You're lucky you didn't lose Alice or you'd be facing a murder rap as well as kidnapping and conspiracy," I said.

Chief Running Deer rose to his full six-foot-one and slammed his right fist on the table so hard the coffee mugs bounced. "Goddamn it!" he shouted. "Stop talking in riddles and tell me what the hell you know about the theater, my OCC partners and Alice Prewitt. Start from the goddamn beginning and go through to the goddamn end!"

"Gladly," I said. "Sit down and listen." After the medicine man was seated, Al and I took turns relating the events we had observed and the incriminating facts we had gathered, right on through the boat chase and the fire in my cabin. When we finished, the always-squared shoulders of the statuesque Chief Running Deer were sagging, and his chin was hanging near his chest.

"I'm having trouble believing all this," the medicine man said, barely above a whisper. "There's so much I didn't know."

"You really expect us to believe you didn't know what your business partners were doing?" I asked.

"Please, Mr. Mitchell, you must believe me. I was not a party to these crimes."

"Then why did you take Alice out to Glanz's lake house where they were planning to kill her."

"I thought it was a safe haven. Mr. Glanz has invited me to use the house for my own rest and relaxation whenever he or someone in his family isn't there. He even gave me a key to the place, for god's sake."

"What about Maggie?" I asked. "Who is she?"

"I hadn't met Maggie before, but she said she was the housekeeper and would be glad to look after Alice. Oh, my god, I delivered the poor girl right into the hands of the killers!" The medicine man buried his face in his hands and wagged his head from side to side in anguish.

Al and I looked at each other for a moment before Al nodded toward the doctor and asked the obvious question: "Do we believe him?"

"I think we do," I said. "It's crazy as hell, but it's hard not to believe him when he says he didn't know what his partners were doing."

"White men speak with forked tongues?" said Al.

"When white men speak at all," I replied. To the doctor, I said, "Okay, chief, suppose we believe that your pale-face partners kept you out of the loop and in the dark? Where do we go from here?"

Chief Running Deer slowly pulled himself erect to his full height in the chair. "You have to go to the sheriff with this," he said. "They have to be arrested."

"They'll probably try to involve you," I said.

"I'll take my chances," he said. "My god, if I'd had any idea they were wrecking Herman Glock's theater and trying to kill my receptionist ..." His voice trailed off again in agony; then he asked, "You say Alice is now some place safe?"

"Yes, sir," I said. "And we have the best lawyer I know coming up from St. Paul to represent her. Maybe you'll want to hire this lawyer, too."

"Maybe. But if what you say is true, Mr. Olson and Mr. Glanz may be leaving town. You've got to call the sheriff."

"I have a feeling that they're the kind of arrogant bastards who will stick around and try to beat the rap," I said. "They don't know we have a tape of the theater board meeting in which they voted poor Herman out of his theater."

"Tell us a little more about OCC, Inc., before we blow the whistle," said Al. "What do the letters stand for?"

"OCC stands for Ojibway Casino Company," the doctor said.

"I told you!" said Al. "Was I right or was I right?"

"You had two letters out of three," I said.

"They were the two most important ones. Anyway, doctor, how long has OCC been in business, and how much money have you raised?"

"We formed the corporation about a year ago," said Chief Running Deer. "I went to Mr. Olson for advice on raising money, and a week or so later he and Mr. Glanz approached me about forming a three-man, fundraising corporation. They said they could arrange for substantial support from a wealthy party in Providence, Rhode Island."

"Providence?" I said.

"Holy shit!" said Al. "The organized crime capital of America. We've been playing hide-and-seek with much bigger boys than Olson and Glanz."

"You believe that the Providence group might be financed by organized crime?" asked the doctor.

"I'd bet every damn chip in your casino on it," Al said.

"We'll never see that casino," Doctor Stone said. "This will kill it for sure."

"It won't be built where the Glock Family Theatre stands, that's for sure," I said. "In fact, Ingeborg Glock will probably be getting the theater back."

"I can't imagine her running it as a theater," Al said. "Every time she walked in she'd be reminded of Herman Glock's final act on that stage."

"Hey, doctor, maybe she'll turn around and sell it to the Ojibway," I said.

"The Ojibway have no money," said Chief Running Deer. "And if everything you've told me is true, OCC won't have a dime left after the district attorney gets through prosecuting us. Now is it time to call the sheriff?"

"I'd like to wait until the lawyer is here to protect Alice," I said. "How about we get together tomorrow morning and make that call?"

"Whatever you say. Where is Alice? I'd like to talk to her — tell her I wasn't the one who tried to kill her."

"Go to your office and we'll have her call you," I said.

"You still don't trust me, do you?"

"I trust you, doctor, but not quite enough to tell you where Alice Prewitt is."

"Fair enough," he said. "I'll be waiting for her call."

Stage Fright

Heather Rondeau was at her desk when I phoned. After uttering some expletives and asking a couple of questions, she said she would tell Alice to call Doctor Stone. "I have to go to the apartment to do it," she said. "I told Alice not to answer the phone."

"After you see Alice, get your butt out here," I said. "We have got a story that will uncurl your hair."

Less than an hour later, there was a knock on the cabin door. Al took a look out the window before unbolting and opening the door to admit both Heather and Alice. "I've got to hear this hair-straightening story, too," Alice explained. "Then maybe I'll call the doctor after that." I noticed that she was still wearing Martha Todd's running suit and I wondered whose bra and panties were underneath.

The women listened while Al and I reconstructed our interview with Doctor Henry Stone. When we finished, Heather asked, "Do you really believe him when he says he's clean?"

"If he was lying to us he's a better actor than anybody I have ever seen anywhere on any stage," I said. "His face looked positively gray when we told him about those assholes planning to drown Alice."

"Well, I've got some news, too," Heather said. "I checked with the sheriff on the three bozos who wiped out in the boat. He still doesn't know who any of them are. One of the survivors is still unconscious, and the other one won't answer any questions. They haven't had any visitors, and the one who's awake can't make any calls."

"You mean he can't reach a phone?" I asked.

"I mean he's paralyzed from the waist down with a spinal injury. They won't know if it's permanent until the swelling goes down."

"Are they under guard?" I asked.

"No reason to be. As far as the sheriff knows, the only thing they're suspected of is careless boat driving, which isn't a crime unless you're drunk or hit somebody else."

This was troubling. If the injured thugs really were hit men hired by the Providence mafia, their lives could be in danger. The fat guy in the pinstripe suit might decide to clean up after himself and get rid of these two before they could be questioned.

While I was turning this over in my mind, Alice Prewitt said, "I'd like to call Doctor Stone now." I handed her my cell. She punched in the number, spoke briefly, and switched off the phone. "He's not there," she said. "Sylvia goes, 'Doctor has cancelled all his appointments, and he is out for the day.' She didn't even ask me how I was."

"He's gone for the day?" I said.

"What was that you said about the best actor you've ever seen any where on any stage?" Al said.

"Okay, so this guy tops them all," I said.

"The son of a bitch is warning his partners. They're all three going to haul ass."

"Call that frickin' sheriff right now!" said Heather. "We can't wait for your lawyer friend to get here."

Naturally, Sheriff Einar Anderson was out on a call. Next I asked for Detective Bergquist and was told that Monday was his day off. In desperation, I asked to talk to any available deputy so I could report a crime. After waiting on "hold" for what seemed like an hour, I heard a laconic voice say, "This is Deputy Lapierre. How can I help you?"

"Deputy Lapierre?" I said. "Are you any relation to Rhonda and Frenchy?"

"I'm their son," he said.

"That's great," I said. "You have a personal interest in what we're going to tell you. We'll be there in — how long, Heather?" She held up all ten fingers, closed her hands and did it again, so I said, "Twenty minutes. And if the sheriff comes back while we're on our way, we want him to listen, too." I hung up before the deputy could say no.

It was twenty-three minutes, actually, before the four of us, and my tape recorder loaded with the Glock Family Theatre board meeting tape, arrived at the sheriff's office on the outskirts of Alexandria. Al and I in my Honda Civic followed Heather and Alice in the Tracker, holding our breaths all the way as the Alexandria reporter weaved her way through the traffic on I-94 at seventy-five and eighty miles per hour.

We were ushered into an interview room, where we were greeted by Deputy Armand Lapierre. The deputy was built like a beer barrel with pony keg legs, having inherited his mother's genes rather than those of his skin-and-bones father.

"You say I have a personal interest in whatever it is that you're going to tell me?" Deputy Lapierre asked.

"It involves your parents," I said. "It's about all the crap that went on at the Glock Family Theatre, including your mother's fall and your father's gunshot wound."

Stage Fright

This did arouse the deputy's interest. We had barely begun when Sheriff Einar Anderson joined us. With everyone taking turns talking and me making judicious use of the tape, we put on an impromptu dog and pony show. Any critic reviewing our performance would have said we wowed 'em.

Chapter 29
A Hunting We Will Go

"If you get a warrant and search Gordon Glanz's place on the lake you might find Alice's clothes, which would prove she was there," I said to Sheriff Anderson.

"And if you send the troops to all three homes, you might catch those bastards before they bail out of Alexandria," said Heather.

"Okay! Okay!" the sheriff said. "Let's take this one thing at a time. I'll send Deputy Lapierre to the court for a warrant and I'll call Alexandria police for some backup at the residences. Meanwhile, I'm placing Ms. Prewitt under arrest for aiding and abetting the crimes committed in the theater."

"I knew it," Alice said. "They're going to hang my ass."

"You'll be talking to the best lawyer in the Twin Cities before bedtime," I said. "I'm sure she'll be able to work out a deal with the D.A. for your testimony."

"You'll be in court first thing in the morning, and if you make bail you'll be able to go right home," said Anderson.

"She won't dare go home until you guys nail those three casino builders," Al said.

"Which reminds me, you'd better put some kind of guard on those two clowns in the hospital," I said. "They're both potential witnesses."

"The Alexandria police can take care of that," said the sheriff. "Sit tight while I make some calls. Then you can stay and visit with your friend here in jail while my deputies and I go hunting."

"We'll be right behind you," I said.

"I can't stop you from following us, but I don't want you going anywhere near those houses," said Anderson. "You stay the hell out of the way."

Sheriff Einar Anderson proved to be a damn good organizer. He set up a simultaneous raid of all three houses, with him and two of his deputies taking the doctor's house because it was outside the city limits, and the Alexandria PD moving in on the Glanz and Olson abodes. At the same time, Deputy Armand Lapierre would be leading a three-man search party at Gordon Glanz's lake home.

As for the three of us, we decided that Al and I would follow the sheriff to Chief Running Deer's house while Heather met the city cops at Oscar Olson's place. Not

Stage Fright

wishing to leave anybody out, we also planned to get pictures of Gordon Glanz in custody at the police station.

The arrests were to go down precisely at 3:30 P.M., when all three parties would cover every exit, ring their respective doorbells and clearly announce themselves as the police. It looked like a masterful plan.

However, at Chief Running Deer's house, we discovered one small flaw. There was nobody home to respond to the bell and the bullhorn. Anderson confirmed the absence of the owner by kicking in the back door and conducting a room-by-room search, including all the closets and bathrooms.

"Shit!" was the sheriff's comment when he allowed Al and me to join him.

"Maybe the others had better luck," I suggested.

"Let's find out," Anderson said. He slid into the cruiser and called the squad raiding Oscar Olson's house.

"There ain't nobody here," came the reply.

"Not even his wife?" asked Anderson.

"Place was locked up tight. We busted in and checked every room."

"Ten-four," said Anderson into the mike. "Shit!" he said to Al and me.

The sheriff received a similar answer when he queried the troops at Gordon Glanz's city residence. No Gordon and no wife. Anderson's verbal reaction to this report was another instant replay.

"Think they could all be at the lake place?" I asked.

"Son of bitch! If they are those three deputies with the search warrant are going to have their hands full," Anderson said. He called on the radio for Deputy Lapierre and got no response. "They're out of the car and they haven't called for backup," said the sheriff. "I hope that means everything is under control."

He was about to get out of the cruiser when the radio crackled and an Alexandria police officer asked for the sheriff.

"This is Sheriff Anderson," he said.

"Sheriff, we just got a call from the desk sergeant at the station downtown," said the cop. "He's requesting that you come down there immediately. Says they've got something kind of crazy going on there and it's related to your case."

Seconds later, Anderson's cruiser and two others were on the way downtown with lights flashing and sirens wailing, followed as closely as possible by a blue Honda driven by an inquisitive reporter with a white-knuckled photographer as a passenger.

What we found at the station was as crazy as the desk sergeant had claimed.

185

As we followed Sheriff Anderson through the door, the first thing we saw was a circle of American Indians — six of them dressed in buckskin shirts and blue jeans. Each of them also wore a grim expression on his face and some sort of feather combination in his hair. The biggest, most elaborate of these headdresses was worn by the one man we recognized — Chief Running Deer. It was the same one he had worn at the exorcism.

We moved into the room, passing a couple of Alexandria cops who were watching with their faces blank and their hands resting on the butts of the weapons in their holsters. Inside the circle of Indians were two white men with flushed faces and frightened eyes. At first glance, we saw that their hands were bound together at the wrists. Closer examination showed that each man's ankles also were connected by a short length of rope, creating an effective set of hobbles, and that the right leg of Gordon Glanz was lashed tightly to the left leg of Oscar Olson.

"They were leaving town," Chief Running Deer said to Sheriff Einar Anderson. "We thought you'd like to talk to them before they went away." The medicine man handed the sheriff the loose end of the rope that was wound around the prisoners' legs.

"This is a goddamn outrage!" yelled Oscar Olson.

"Yes, it is," said the sheriff. "You're both under arrest for conspiracy and attempted murder." Olson started to reply but Glanz told him to shut the hell up. They both stared silently at Einar Anderson while he read them their Miranda rights.

Al got some great pictures of the captives and their colorfully costumed captors. Heather Rondeau arrived in time to get a shot of Olson and Glanz being untied by the sheriff and his deputies. Together, she and I approached Chief Running Deer after he finished answering the sheriff's questions.

"Congratulations, doctor," I said. "We misjudged you again. When you weren't in your office to take Alice's call, we were sure you were on the run with your partners."

"They were going to take off and leave the Ojibways holding the bag," said the medicine man. "We decided that just this once the white man should pay the price for what he did to the Indians."

"You couldn't have picked a better time," I said. "But what about you? Is the sheriff letting you off the hook?"

"For the time being. He is withholding charges pending further investigation. I am not to leave Douglas County, as if I would after this."

"You're luckier than Alice. He's got her in a cell in the county lockup."

Stage Fright

"Oh, god, can I do anything to help her?"

"She can probably use some bail money in the morning," I said. "Meanwhile, why don't you go out there for a visit? She did want to talk to you."

A deputy who had been waiting outside in a cruiser poked his head in the door and announced that Deputy Lapierre was on the radio calling for the sheriff. Al, Heather and I followed Anderson to his cruiser in time to hear the report.

"We found the house occupied and were admitted by two women who identified themselves as Mrs. Gordon Glanz, who said she owns the place, and Mrs. Oscar Olson," the deputy said. "They told us their husbands were going away on business and had dropped them off at the lake for a few days' vacation while they're gone. We executed our search warrant despite Mrs. Glanz's objections, and we did find a pair of women's jeans and a T-shirt that are way too small to fit either of those ladies."

"Good work, Armand," said the sheriff. "Inform those ladies that their husbands aren't going anywhere but court tomorrow morning, ask them if they need a ride home, and bring the jeans and T-shirt into the office."

"Ten-four!" said Deputy Armand Lapierre.

Back at the resort, I e-mailed a super story and Al's photos to the desk. I followed with a note that said we were both too pooped to drive home. "We'll hit the road for St. Paul right after Herman Glock's funeral tomorrow," I concluded.

Gordon Reynolds, the night city editor, replied that it was okay with him but that Don O'Rourke was ready to cut off our expense accounts if we stayed one minute longer than necessary. "He suspects you're out there catching walleyes," Reynolds wrote.

"Tell him we're not doing anything fishy," I replied. A minute later there was a knock at the door and Al opened it to find Linda L. Lansing standing outside.

"Come on in, Triple-L," I said. "You know Al Jeffrey, don't you?"

"Hi, Al," Linda said. She looked around and asked, "Is my client here, too?"

"Your client's in the county lockup," I said. "A lot of things have happened."

Chapter 30
No Rest for the Angelic

Any notion Al and I might have had that our last day in Alexandria would be relatively uneventful was dispelled immediately after the 8:00 A.M. court appearances of Alice Prewitt, Oscar Olson, and Gordon Glanz. The two of us, along with Linda L. Lansing, had accepted Doctor Henry Stone's invitation to stay overnight at his spacious home. In the morning, Al and I were looking forward to spending a few routine minutes in court followed by some relaxing moments with Triple-L and her client in a coffee shop before filing our story and photos.

The moments in court went as routinely as we had hoped they would. Alice pleaded not guilty and was released on $25,000 cash bail put up by Doctor Stone. Because Olson and Glanz had demonstrated their desire to be elsewhere the previous day, the district attorney had no difficulty convincing the judge that those two were flight risks. Consequently, it was ordered that they be held without bail after their lawyers entered pleas of not guilty.

The quiet routine didn't last long after that. Heather Rondeau, Al, and I were almost to the courthouse door when Sheriff Einar Anderson came running up behind us in the lobby. "Mr. Jeffrey, have you still got the photos you took of Herman Glock's body hanging on the stage?" he asked.

"They're in Mitch's computer," Al said, pointing at the encased laptop I was carrying in my hand.

"I'd like to look at them, if you please," said the sheriff.

Both Heather and I perked up our ears at this, and in unison, we asked, "What's going on?"

"Set up your computer in the DA's office and I'll tell you while we're looking at the photos," Anderson said. We followed him to that office, and while the computer was booting up the sheriff told us that the medical examiner had found something unexpected while performing the autopsy on Herman Glock's body.

"He found a bruise at the base of Herman's skull," said the sheriff. "The M.E. says it doesn't fit into the established pattern of injuries sustained in a death by hanging."

I opened the photo file, and we flipped through the grotesque images of Herman's body dangling from the rope. "Looks like a normal suicide to me," said Anderson. "I can't see any way he could have got that bruise."

"Wait a minute," Al said. "Look at the chair."

"What about it?"

"If you're going to hang yourself onstage, facing toward the audience, how would you set the chair?" Al asked.

"You'd most likely set it facing toward the audience," said Anderson.

"With the back of the chair upstage?"

"Yah, I suppose so."

"And how would you get the chair out from under your feet?"

Anderson thought a moment and said, "I'd kick against the back of the chair so it either slid backward or tipped over."

"Right. And where would that leave the chair in relation to your body?"

"The chair would be behind me, I suppose."

"Right again. And if the chair tipped over, which way would the legs be pointing? Away from or toward your body?"

Again the sheriff thought for a moment. "They'd have to be pointing toward me. Oh, shit, I see what you mean." The chair in the photo on my computer screen was lying to the left of Herman Glock's feet, and the legs were pointing away from his body.

"Somebody helped Herman get off that chair," Al said. "In fact, Herman probably was never on the chair."

"And that same someone must have conked Herman on the back of the head before sticking his neck in the noose," I said.

"That might explain why we never found a suicide note," said Einar Anderson. "Whatever you do, gentlemen, take care of those photos. I'm going to be asking Oscar Olson and Gordon Glanz some very tough questions this morning."

Anderson practically galloped out of the room, leaving Al, Heather, and I staring at each other. "Jeez, I need to go write a story!" said Heather.

"Me, too," I said. "But first I need to find Alice Prewitt and tell her she doesn't have to feel guilty about Herman Glock's suicide anymore."

Alice and Linda were standing beside Triple-L's silver Mercedes when we got to the parking lot. "What the hell have you been doing in there?" asked Linda. "We're ready to go get that coffee."

"We've got something a hell of a lot better than coffee," I said. "Let's find a restaurant and Al can tell you all about it while I write today's story on the laptop."

Because the M.E. could not release Herman Glock's body until Monday evening, the funeral was not held until Tuesday afternoon. The service was set for 2:30 P.M., after a two-hour visitation period. Al and I arrived at the funeral home a few minutes past 12:30 and found people lined up out the door and at least fifty feet up the sidewalk.

"Holy shit!" Al said. "Looks like Herman had a few friends."

Ignoring dozens of dirty looks and a few uncomplimentary under-the-breath remarks about our parentage, Al and I crashed the line and went inside. The casket, heaped with flowers, was at the front of the largest room in the funeral home. In the receiving line to our right as we faced the casket stood Ingeborg Glock, her son and daughter-in-law, her daughter and son-in-law, Herman's older brother and his wife and — at the end — Ding Dong Bell.

I wormed my way to Ding Dong's side and said I needed to talk to him in private. He grumbled something about a "goyisher schmuck" but followed me to a side room where I told him what we had learned about Herman Glock's death.

"Son of a bitch!" Ding Dong roared. "You mean those sons of bitches killed the poor schmuck and made it look like suicide?"

"It looks that way," I said. "The sheriff is grilling Olson and Glanz even as we speak. I'm wondering if there's a way to tell Ingeborg and the family before the funeral."

"Sure there is. I'll take care of it. Son of a bitch!"

Al and I sat off in a corner while Ding Dong brought the family members — beginning with Ingeborg — into the side room one by one and told them that Herman's suicide was a fake. As each family member got the word, it appeared as if a weight was being lifted off his or her shoulders and a dark overhead cloud was rolling away. The mood of those in the receiving line remained somber, but the knowledge that their husband, father, and brother had not destroyed himself made it easier for Herman's survivors to respond to the well-wishers' words of sympathy.

The start of the service was delayed more than half an hour because of the number of people passing by the casket. When the funeral finally began, there weren't enough chairs for all who stayed, so Al and I joined a couple of dozen mourners standing in the back and along the sides of the room.

Midway through the service, Ding Dong delivered a delightful eulogy about his days in college with Herman. Everyone was smiling when Ding Dong came to the end and said that he had an important announcement to make before he sat down.

Stage Fright

"Thanks to the diligent efforts of the medical examiner, the county sheriff and my two dear friends from the St. Paul newspaper, we have learned that Herman Glock's death did not come by his own hand." He gestured toward where Al and I were standing, and every head in the room turned toward us. Until then, my eyes had been dry.

We followed the procession to the cemetery and watched as Herman Glock's body was committed to the earth. Then it was back to the resort dining room for the customary post-funeral lunch. At least a hundred people showed up to partake of the goodies, but Ingeborg had her troops lay out a spread that would have fed twice as many.

Al and I were in a corner consuming pastrami on dark rye sandwiches and softball-size scoops of potato salad when Heather Rondeau joined us. "Where's Alice and her lawyer?" she asked between bites of smoked turkey on whole wheat.

"Alice couldn't face going to Herman's funeral, even after she found out he didn't commit suicide," I said. "Triple-L took her home for a shower and clean clothes."

Next we were joined by Ingeborg Glock and her son and daughter, who came as a group to thank us — Al in particular because of his photos — for helping remove the stigma of suicide from Herman's death. "You and your families can stay here at the resort for free any time you want to, and for however long you want to," Ingeborg said.

I wanted to ask if she would reopen the theater when it was returned to the Glock family, but I was afraid the wound was still too raw. Ingeborg seemed to read my mind.

"When everything gets settled, I'm going to donate the theater and several acres of land around it to the local Ojibway tribe. They can build a casino or do whatever they want to with it," she said. "Personally, I can never go into that building again."

"It's very generous of you to give it away," I said.

"It's the least I can do after what Chief Running Deer and his men did to keep those monsters from getting away. The sheriff told us that Oscar and Gordon had plane reservations to the Dominican Republic. Apparently they were just going to skedaddle and leave their poor wives to pick up the pieces."

Glenn Ickler

"Nice folks," Al said.

"Salt of the earth," I said.

"Let's hope the sheriff is peppering them with questions."

In fact, Sheriff Einar Anderson shook some spicy answers out of his two prisoners. Al and I were back at his cabin, packing up our stuff, and preparing to head for St. Paul, when the sheriff knocked on the door.

"Glad I caught you before you left," he said. "The D.A. wants you to preserve those photos of the body and the chair. He plans to subpoena them if there's a trial."

"Did you get anything new from Olson and Glanz today?" I asked.

"Oh, man, did we! They're blaming each other for everything and singing like canaries in order to cut their own deals with the D.A. They've been talking so much that their lawyers have pretty much given up on putting together any kind of defense."

"So, fill us in on the words and music."

"From what Olson says, the idea to sabotage the theater started with Glanz after Herman Glock flat out refused to sell it to OCC, Inc. Of course Glanz says Olson was ready to go along with anything and everything, right from the start. In fact, it was Olson who thought of approaching Alice Prewitt because Doctor Stone had been talking to him about his good-looking new receptionist who was in terrific shape from working out and was broke because she was paying off her college loans."

"Did Oscar demonstrate his phony Norwegian accent for you?" I asked.

"No, I'll have to ask him to do that," said Anderson. "Anyhow, through his bank dealings, Glanz knew some people in Providence who were willing to put up money to build a casino if OCC could come up with the land. This is where they really got themselves into deep shit because they went into business with people who don't mess around when they want something done."

"I assume it was the Providence bunch that decided Alice was a threat and needed to be silenced?" I said.

"It was," said the sheriff. "Oscar and Gordon both swear they didn't want to hurt Alice, but Providence sent up a crew to convince them that it was necessary — and to do the job. This was the three guys who were in the boat that crashed, the boss man you called Fatso when you gave me your statement, and the woman they called Maggie. Gordon thinks she's the fat guy's wife, by the way. They took over his lake place and a house Oscar owns out in the country somewhere."

Stage Fright

"The house in the country must be where they took Alice the first time they grabbed her," I said.

"What about Herman's murder?" Al asked.

"Same guys," said Anderson. "Providence was pissed because Herman swore to Oscar and Gordon that he would go to court to fight the sale of the theater to OCC. That happened in the board meeting after your tape ran out. They figured a court case could tie everything up too long, so they decided to eliminate the plaintiff. With Herman in the state of mind he was in, faking a suicide looked like a good scam. The trouble was the fakers were too dumb to set the stage properly."

"They needed a good stage manager," I said. "How about torching my cabin? Who did that?"

"Your fat friend and his wife. That was an act of revenge, actually. They were really pissed when they read the story about the boat accident in your paper, and they figured out that it must be you who stole Alice from them."

"Was it our discovery that Alice was held prisoner in Glanz's lake place that made him and Olson decide to leave the country?" I asked.

"Partly, but not entirely. The people in Providence were so fed up with the way Oscar and Gordon were losing control that they threatened to take them out of the picture if they made one more mistake. They weren't sure if that meant cutting them out financially or cutting them off permanently, like Herman, so they decided it was a good time to haul ass out of town."

"And leave their wives to face the music in Alexandria?" Al said.

"They were going to send for the women later," said the sheriff. "But they hadn't told the women where they were going, just in case somebody — either us or the boys in Providence — started asking questions."

"What happens next?" I asked.

"Next the D.A. works out a deal that will put Oscar and Gordon away for awhile but not forever," said Anderson. "We also will be charging the two guys in the hospital with Herman's murder and Alice's kidnapping. And we'll go looking for the fat guy and his wife, who are now long gone back to Providence or wherever they hang out. I doubt like hell we'll ever catch them, even with the help of the authorities in Rhode Island."

"What about the theater?" I asked. "Does that legally belong to Ingeborg?"

"If not, it will shortly," the sheriff said. "That's another interesting thing. We got a warrant and searched Glanz's files — he was treasurer of the theater board, you know — and found out he was keeping two sets of books. The figures Herman saw showed that the theater was losing money. The real set of books showed a small profit."

"As the famous director, Ding Dong Bell, would say: that son of a bitch!" I said.

We loaded my car and went looking for the famous director, Ding Dong Bell, so we could say good-by. We were not surprised to find him in the bar, which had been opened during the lunch after the funeral. He was sipping his usual scotch on the rocks.

"Son of a bitch!" he said. "For a couple of newspaper schmucks, you guys did a hell of a job."

"I'm not sure that's an unqualified compliment, but thanks anyway," said Al.

"We're heading for home," I said. "How about you?"

"Tomorrow morning," said Ding Dong. "And this time I'm staying there. I ain't taking on any more projects to save any more old buddies' asses. Buy you a drink?"

"Sure," I said. "Make it a ginger ale with no ice for me." Al, who could sleep all the way to St. Paul, ordered a brandy Manhattan. We were rehashing the events of the past few weeks when Linda L. Lansing and Alice Prewitt appeared. Alice was dressed in her own clothes — black stretch pants and a lime green muscle shirt — and was carrying a plastic grocery bag.

"I knew we'd find you in here," Alice said. She held the bag out toward me. "Here's your girl friend's clothes. Tell her thanks and that I'm sorry I didn't have a chance to run them through the wash."

As I took the bag, Alice caught my hand and said, "Can we talk over there alone for a minute?" I followed her to a small round table in a quiet corner, and we sat facing each other. "Do you really have to go home tonight?" she asked.

"I really do, if I want to keep my job," I said. "My editor e-mailed me a note after I filed my story today, and he made it very clear he wants to see me sitting at my desk bright and early tomorrow morning."

"That's too bad. I still owe you that ride I promised and I was hoping I could give it to you tonight."

"Guess I'll have to take a rain check. Is the offer good until next summer?"

"It is if I'm still here," she said. "There's no expiration date, but I'm not sure I want to stay in Alexandria after all the shit that's happened to me here."

"Come to St. Paul. I've got a bed you can sleep in any time you like."

"I'll think about it," Alice said. "Right now, I'll say good-by if I can't talk you into staying around tonight." We stood and hugged each other, and she gave me another flick of her hot little tongue as we kissed each other good-by. At that moment I was ready to say to hell with my antsy editor and yes to the sexy redhead. I think I might have taken the risk if Alan Jeffrey hadn't been counting on me for a ride to the arms of his wife and kids.

"What were you and Alice whispering about over there in the corner?" Al asked as we pulled out of the parking lot in my Honda.

"Oh, I was just filling her in on the details we heard from the sheriff," I said.

"And what was her reaction?"

"'Curiouser and curiouser,' said Alice."

"What now? Have you suddenly become the poor man's Lewis Carroll?"

"Wonders never cease," I said.

"Off with your goddamn head!"

Chapter 31
Home Sweet Home

Al and his family lived in a too-small, two-story house in the Midway district of St. Paul. They were planning to build an addition with the proceeds from the sale of a sprawling ranch house in suburban Roseville that Al had inherited from his uncle a year earlier. They decided to sell the Roseville house because the inheritance included a $200,000 mortgage. The $400,000 selling price left the Jeffreys with enough to build a modest wing, even after they paid the taxes.

We stopped for a quick dinner along the way, so it was after ten o'clock when we pulled up in front of Al's house. I went in and said a quick hello to Carol and the sleepy-looking kids, then made the six-minute drive to my apartment on Grand Avenue.

Before leaving Alexandria, I had called Martha Todd and told her she could take Sherlock Holmes back to my apartment because I was coming home. Therefore, I wasn't surprised when the burly tomcat trotted up and greeted me with a meow and an ankle rub when I opened my front door.

What did surprise me was the next greeting, which came in the form of a hug and a kiss from a black-haired, brown-skinned woman clad in a pale blue, almost see-through nightgown that covered only the territory from lower-cleavage to upper-thigh.

"I thought you'd never get here," said Martha Todd when our lips finally parted.

"If I'd been expecting this kind of a welcoming committee I wouldn't have stopped for supper," I said.

"Sherlock Holmes and I thought you deserved more of a welcome than you'd get from a sleepy old tomcat."

"You've forgiven me for sharing my cabin with two beautiful young women?"

"Tell me the truth. Did you go to bed with those two beautiful young women?"

"No, Martha, I did not."

"Did you want to?"

"Yes, I did," I said. "I can't deny that."

Stage Fright

"Do you want to go to bed with me?" she asked with her hundred-degree lips one thirty-second of an inch from my ear. This was a Martha I had never seen before.

"That's why I invited you to my cabin up there in Alexandria."

"Would here in St. Paul be okay?"

"Lead the way," I said. She uncoiled her arms from around my neck, took my right hand in hers and led me into my bedroom. In the dim light of a bedside table lamp, which had been reduced in wattage since last I used it, I could see that the covers were turned down, and the bed was ready for occupancy.

Martha stretched luxuriously on her back with her arms spread as wide as the wings of a soaring eagle and her thighs held invitingly apart while I hastily removed my clothes. For a moment I considered taking a quick shower, but the sight of Martha's strategically-positioned limbs, with the hem of her diaphanous nightie pulled up almost to the wondrous Y where her belly curved into her thighs, was more enticing than any man could resist.

Naked, I finally laid down beside the woman with whom I had been yearning to make love all through the fall, winter and spring. As I sank full-length onto the mattress, my body suddenly sent my brain a message that said it was bone tired from the days and nights of whirlwind, round-the-clock action at Alexandria.

Physical exhaustion be damned, I said to myself, as Martha drew me close against her sweet-smelling breasts and belly while pressing her soft lips onto mine.

"Does this mean we're committed?" I asked. I felt royally relaxed as I wrapped my arms around Martha, slid my hands up under the nightie and traced the curves of her marvelous ass with both hands.

"It means I want you here with me, not roaming around lusting after other women," she said softly.

"Me, too," I whispered with my eyes closed. I gave the buns I loved a gentle squeeze, nuzzled her silky neck just below the ear lobe with my lips — and slid helplessly into the darkness of a long, deep sleep.

The End

1690

NORMANDALE COMMUNITY COLLEGE
LIBRARY
9700 FRANCE AVENUE SOUTH
BLOOMINGTON, MN 55431-4399